Epiphany

Susan Slater

Epiphany

Dan Mahoney Mysteries, Book 4

Susan Slater

Secret Staircase Books

Epiphany
Published by Secret Staircase Books, an imprint of
Columbine Publishing Group LLC
PO Box 416, Angel Fire, NM 87710

This book is a work of fiction. Names, characters, places and
incidents are either the product of the author's imagination or are used
fictitiously. Any resemblance to actual events or locales or persons, living
or dead, is entirely coincidental.

Book layout and design by Secret Staircase Books
Cover illustrations © Tamara Ray, Jon Bilous,
Andrey Puzanov

Publisher's Cataloging-in-Publication Data

Slater, Susan
Epiphany / by Susan Slater
p. cm.
ISBN 978- 1945422676 (paperback)
ISBN 978- 1945422683 (e-book)

1. Mahoney, Dan (Fictitious character)—Fiction. 2. Insurance
investigation—Fiction. 3. Florida—Fiction. 4. Religious relics—
Fiction. 5. Human trafficking—Fiction I. Title

Dan Mahoney Mystery Series : Book 4
Slater, Susan, Dan Mahoney mysteries.

BISAC : FICTION / Mystery & Detective.
813/.54

Acknowledgements

Yes, it really does take a village. All that inspiration for *Epiphany* didn't just magically happen. I love it when friends start a sentence with "why don't you consider writing about ..." So, thank you Mary Russell for taking me to a table tipping. A thank you to the real M. Mahoney, certified psychic medium, whose insightful reading helped me get my own Maggie Mahoney's cards right.

And to all those who offer encouragement and help with research—Karen Wolford, those once-a-month beer and pretzel consultations are necessary, and to Maria Sayers, who thinks I tell a good story and always insists on more, a special thank-you!

Chapter One

Stupid. Stupid. Stupid. There she went again, thinking in threes. Her mind was spinning, repeating itself—repeating the warnings. The internal voice was getting louder, first the words then a buzzing so loud that she heard nothing else but this threatening high-pitched hiss. She *needed* to give this up. Walk away. Now, before something terrible happened. She couldn't be responsible … not even involved. But the money. She made more than she had ever thought possible. So, there was right and there was wrong. Which side did she want to be on? Which side *should* she be on?

Suddenly the driver hit the brakes, just a tap before

accelerating again. Had there been something in the road? She couldn't see; the night was almost pitch black. She looked down at the young girl sleeping beside her stretched out across the vintage limo's wide back seat. Good, she was still asleep. She would need her rest for what lay before her.

It was wrong handing this child over to who knew what. But how could she say no? Would she still be his chosen one, his right hand, the one he depended on? He had reassured her. Said yes. She knew, of all the women he could have turned to, she had been singled out because she was bright, knew how to be discreet and she loved him unconditionally. No, she couldn't leave him, nor could she betray him. He knew that. But hadn't he offered to help? To free her, yet keep her close? Offer her a much coveted position among his disciples? She smiled, an office job maybe? Or would marriage be offered? She knew he loved her.

It was her recruiting that had earned her accolades, caught his attention. She was persuasive but, better yet, she knew who would be receptive, whose family needed the money, who would be strong enough to play the game and walk away when the time came. Until this last one. Could she be losing her touch? Her insight? Her intuition? Was it too late to save this young woman asleep next to her? Beg for her release? Take all the blame for misguided information? It was one thing to enslave an eighteen or nineteen-year-old—they were young adults and often chose the life willingly. But, a sixteen-year-old, perhaps fourteen? Maybe thirteen? No. That was simply wrong.

There was a distinct line between children and adults—to her way of thinking and in the eyes of the law. There were stiffer penalties for working with children, as there should be. But this new demand for virgins, in and by itself, lowered the age of recruits but upped the reward. She couldn't overlook that. The more danger, the higher the risk but also exponentially, the greater the reward.

She knew she was invaluable. She spoke the language of the fearful … the downtrodden. Literally. And she wore the trappings of a Bride of Christ. How could she not be trusted? She was a fraud, but a good one and worth the money, the finder's fee, if you will. Her bank account was growing by tens of thousands. Maybe she should stay in the game—even raise her prices. She felt other "stewards" were getting more. What sum would be fair for the research, the meetings, the handholding—she was thorough. No one could take that from her. She made more money than she could have ever imagined. But she had a conscience. She cared. Would this job last forever? Did anything? She needed to take care of herself.

Recently, she felt overlooked, taken for granted—certain, more mundane, things were expected of her. For example, babysitting, like tonight. Had she been passed over for the more plum jobs of negotiating with the brokers who represented buyers? It was let known in whispers and side-long glances that she had competition—someone was vying for her spot, would soon openly challenge her. Would she be ready? More importantly, would she have the backing needed to overcome this show of power? This play for position? Would he be there for her? She was counting on him. Was her trust misplaced?

"Are we there yet?" The young girl beside her had startled awake when the car strayed to bump over the rumble strips along the side of the highway.

"No, sweetheart, go back to sleep. I'll wake you when

it's time." Whispered, but in tonally perfect Mandarin. She marveled at how quickly her native language had come back to her. She gently brushed a wayward strand of hair out of the child's eyes and tucked it behind an ear returning the wan smile as the girl readjusted the pillow beneath her head and once again closed her eyes. Yes, she was a child—so beautiful, so innocent. She should ask for more money for this one. But the age—could she even trust the man who posed as her protector, who swore on the life of his mother that she was fourteen? Then pocketed the five thousand dollars the Leader offered and slipped back into the oblivion of the tent city provided by the community for its homeless.

And maybe she *was* fourteen, but something just didn't feel right. Yet, she'd been told that there would be a bonus. The benefactor was so pleased with her pictures that he was expected to "tip"—handsomely. This child was truly a prize, not something she'd wrestled from a soup kitchen or rescued from begging on a street corner. This one was not born on the streets but simply had ended up there with nowhere else to go.

That's where her pretend vocation gave her an edge—she could move freely among the less fortunate singling out those who would add to her bank account. But this child was a runaway. Refusing to be restrained by a desperate father new to this country. Brought here with her parents by a Jesuit order and sheltered by the Church. Her mother had died and her father had fallen on hard times—there was no money or even interest in trying to raise, let alone control, a wayward teenager in a new country full of temptations. He had sought her out because she spoke his language and he knew she would help him do the right thing. No, this wonderful example of an opportunity had simply fallen into her lap. But a father selling his only child? So that he could go home? Support and protect his own parents who were too old to work? Sacrifice one to save three? It would not be the American way of doing things. But she understood the need to preserve honor.

She sighed and tried to make out landmarks as the driver accelerated in the darkness. The night was black with the headlights of the large car barely piercing the thick curtain. The air, heavy with moisture, seemed to weigh down the clouds hugging the horizon while high cirrus wisps obscured all but just a glimmer of light from moon or stars. Along this stretch of ocean, there were no streetlights or illuminated signs praising Morgan & Morgan Law offices or suggesting happiness was owning a Harley Davidson.

The air-conditioning in the car made her shiver. Was there a reason it needed to be on? December and all of Florida took a deep, cool, humidity-free breath. Light jackets were needed, not blasts of cold air. Or maybe the air wasn't on. Could it be her nerves—just knowing what was about to happen? How her young charge would soon be swallowed up in a world on the fringe—the edge of decency, of morality, of life itself. If she were lucky, she wouldn't be sacrificed. Her beauty and youth might save her from that. No, at the very worst the girl would become the plaything of an old but very rich man who would give her everything but demand even more in return.

Eventually the car slowed and pulled onto an overlook. The driver sat silently scanning the beach before opening his door and getting out.

"OK, this is it. Move. They won't wait on us forever."

He pulled the back passenger-side door open.

She barely had time to waken the girl and whisper, "We're here."

"Speak English. I don't want to hear no mumbo-jumbo."

The man was not a native speaker himself, but seemed to be trying hard to appear American. And he'd probably been instructed to report on any conversations. She would be careful. He could be mean and threatening—she'd found that out earlier in the evening. He had demanded money—he would let her buy her way out of doing what she was doing. She had turned to him but now wasn't so certain. He had named a horrendous sum. But she found a way of producing it. If she decided to leave, he would help her. She played the game well; she was a good follower and most importantly? She pleased the Leader. She had his protection. Didn't the offer of help from this man prove it? Wasn't it the Leader who sent this man to her?

Then this had to be it. The last girl. The last midnight trip to hand over flesh and blood to who knew what end? She would finish her involvement this very night and begin a new life. If the Leader wasn't there to support her, she had a nest egg. She would survive. But most importantly she would do the right thing. She couldn't be wishy-washy; she had already paid for her freedom. Some would say she had earned it.

She bowed her head ever so slightly, nodded to the driver, averted her eyes and followed the girl out of the car. The girl held tightly to her hand. His guttural tone had frightened her. Would she be able to walk with her to the water's edge? Hold her close, reassure her? Whisper words of courage?

She barely had time to pull the girl's down vest in place and snap the metal buttons closed under her chin before the driver grabbed the child around her waist. He tucked her slight frame neatly under his arm and started toward the boat gently rocking in the water some twenty-five feet from shore. The child's cry was quickly muffled by the hand clamped down roughly across her nose and mouth. He paused and turned back.

"That's enough of that. Tell her to stay quiet. Good girls who follow directions don't get hurt. As her caretaker you should have instructed her."

Quickly she translated, though she knew the girl had already understood, adding, "This is for your own good. Soon, you will be able to help your father and grandparents. Think of your family. Do what he says." The girl nodded and ceased to struggle.

The driver hoisted the girl higher so that her head rested on his shoulder, holding her securely against his broad chest. He placed her right arm around his neck and with gestures, indicated she place her left arm on the other side.

She almost called out, "She speaks English, you know." But she didn't. The girl was smart; she would realize how valuable that secret might be. Learn and process information without telling anyone that you could. She had survived that way herself—always appeared a step ahead. Something that was mistaken for uncanny intuitive abilities, not merely second language proficiency.

She took a step forward around a clump of sea oats only to see better but he motioned for her to get back in the car then moved quickly again across the sand with his captive. She watched as he held the child above the water, cradled in two strong arms before wading toward the skiff. The twinkling lights of a larger boat, perhaps a yacht, blinked against the horizon. More proof of the vast amount of money there was in this business. But had the rewards ever offset the peril? Perhaps, unless you had a conscience. And she felt a sudden wash of relief. Her decision had been made. She would never watch someone be taken against her will into a life unknown. She took a couple deep breaths. It wasn't her imagination; she felt lighter.

She checked her watch. One a.m. She needed to get back. Safely, she could be gone between eleven p.m. and four a.m.—not sooner and not later. The dormitory held twenty-three women who would descend the stairs to the dining room, single-file, at precisely six a. m. after the five-thirty mass held in the chapel on the second floor. Every weekday morning. Routine. A bother, but also comforting.

She settled against the cushiony, padded leather of the Lincoln's backseat and adjusted her seatbelt. Odd. But there was always more demand for deliveries during the holidays. Christmastime. Maybe if she thought of her young wards as gifts—presents for the very wealthy, she would feel better. A person would be less likely to mistreat a gift. But that wasn't necessarily logical. She sighed. She was too tired to wonder about that. Tired? Or was it a complete relief that she felt? Relief at the finality of this one last delivery.

After a delivery there was always a quiet time. But tonight was different. All the fear and angst seemed to be draining away. And there were so many demands this time of year. She would be able to throw herself into holiday preparations—distance herself and begin to heal, put behind her what some might call atrocities. She had never lost her child-like wonder at the Church's pageantry. Christ's birth. Such a joyous time of celebration. It always gave her a renewed faith in the world. She needed to recapture that belief now.

She would whole-heartedly take advantage of the opportunity to start over. She was still in her twenties; a full life was ahead of her. She had choices. She might have to disappear for a while but the Leader would help her—would be there for her. She could leave the country. She had learned the language of her parents but could she go to some obscure village where prying eyes wouldn't follow? Probably not. She had been spoiled by convenience, by the modern world … by a laptop and a smart phone. She smiled. She and Father. Now *there* was someone addicted to instant communication. The slamming of the car door startled her. A quick check of her watch. She would get back on time. She turned her head away from the window, relaxed and closed her eyes as the car rolled forward and navigated a short incline to reach the highway.

"Hey, Sister … you want anything? I'm gonna get a beer."

She opened her eyes. Had she been asleep? She toyed with asking for a soft drink but shook her head. They had pulled up in the back parking lot of a bar; its flashing neon invitation to 'Come On In' reflecting in pools of water around the car. She had slept so soundly she hadn't realized it had rained. She watched as her driver got out and talked briefly with a man smoking outside the back entrance. He bummed a cigarette and took a few drags before following him into the building. Then she curled her legs up under her, snuggled against the plush leather upholstery and, once again, closed her eyes.

Suddenly she was jolted awake. She'd lost all track of time but the car had abruptly stopped—when had the driver come back? Where were they? She sat up straighter and peered into the darkness before checking her watch. They had been traveling for half an hour but there was no landmark that she recognized. They were beside the highway that ran alongside the ocean, but they should be back within the edges of civilization by now. The blackness of the night was complete; it was impossible to get her bearings even though she'd traveled this route many times before.

The driver was outside the car talking on his phone. Bursts of anger punctuated by a fist slamming down on the front fender. What did it mean? He was relatively new. This was maybe the second or third time she'd worked with him but that didn't mean he wasn't a legitimate mule. Wasn't that the word that was used to describe those in the step 'n fetch-it ranks? Underlings who made a lot of money looking the other way? Delivering contraband? Collecting money … killing. He had known the codes, those passwords she was sworn to protect with her life. Just because he wasn't her regular driver didn't mean that he wasn't the real thing. And just that—a driver. Yet, she was uneasy. She had trusted him with the opportunity to make a large sum of money in exchange for her freedom. She was certain that the Leader had sent this opportunity to her. She had no need to worry. She was safe.

He walked to her side of the car, in the back behind the driver's seat and just stood looking at her. She held her head up and met his gaze. Then he jerked the door open and grabbed her arm. With his right hand he crossed himself.

"This is not my idea."

A stab of fear. She could hardly breathe. "Let me go."

"No, Sister." He twisted her arm behind her and pressed her sideways, dragging her to the back of the car. Leveraging her against the cold metal, he held her immobile while he fumbled with a key ring in his free hand finally leaning forward to insert a key in the trunk's lock. She heard the lid pop open.

Chapter Two

Sister Angelica opened the door quietly. These younger girls liked to sleep in—get their beauty rest—right up until the moment they needed to be at Mass. She stifled a snort of a laugh. Beauty rest? Didn't that smack of vanity? Sister Leah was one of the young, foreign nuns with heavy, straight black hair that reached past her waist. Even drawn up under her veil, strands would escape to dangle alongside her face. It needed to be cut but Sr. Leah seemed to take pride in its luster and abundance. Sr. Angelica had left pamphlets containing bits of scripture warning against the sins of the overly proud. But they were ignored. And those rosebud lips—did she use color? More than gloss to make them shine that way? The girl seemed obsessed with carnal beauty, and Sister knew enough of the world to know men would find her irresistible.

Quickly she admonished herself. She had no right to criticize or ponder what men might be attracted to. She was certainly not one to judge God's chosen or cast aspersions. Didn't she know how very precious every maiden of Christ was? How very few chose this path nowadays? And for those who did, each was to be cherished and fostered along her journey, not discouraged, or criticized. Sr. Leah was compassionate and caring. The Church was right to open its arms to Filipino, Hispanic, Indian, Chinese—any and all young women who professed a love for Christ. After all, wasn't it written in Genesis 1:27 ... *So God created man in His own image.*

Scripture always comforted her—reminded her of what was right. In the old days ... ah, a phrase she too often uttered anymore—the result of being on this earth some eighty-seven years ... but when she was young, the choices were few—an unwelcome marriage to an older, pious but excruciatingly dull widower. Or, as the oldest girl, maybe it would be years of taking care of her parents, staying on the farm in Nebraska, no chance of college, of travel, seeing the world—learning about it. What is that phrase used today? It wasn't rocket science to know that her choice of the church had been the right one—the only one. She truly wasn't sorry. Her life had been good. There had been no corporeal husband, no children—Oh dear, there she went again thinking in the past tense. She hadn't been called yet; she had a few good years left. Years to devote to new young women following their calling. She shouldn't dwell on what hadn't been. The church could still use her wisdom, her experience—as with these young sisters.

Sister Leah, for example, was an oddity. She would stop short of calling her a misfit—not everyone who answered the calling had to fit a certain mold. Still, a Chinese young woman, an orphan, to hear her tell it, from the streets taken in by Christians—wealthy, educated ones that gave her opportunities she could have only dreamt of. She certainly had different interests, different values—different experiences. The other girls were welcoming; it wasn't that. And she certainly spent adequate time in prayer … and volunteered to do more than her share of helping in the kitchen or cleaning the vestry. Or doing mission work among the poor or homeless. Maybe if she weren't so shy. A conversation was almost impossible. The word "inscrutable" came to mind. Oh dear, wasn't that word ethnically inappropriate? One had to be so careful these days. But still, Sr. Leah just wasn't very forthcoming.

She poked her head into the young woman's room then pushed the door wider open. That was strange. The bed was perfectly made. All folded hospital corners, taut sheets, perfectly draped quilt, pillows fluffed without the indentation of someone having slept on them.

And that was just it. No one had. She felt sure of it. But then, perhaps, Sister Leah had gone out very early. But it was only five-thirty now. The sun wasn't up. Why would she have left the house in the dark? Could she even remember when Sister Leah had gone up to bed? *Dancing with the Stars* always put her to sleep. Such frivolity, such nonsense. But she allowed the show. She only drew a line at *American Idol.* Young people in skimpy costumes strutting around singing off-key. There was absolutely no value in it. But possibly it was the lesser of a multitude of evils— so many shows on TV were merely indecent. Nothing to offer whatsoever. Certainly not intellectually challenging.

Should she tell someone about this breach in rules

of conduct? No, she wasn't punitive. Not a word would be uttered until she'd first confronted Sister Leah. There might be a very good reason for her absence. Still, she felt unsettled. Some vague feeling of foreboding. She quickly drew the door toward her and softly closed it. All the girls were now at Mass. She turned and walked briskly toward the chapel.

The jangle of the phone in the downstairs foyer echoed through the quiet house. Oh dear, would the cook be able to pick up before it interrupted Mass? Sister Angelica turned and hurried toward the stairs as the second volley of bell tones seemed to impart urgency. No one in this close-knit religious community had a cell phone. All relied on this single landline for messages. Well, that was not exactly true. Father seemed overly proud of his iPhone—overly intrigued by that sweet-voiced woman who would give him the Yankee's scores without him having to look them up. It didn't seem right but it was the way of the world. She sighed. She remembered picking up the receiver when she was young to hear a pleasant voice say, "Central." And she knew she had a real person on the line—often more than one, as the term "party line" had real meaning. But today? She had no idea how things worked anymore and certainly one needed an entirely new vocabulary to just function. She paused at the bottom step to take a breath before answering.

"St. Augustine Convent—Hand Maidens of the Precious Blood." She knew she sounded wheezy. It was those stairs. An electric lift would be so helpful—a chair that ran on rails which followed the bannister; she'd seen pictures. Pie-in-the-sky, perhaps, but maybe if she prayed.

"I'm sorry. Could you repeat that?" She needed to

pay attention. Too often any more her mind wandered. "Cai Ling? I think you mean Sister Leah. Yes, yes, this is her residence. She's not here at the moment. Who is this again?"

Local law enforcement? She glanced at the wall clock, just past five-thirty—what could be so important that it couldn't wait until after breakfast? Or at least until after Mass.

"You need someone to identify … to identify a body?" Sister Angelica now held the receiver with two hands but felt her knees give way just as the cook stepped out of the kitchen.

"Sister?"

She waved the cook away and managed to whisper, "Father … get Father," before slumping against the wall.

Chapter Three

"I just knew I'd love St Augustine. This is Santa Fe by the sea. We're not in Daytona anymore, Toto."

Their introduction to Florida had been to chase down the supposed death of five very expensive and well-insured racing dogs. But the NASCAR supporting, bike-week promoting community of Daytona Beach couldn't hold a candle to the absolute ancient majesty of St. Augustine. Elaine was right, this city was special but that didn't mean he couldn't tease her.

"Be fair. You're going to miss Sadie and Fucher and the Greyhound track."

"Okay, maybe a little. But this place is magic."

Elaine grabbed his hand and pulled him across George Street to look in the window of yet another tourist trap.

Well, maybe that was a bit harsh. Dan had to admit that the street was fun—especially if you were a people watcher. Closed to traffic, cobblestone walkway, old trees shading park benches, storefronts a study in quaintness—actually, what was not to like? And the holiday season made it magical. Strings of lights defined rooftops and doorways, trees and lampposts. It seemed these bright dots outlined everything. It was no wonder that the trolleys were full of sightseers night after night. It must feel like rolling along through wonderland. Didn't Tourist Advisor magazine rank it as the number one holiday destination in the USA?

And speaking of people watching, he noticed the glances and they weren't directed at him. The woman on his arm was a looker—wavy dark hair pushed back from her face by a red and green paisley scarf to spill out across her shoulders, jeans that hugged her curves like a second skin, short faux fur vest in bright red … forty-six didn't look half this good on other women. And as of one month ago, she was his wife.

Elaine didn't drop his hand but pulled him toward her for a quick kiss. "I'm glad we have some time before you have to report for work."

"Yeah, United Life and Casualty has a heart after all."

"C'mon, they're not going to be mean to their lead investigator. Not on his honeymoon."

"Doesn't look like it." Dan turned back to the store window and studied the display of antique toy soldiers. Then, a sideways glance at Elaine, "Well, actually …"

Elaine didn't wait for him to complete the sentence before stepping between him and the display, making him look her in the eye, "Actually, *what?* Why do I get a feeling that you know something that I don't?"

"Got a text this morning. One of those 'as long as you're there' sort of things. It seems that the St. Augustine Basilica is missing some very expensive, very precious artifacts."

"I knew it!" Elaine pulled away and moved to a bench near the store's entrance and sat down heavily in feigned exasperation, slumping back and stretching her legs out in front of her before crossing her arms. "This was all just too good to be true. Renting a motel room for a couple weeks was just a ruse—keep the new bride from catching onto 'this is work, not play'—a make-believe honeymoon."

"No ruse, no make-believe. I don't think we'll be here any longer than a couple weeks. A few interviews, make sure the church custodian didn't pocket an apostle's distal phalanx—still leaves lots of time for sightseeing and good restaurants. I don't think we could get stuck in a better spot."

"Wait. An apostle's what?"

"Tip of the thumb. In this case surrounded by other relics in a lined, carved, bejeweled box of elder bark. Street value of over a million. Insured value $1.2 million and that's based on an old appraisal. "

"You'd think something like that would be protected— kept in a safe, at the very least."

"This one was traveling, being passed among designated churches across the states. I agree; one would think that better safeguards would have been in place, but that's for me to find out. I wanted to stop by the church today. Just informal, get the lay of the land—so to speak."

"We're walking?"

"It's on King—between George and Charlotte Streets. Not far."

"When did this happen?"

"Day before yesterday—well, it was discovered then and reported the same day."

"Truthfully, I really wouldn't mind visiting the Basilica. It represents the oldest Christian congregation to continuously worship in the same parish in the U.S.—dates back to 1565. Let's see, it's survived being burned to the ground twice, deterioration by salt air another couple times, and a sacking by Sir Francis Drake."

"Somebody's been reading the tourist brochures."

"Hey, I like to keep up. It *is* the seat of the Catholic Bishop of St. Augustine. Not every church gets to be called a Basilica."

+ + +

And somehow, Basilica was the better name, Dan decided as he opened the heavy, double doors to the entry. Vaulted ceilings, polished wooden pews and flooring, stained glass, paintings depicting the stations of the cross dueling for recognition with the carving of Christ on a giant cross hanging above the dais. The nave was enormous with two alcoves jutting out to either side of the center aisle. Would three hundred people fit within these walls? Four hundred? More? The choir loft alone could accommodate thirty, at least.

"It's beautiful." Elaine spoke in hushed tones. "This part was completed in 1797."

Dan nodded. What was it about a church like this that somehow, silently demanded reverence? But he whispered back, "I noticed an office off the foyer. I'm going to see if I can talk with the person who called in the claim."

Dan walked back up the aisle counting some twenty-five people either kneeling or sitting with clasped hands and bowed heads in pews close to the front, seemingly in prayer. Dan stole a look at the confessionals. Again, several people appeared to be waiting their turns. The church was popular. And that was the problem with a public place such as this. It couldn't be locked up, removed from its parishioners. It was here to be used. Open, unprotected, inviting to the nefarious as well as the religious. Was there any verbiage in UL&C's policy that specified how the relics were to be stored when not being used? Relics were often displayed at the end of a service, made available for the devout to come forward and pay their respects—some touching, even kissing the bit of antiquity purported to be a part of an apostle or saint. Were they on display before and after a service? In plain view? A lot of questions needed answers.

He pushed the office door open to find yet another group of people waiting to speak to the single woman sitting at a desk behind a waist-high partition. She looked harried and Dan counted three separate calls that came in during the first five minutes he was there. But finally it was his turn. He presented his card and succinctly reiterated the reason for his visit.

"A name? Someone to speak to? That would be Father Al. He's not one of our regulars, just on loan for the Christmas season. He was, however, the one traveling with the relics. Let me take your card; I'll see that he gets it." With that, he was dismissed, she clearly called out, "Next," and he felt a rush of annoyance.

He was not about to relinquish his spot in line—not after a fifteen minute wait. "I'm sorry I need a little more. I need to set up interview times, contacts, photograph whatever safety measures had been taken. Please understand, whether or not the policy holder can recoup some one million two hundred thousand dollars in insurance money depends upon it. I suggest you don't want to impede an investigation."

He was startled when the woman whose nameplate said she was Alice burst into tears, jerked open the middle drawer of her desk, brought out a wad of Kleenex and loudly blew her nose.

"Well, I don't know what right you have to be so demanding, right on top of the murder. That poor girl. Thank God, she had been chosen by Christ. They said she'd been mutilated and even …" Here her index finger pointed to her own anatomy beneath the desk. "You know …" More pointing, a wagging back and forth of her finger.

But Dan was getting the idea of molestation, maybe rape. He also felt like he'd just been dropped into a conversation on Mars. What was she talking about?

"I think I can help here." A man sitting along the wall handed him a folded newspaper. "Morning headlines. Keep it, I'm finished."

"Thanks." Dan stepped out of line and opened the paper. Body of Nun Found in Gamble Rogers Preserve. The entire front page was devoted to the incident.

Related? A connection to the missing relics? Doubtful, but something he'd probably have to rule out. Sigh. That just added a week or more onto their stay. It probably made sense to rent an efficiency. Or, just bite the bullet and take a vacation rental, some Airbnb if they could find one at this late date during the holidays. Cheaper in the long run if this dragged out for a month. It would go on the expense account but that didn't mean he could be frivolous.

"Alice, do you have a number for Father Al?"

Alice glanced at him, excused herself from helping the family standing in front of her and scribbled something on a scrap of paper. "This is the rectory number. Use it. I'd make an appointment first if I were you—not just show up. There is protocol and this is the Basilica."

Dan vaguely felt something more was expected of him—a bowing of the head, genuflection, the sign of the cross? Ah, now he was just being snide, but overly pompous, front office gatekeepers irritated him. He offered a "thank you" and felt her watch him until he'd gone back through the door to the foyer.

"Thought I'd lost you." Elaine motioned for him to follow her outside. She pushed open the heavy front door. "Whispering drives me nuts. Ok, you don't look very happy. What happened?"

He told her what Alice had shared, going lightly on the rape and mutilation parts but added, "Looks like one investigation is going to impact the other."

"You can't be certain."

"Certain enough to want to look for more comfortable quarters. I'm worried that a murder investigation might interfere—keep me from interviewing witnesses in a timely manner, for example. I'm going to be low man on the totem pole. So, I don't rule out our being here past New Year's."

"You know, I won't really mind. I want to invite Jason to spend the holidays with us. There's probably some unwritten rule about taking children on honeymoons, but he loves the ocean. And I think he needs a real break from school. He seemed tired and preoccupied at the wedding."

"I think that's a great idea. The kid's twenty; I bet if we provide a bed we still won't see much of him. A little salt air might be just the thing."

Chapter Four

There's luck and then there's that kind of good fortune that defies logic. Dan held no hope that there would be a rental available, spur-of-the-moment for three people and maybe a dog, one block from the ocean. But a change of plans had led to a couple's last minute cancellation and the travel agent had gushed her approval of the townhouse—great neighborhood, quiet, gated and safe, *and* the owners would allow a pet. Dan crossed his fingers that there wouldn't be a size/weight limitation. Simon was a one hundred and forty pound Rottweiler. Wasn't that breed at the top of everyone's scare list? Well, maybe number two after Pit Bulls. Simon was with Dan's mother at the moment and there was every possibility that she might want to keep him for a while. Dan wasn't sure Maggie was over her recent near-death experience and a big furry alarm system might be just what the doctor ordered.

"I think we're in luck." He reiterated the specifics to Elaine.

"Oh my God, two baths/two bedrooms, a study, large kitchen and living room—it sounds perfect." Elaine was ecstatic. "When can we take a look?"

"I've arranged for us to meet the agent there after lunch."

+ + +

And it *was* perfect. The furnishings tasteful and new—right down to a full array of Le Creuset cookware. Until the day when the two of them could empty the storage unit in Hobbs, New Mexico and move their joint household goods to somewhere permanent, this kind of temporary housing more than made life comfortable. They took it for two months with a right to renew up to six months on a month-to-month basis.

"I'm feeling pretty lucky about now. New wife. New digs. The ocean about a block away. But here's the tough question—think you can share an office? We may be here long enough for you to take an online course or two."

Having a partner was new for him but Elaine had started certification coursework at Daytona State College to become a private investigator. A far cry from her first career as a university professor, but he was impressed with how much she seemed to like it. If she stayed on track, she'd have the compulsory AA degree in criminology and a PI license by spring. He'd wrangled an unpaid internship for her from UL&C. So, he'd just married the love of his life and now they were hanging a shingle together. Too much together time? He didn't think so, but guessed he'd find out.

"I don't know. Should I have read the fine print on the marriage license? Are there going to be other challenges?" Mock-seriousness but the grin said she was kidding. "We haven't even discussed whose name goes first on any shared stationery. If we do it alphabetically, I win by a hair—Linden before Mahoney."

"Hey, I thought you were a Mahoney, too. Guess we'll have to arm wrestle over position."

"Don't be so sure you'd win." But she pulled him toward her for a quick kiss before continuing down a short hallway. "Dan, look. The second bedroom is next to the back entrance. That's perfect for Jason. His comings and goings won't bother us at all. I know he'll appreciate the privacy. I'll call him today."

"He could even have company and we'd never know." Dan waited for Elaine's reaction.

"Oh. I'm not sure I'm ready for that, but, yes, guests would be welcome. Is this some kind of modern parenting test?"

"No, but you passed."

He was going to suggest that they christen the master bedroom when his phone rang. He wondered what it said about him that the ringtone sounded like it belonged to a 1950s rotary. He pulled his phone from his back pocket. He was fifty-two years old but the sleek, modern phones that could do everything on verbal command made him feel old. Even this one at three years of age was old by modern standards. He checked the screen. Not a number he recognized but, at least, it was a local prefix. Of course, anymore that could mean a robo-call.

"Mahoney here ... Father ... thanks for returning my call." Dan caught Elaine's attention and held up four fingers mouthing "today" then waited for her to nod. "Four o'clock it is at the rectory."

Chapter Five

The rectory of the Cathedral Basilica of St. Augustine connected to the church on the left and blended perfectly with the cut stone edifice of the older structure. The building's spire rose majestically drawing the eye upward beyond the curved dome of the parish center. A private parking area was discreetly out of sight from the street. The word 'serene' came to mind, or maybe 'tranquil' was a better fit. Dan guessed both words were appropriate but odd to include a parking lot in the assessment. Double seven-foot carved wooden doors topped the six front steps. A small, stenciled, copper plaque inviting them to "Come In" hung from a hook beneath a tiny, shuttered window in the center of the door protected by decorative wrought iron.

"Is there anything that isn't grand about this parish?" Again hushed tones as Elaine took in the shiny marble floors and seemingly endless polished wood accents in the foyer—doors, stained glass transoms, upholstered benches along the walls, oils depicting scenes from the days of Ponce de Leon. According to a schedule prominently posted inside a glass case in the entry, there were tours of the grounds and buildings every afternoon at two.

This time, however, the woman behind the information desk was briskly efficient and even offered a welcoming smile. "I'm Janice, Father's secretary. He's expecting you, but just give me a moment to tell him you're here."

Funny, Dan thought, no Administrative Assistant title. One rarely heard the term "secretary" any more. But it was somehow more in keeping with the trappings of antiquity that surrounded him. Hadn't Elaine pointed out that this was one of the first places of worship, of dedicated churches, in the United States?

Janice rose from behind the desk and tapped on the closed door to her right. She opened the door, said something that Dan couldn't hear before turning and motioning them forward. "Father Pete will see you now." She remained at the door until they had entered, then pulled it closed. Certainly a nice personal touch, Dan observed, but the door hadn't shut before he'd seen two plainclothesmen and a female police officer enter the foyer behind them. The paper hadn't given many facts about the nun's death—mainly that it appeared to be an abduction and murder. Rape wasn't mentioned but Dan figured someone who worked on the inside would have better knowledge. He trusted the information shared by the office matron next door.

The priest stood behind yet another grand antique piece of furniture and gestured toward two equally handsome carved wooden chairs in front of him. He was a synonym for the word gangly, Dan thought. Over six feet tall, he was wearing baggy brown robes with a hood in the style of a medieval monk and an honest-to-gosh rope tie was at his waist. His hair was dark fringe rounding his egg-shaped head and just dusting his ears at the edge of a self-made tonsure. A step back in time—that was for sure. How odd. Of course, in a town that prided itself on having the best alligator farm on the planet, a Ripley's Believe It or Not, and sponsored daily ghost-detecting tours, perhaps, the priest was dressed appropriately.

"Have a seat. Oh, sorry, looks like we're going to be interrupted before we get started." The door had opened again and Janice motioned for Father to join her in the hallway. "I'll try to keep this short." A forced smile before a more grim resolve replaced it.

Small town, huge Catholic influence, the diocese of the Bishop and one of their own brutally killed … Dan could only imagine the horror, the fear. It certainly seemed to push the theft of an artifact to the back burner. He'd found a mention of an investigation into the disappearance of the "traveling relics" on page three of the *Record*.

When the priest returned, he seemed distracted but apologized for the interruption without a comment as to why he'd been called away.

"Mr. and Mrs. Mahoney, I believe? I'm Father Pete. Let's hope we don't have any more interruptions. I'm anxious to move our claim forward."

He pulled a folder of papers and pictures from a desk drawer but assured Dan that he'd have Janice follow up with electronic copy if he would leave his email address.

"These are older photos that I've had scanned. Pictures of the container and contents both. This was the second time the Tour of Saint Bonaventure's Relics has visited us in the last five years. We're such a strong Catholic community—several churches, the convent—the relics tour is popular. It's highly publicized and there are several events taking place during the month the exhibition is with us. Celebrations that underscore the strong ties the parish has to St. Bonaventure."

"Ah, Giovanni di Fidanza." Both men turned in unison to stare at Elaine.

"A Scholar of the Church, I see." Father Pete looked pleased.

"No, nothing so grand—my master's was in Medieval Literature. Not a degree that's even offered any more. I was raised Catholic but I am what I believe you refer to as 'lapsed'."

"You're in pretty hefty company, though, I dislike the term. Always sounds to me like something you get if you don't keep your inoculations up to date." A nervous laugh and clearing of the throat. "So you're familiar with the man's life?"

"Let's see, he studied with Thomas Aquinas at the University of Paris, and later he became a lecturer on *The Four Books of Sentences*; Peter Lombard's writings on theology." Elaine gave a quick laugh, "I know I'm showing off here but my thesis was on tracing the rhetorical devices, including references to the influence of Christianity from the eight hundreds—the first recorded Anglo Saxon writings to roughly 1250 after the Church was more established and religious treatises more prevalent. My study began with *Caedmon's Hymn* as translated by the Venerable Bede down to several of the collected works thought to be by St. Bonaventure."

"I'm assuming you still might be involved with university life?"

"I've taught on the college level for more years than I care to share. I've currently just finished a sabbatical. In fact, I'm looking into a degree in investigative science. Possibly becoming a business partner with my husband." Dan returned Elaine's smile.

"What an interesting plan. I wish you well. If you'd like to make use of that previous degree, I hold seminars on church history once a month. Perhaps, you would consider sharing your expertise with our group?"

"I would enjoy that. Keep me in mind."

If Dan hadn't felt like a fifth wheel before, he certainly did now. But secretly he was pretty proud of this smart woman he called wife. And hadn't she just more than established their credentials? Convinced the man in charge that they knew what they were doing—well, that made one of them anyway.

"I'm sure you've put two and two together—why the Bonaventure relics are of such interest to us here—the Franciscan connection, that is."

"Yes, I believe St. Bonaventure was the founder of the Franciscan order only to be replaced in importance by the Jesuits. St. Augustine is the oldest continuing Franciscan parish in the States," Elaine volunteered.

"Ah, another A+!" Father Pete could not look more pleased, Dan thought; he was fairly beaming. "But there was little enjoyment in accomplishment. He was yet another churchman to be struck down at the height of his career—

most of the history books seem to suspect poison. I'm sorry to say competition was often deadly—even among the church's hierarchy. Jealousy as a sin has been around for awhile."

"Poison was popular in those days. It's interesting that it's had somewhat of a resurgence today." Dan finally offered something, innocuous though it was. "Correct me if I'm wrong but I believe St. Bonaventure's right arm and hand are still extant and can be viewed in Bagnoregio, Italy? Not far from his birthplace? I haven't found anything that says a part of those skeletal remains have been divided or parceled out. Is there a written history of the bones that were here on tour?" More than one person could do the research, Dan thought smugly even if United Life and Casualty had emailed a crib sheet of facts when he took the job.

"Yes, and no. Faith is an important element of the Church and its teachings—I might add, that's an understatement. But the written history dating to the gift being made to the chapel near his birthplace in 1491 *is* well documented. It was timely because his tomb in Lyon was plundered by the Huguenots some seventy years later and his remains were burned in the square. His head, however, according to most accounts survived only to disappear during the French revolution."

Dan was beginning to think that some of this came under the heading of too much information. He needed to bring Father back on topic. "So just what bones were a part of the tour?"

"Proximal and distal phalanges. An oral history has them being given to Pope Sixtus IV when St. Bonaventure was canonized April 14, 1482. That would not have been out of the ordinary. In fact, it's very believable, and the hand-carved box holding the relics has been dated to the latter fifteenth century which gives further credence to that time frame."

Dan leaned forward and picked up the stack of photos Father Pete had placed in front of him and rifled through the pictures selecting a close-up of the box. Plain, yet striking in its simplicity, it was, in fact, a rectangle—not a mock cathedral or intricate crown. A cross ran the entire length of its flat top. The one color photo showed the cross to be of heavy gold set with cabochon cut precious stones about the size of his thumbnail. Rubies? Dan thought so. The color photo captured their deep red glow. Silver scrollwork softened any sharp corners and preserved the integrity of the wood frame to the point of the box being almost solid metal. There was a Latin phrase that seemed to run the length of the box and continue across the side, back, and end opposite where it began. The carvings were worn and the box seemed in poor repair. But then wasn't it over six hundred years old? There were no hinges, or latches. The top was really a lid indented and carved to snugly fit on top of the container. Dan made a note to get a translation of any writings. But he suspected they supported the carvings, which appeared to be the Stations of the Cross—in number, at least.

"I know you can't tell from the photos but the inscription is inlaid with gold foil. A lot of it is missing." Dan thought Father Pete was going to add something but then changed the subject. "We were lucky to get the relic this close to Christmas—it's a special treat—a bigger draw even than our usual pageantry."

"What is it about relics that speak to people today?

What do you think they walk away with?" Dan paused. Was the question too non-Catholic? Maybe showed heretic leanings?

Father Pete didn't seem offended, "Relics can form a bridge, help people by offering something tangible to overcome the abstract. Saints can intercede, not perform miracles per se, but make the path easier to receive answers to prayer directly from God. In the Middle Ages, Funerary Halls were erected near the burial sites of saints for the devout, as it was felt just being buried near a saint could aid in the struggle to enter the world beyond death."

"I'm assuming there's a well-established black market for these things?"

"I'm afraid so. A thriving, very lucrative one, unfortunately replete with forgeries. And very difficult to trace the guilty. For those privy to the secrets of the 'dark net', inquirers can remain invisible. Relics can be bid on and exchange hands and never be detected.

"Yet, I'd like to give man the benefit of the doubt. The more complex and confusing our modern world becomes, the more people want a simpler way to connect with God. People want to be heard and protected. They want life to be simple but have meaning. The bartering for relics is rife with those willing to spend a fortune to create this for themselves. Not unlike royalty in the Middle Ages— collecting and dealing in relics was big business back then, too.

"Of course, relics did their part for commerce. Villages with churches known to house them gave rise to our present day inns—the first motels and hotels across the countryside. And the first known mass transit, so to speak. The pilgrimages became sources of revenue for villages along the way. The community often accepted donations on behalf of the saints. But the feeding and housing of the visitors turned into the really prosperous business."

"Interesting that this practice continues today—visitors from around the world traveling to view celebrated artifacts of Church history. What is the best known relic we have today?"

"There are many relics touted as representative of Jesus—the Shroud of Turin is, perhaps, the most famous."

"Of course." He should have known that. Dan referred to his notes. Time to rein in the chit-chat. "I need to know when your loss was discovered and where the box was kept while it was here."

"It seems like a year but only seventy-two hours ago. The box was kept in a glass-fronted, three-foot square, shadow-box to the right of the altar in the vestry, bolted to a steel frame, I might add. And the frame was then in turn bolted to the floor. It's a permanent fixture. We refer to it as a 'relics safe' and use it for up to six different displays during the year. The glass is known as 'blast-proof'—stronger than bullet resistant. The very elaborate safe can be on full display for parishioners, but it cannot be moved and only opened by those with the combination. It was in complete compliance with UL&C's regulations."

"I'm not understanding—then, how was the safe compromised?"

"It was opened. Someone had the combination to the lock."

"Are you saying there was no forced entry?" Father Pete shook his head. "Who was privy to the combination?"

"Myself, of course, and Willis Johnson our grounds man and custodian, Father Al who traveled with the relics, of course, and the young nun who supervised our basic housecleaning chores."

"I'll need to speak to each person. Will Janice be able to set up individual appointments for me?"

"Yes, I've already alerted her that you would be using the conference room here at the rectory. It would be possible to begin tomorrow if that time agrees with your schedule?"

Dan nodded, the sooner, the better. "Have all of these people been alerted to the fact that I will be interviewing them?"

"Yes, well, not exactly everyone …" Father Pete paused and seemed agitated twirling a massive gold ring on his left hand. Dan waited. Finally, the priest leaned forward with elbows on the desk and his face in his hands. "A moment, please …"

"Of course."

When he looked up, he took several deep breaths. "I'm sure you've read about our loss. Sister Leah was an important part of our community. She'd been with us less than two years but I've never met a harder worker—someone so responsible, so compassionate—unusual in someone so young. She was in charge of housekeeping and had access to the relic safe"

"My condolences. I can't imagine how shocking this has been, so unbelievably sad." Elaine added, "I'm sure the community is strong but the not knowing …"

"There's no word on what happened?" Dan asked.

"None. Frankly, it's baffling, to say the least."

"Do you have any reason to believe that the two criminal acts are related—other than they appear to have taken place within the same timeframe?"

A pause, more fidgeting, then. "I would have sworn before God that the events were not connected in any way … until …"

Dan waited. "I'm sorry that this is painful but—"

"No, no, I understand." A deep breath, "Earlier when Janice interrupted us? It was the very news I would have never expected, but the coroner has reported finding scrapings of gold foil beneath Sister Leah's fingernails on her right hand. The foil, because of its purity and inclusions, is thought to be centuries old. I believe it came from the inscription on the elder bark container."

Chapter Six

Dan was really thankful for the townhouse because instinct told him they would be in St. Augustine for a while. Suddenly a cut and dried investigation had just turned into a whole new challenge—and a lot more work. Gold foil underneath the fingernails? That certainly brought suspicion of wrong-doing home. There was a big difference between chasing down a lead into international black market dealings in antiquities, and a local murder—of a nun, no less. Somehow that last made the crime doubly sinister. As naive as it sounded, a nun should be exempt from torture and murder. Now his life would include coroner's reports, police intervention and God knew what else … probably throwing God into the mix was more apt than he even realized. He just knew he'd need all the help he could get.

His second cup of coffee was getting cold. He was down to making lists of lists—things he had to do which depended on other things he had to do first—and the sooner the better. He had a feeling the lists wouldn't get shorter. Not by themselves, anyway.

"Still here?" Elaine joined him at the breakfast table, a towel wrapped around her head and a terry cloth robe belted loosely at the waist. It appeared she wasn't wearing anything underneath but Dan quickly shut down that way of thinking. He had to get to work.

"Putting off the inevitable. But I need to get going. I have an appointment at the county morgue at ten. It'll be interesting to see what the take is on the gold foil."

Elaine's phone jiggled across the table. "I should have taken it off vibrate last night. I wonder if I've missed any calls." She pushed the answer button and put the phone to her ear. "Yes, this is she. Good morning, Janice. Ten? That would be fine. Thank you for calling."

"Hot date?"

"With Father Pete." Elaine laughed. "He wants to include me in the lecture series he mentioned and share some of the materials they've already covered this year. Sounds like I might get my pick of topics and dates."

"Lucky you. Sounds more like it would be difficult to coordinate lunch today, how about dinner out?"

"Now you have a date. I even have an idea for a dessert that you might like." Elaine laughed and headed back toward the bedroom.

+ + +

Janice grabbed a pad and pen and followed Elaine into Father Pete's office. There were several flyers laid out across the edge of his desk facing one of the chairs for guests. Handouts, Elaine guessed and was right.

"Here's a twelve month history of topics covered this year. We hand out flyers and mail a few, in addition to articles in the newsletter. Turnout has been exceptional."

The materials appeared to be professionally done—good use of color with verbiage kept to a minimum. Elaine picked up the nearest one, which announced a discussion of "Genesis and the Big Bang Theory." There was even a picture of Sheldon, from the TV series, pointing to the title. Another asked the question, "Did Women Write the Psalms?" The topics lacked the stodginess one might expect of the Church. These were "now" topics. No wonder the sessions were so popular. She'd have to keep that in mind when she decided what to talk about.

"I'd like you to be the first presenter for this year's lecture series. We'll begin on January 6—Epiphany. It's a Sunday and there will be other festivities that day, which should guarantee a good-sized audience for you. We often have a pot luck supper, say six to eight and you would have the eight to ten slot—maybe an hour and a half presentation and thirty minute Q and A. How does that sound?"

"Perfect." Elaine entered the date and time in her phone's calendar. "May I borrow some of these?" She pointed to the array of materials in front of her.

"Of course. Whatever you need and I will make certain I'm available if you have questions. I hate to put a deadline on you already but if you could send me a suggested layout for a flyer, maybe by Friday, I'd appreciate it. Thank you again for accepting my invitation. I look forward to the event."

Elaine tucked her phone in a front pocket of her purse and started to stand.

"Uh, Ms. Mahoney, I'd like another fifteen minutes of your time, if I may."

"Yes, of course, Father."

He sat staring at her, hands steepling, index fingers pressed against his lips. "Excuse me, I'm not sure where to start. First, let me tell you how impressed I am with your background—teaching on the college level and now striking out in a totally new direction. I admire people who continue to learn, try new things. It shows character. And, quite frankly, I think it keeps you young."

Elaine wasn't necessarily certain about that but there didn't seem to be a need to say anything. Curiosity, however, was getting ready to choke the cat. It was dawning on her that whatever this was, it was the real reason she'd been asked to meet with him today.

A sigh, deep breath, then, "I need a temporary housemother, for lack of a better word. Well, not me personally," a chuckle, "but someone for the convent. Sister Angelica is elderly—"

"She's eighty-seven." Janice interrupted. "Far too old to have the responsibility of twenty-three young women. They've taken advantage of her. We're fortunate that this is our first 'incident'—the loss of Sister Leah."

"Well, now, we don't want to be sharing gossip, but there's reason to believe that Sister Leah had gone out earlier in the evening ... on that night. And there are whisperings that it wasn't the first time. This is alarming, to say the least and now that she has been linked to the disappearance of the relics ... well, I think you can see the predicament we're in. I need someone who can be trusted to, if possible, find out what was going on. More exactly, find out if she was involved in the theft."

"I see."

"I'm offering the position to you because of your work with young people of this age. I think the oldest of the women with us is thirty-seven. Five have taken their vows but eighteen are novitiates. And you seem to have a very keen interest in investigative procedures. The position is temporary, as I mentioned. I cannot get a permanent replacement for Sister Angelica until after the holidays. She may, at that time, choose to move to Colorado Springs, join a group of retired nuns—we've spoken of it—but until then, you would be her assistant. I also think you would be quite good at being non-competitive. I believe that you would be able to ease into the position without being viewed as threatening."

"Thank you for your confidence."

"You'll join us, then?"

"I think we need to discuss the hours first and when you would like me to start."

"Tomorrow, of course." A laugh, "I really would like you to join us as quickly as you can. You would be compensated for a forty-hour week but the hours would vary. I would like you to, quite unannounced, be able to spend the night maybe once or twice a week. Take one meal a day with us the five days that you are here and work two weekends a month—your choice."

This was not an off the cuff, spur of the moment offer—Father Pete had given this some thought. But the offer was tempting. She might be able to be of help to Dan now that a link between the murder and theft had been established.

"You'll have an office in the rectory closer to Janice who can help you with any secretarial support you might need. Bring your own computer, if you like. Your office would be a safe place to leave anything you don't want to drag back and forth. The rectory foyer is locked at night. In addition, our library is quite extensive and at your disposal. It has a distinct religious leaning but I think you'll be impressed with its size and scope. The pay, of course, might be a disappointment. We'll pay you fifteen dollars an hour. You'll be on the honor system. Keep track of your hours and give the amount to Janice at the end of the week."

"Could you be more specific—I'm still a bit foggy as to what my duties would be."

"Quite plainly stated, I want you to do some snooping. How was Sister Leah involved in the theft? What was she doing out that night? What do other women in the convent know? I want you to build trust—friendships that will make them comfortable and encourage them to talk with you. I don't need to tell you that the diocese doesn't need this kind of notoriety. I blame myself. I should have had better supervision in place. But I'm not sure I thought young adult women would need to be supervised. Still, safety is so important. A group of women together in one place could invite the attention of someone with criminal intent. However I can't lock the doors of the convent from the outside at night, now can I?"

"Father has stressed over this matter for some time. Quite frankly, we're both overwhelmed. This is a very large Parish—responsibility for every aspect of it is mindboggling. I think we've feared something like this might happen. You would be such an asset. Please help us."

Elaine looked from one to the other. Father Pete and Janice were desperate, wracked with guilt. How could she say no?

"What time is breakfast tomorrow? That might be a good time to introduce me."

+ + +

She waited to tell Dan about her new job until they'd both finished the shrimp and grits at O. C. White's, one of St. Augustine's consistently great restaurants. A corner table upstairs, subdued lighting ... finally, coffee and key lime pie.

"I think you'd be good at it. Father is right, that's your age group. I think he's asked the right person." A sip of coffee, a sly smile ... "At least you don't have to masquerade as a nun."

"You think I couldn't be believable?"

"Well, all but the chaste part."

"Why? Because you'd tell?"

"Me, tell? Nope, no way, you're my best-kept secret. Have I ever told you that I think I'm a lucky man?"

"That's endearing."

"I am thinking that I'll need to come up with a better honeymoon though—working fulltime, going undercover in a nunnery wasn't in the plan.

"Convent, I'm working in a convent."

"Kidding aside, I think having you on the inside could be helpful to my investigation, too. The coroner pointed out a couple interesting things."

"Such as?"

"The cause of death was repeated thrusts with a sharp

object. I'm assuming knife but not until after she had been raped. It was also pretty obvious that she'd fought her assailant. It appeared she'd been struck across the face and there were several bruises on her arms. The gold foil under her nails was part of minute wads of wool fabric—the type found in stiff, short-napped carpeting, like a floor mat from a car's interior or possibly the trunk."

"How awful. If the car trunk hypothesis is true, it would seem to negate, perhaps, any first-hand involvement in the theft itself. Sister Leah might have had purely accidental contact with the box."

"That's what I'm thinking, but I'm not coming up with any logical conclusion as to how or why. We still have a young nun beaten, raped, stabbed and left in an ocean-side, wildlife preserve. I think the answer is in that convent. Somebody had to have seen something or just simply knows something. I'm a little envious; you'll have the inside track, so to speak."

"Yeah, maybe. I'm trying not to get my hopes up."

"Something I didn't expect to find out is that she's Asian—probably Chinese."

"That's unusual. Any backstory? Maybe adopted? Or was she actually born in this country?"

"The investigator had received a packet of her papers from the Church to be handed off to the detectives working the case. There's been some difficulty reaching next-of-kin. According to her history she was born in Boston to a Phillip and Chu Hua Tran. Her mother worked as a translator and her father was an academic at Boston College. He had been born in Philadelphia but he did mission work in Tunnan, southern China, as a young man. He met and married her mother while there before coming back to the states. Cai

Ling was their only child and had been raised in the church going to parochial schools all of her life. She would have been twenty-five on January sixth."

"On Epiphany."

Dan nodded. "See it's all coming back, isn't it? I'm beginning to think it's a ruse—Father's getting you involved just to erase that 'lapsed' in front of your name."

Elaine laughed. "Sorry, that's just the day, a Sunday this year, that I start the lecture series with a talk whose topic is yet to be determined. Oh, I completely forgot to tell you that Jason took us up on the invitation to spend the holidays here. He's really excited and he's coming this weekend."

+ + +

The alarm went off at four forty-five. Elaine sat up, turned off the alarm and gently pushed away the arm he'd flung out to keep her next to him.

"Gotta go. I'm a working girl now. You can have this bed all to yourself for the next couple hours."

"Don't want it to myself." Dan wasn't sure what he'd just mumbled made sense. He couldn't go to bed at midnight, make wild passionate love for an hour and then after three and a half hours sleep, wake up chipper and clear-eyed and ready to meet the world. Was she that much younger? Six years shouldn't make a difference. Was he beginning to fixate on age?

"I'll be quiet." She turned and kissed him—a chaste peck in the middle of his forehead. "I'll give you a call later. But not sure when I'll be home."

Chapter Seven

Elaine was standing on the steps of the convent at exactly five-thirty. Father Pete himself opened the door. She had to admit the dark navy skirt and light blue, short-sleeved, silk blouse felt way over dressed for what should be a fun vacation—actually, a honeymoon, one complete with piña coladas, miles of sand and surf, and swimsuits. Was she having second thoughts? Yes, and no. There was something so compelling about the situation. A young person's death was always tragic but this one, doubly so.

"Shall we go up to Mass?"

She smiled and nodded, no grimacing or gritting of teeth—this was just part of the job. At least she knew the routine.

The Chapel was breathtaking. It would probably seat fifty and was half full this morning. She supposed the two people she hadn't seen before were the grounds man and the cook. An older, heavy-set nun was kneeling in the last pew. Sister Angelica, no doubt. A forest had to have been sacrificed to appoint this parish. The carved wooden pews, the dais, the altar, the inlaid beams in the ceiling—for a small room, one could only call it 'grand'.

A devotional niche to the left of the altar held a four foot tall Mary, her plaster-of- Paris blue robes swirling around her feet, her eyes demurely downcast as she looked with adoration at the porcelain baby in a wooden crib before her. The bank of prayer candles, white beeswax votives, flickered in their red glass containers to her right.

Furtive, side-long glances said the young women were curious. She wondered if they had been prepared. Had Father told them someone would be joining them? An Assistant Housemother. She could only hope her appearance was not a surprise to Sister Angelica. If anyone noticed that Elaine didn't follow the usual ritual, they didn't stare. It was amazing how quickly it all came back—the prayers, the responses, the correct way to show deference.

With practiced precision Mass ended at five minutes before six and the women left the chapel single-file to enter the dining room downstairs. Elaine again was accompanied by Father Pete and was shown to a seat at the north end of a long dining table. A place had been set for Sister Leah with a simple cross instead of cutlery and china. A nice tribute and reminder, Elaine thought.

Rapping a spoon on his water glass, Father called the group to attention.

"I know you've noticed we have a visitor this morning.

Let me introduce, Elaine Mahoney. Ms. Mahoney will be working with Sister Angelica, supporting her in general household duties. I know you join me in giving her a warm welcome." There was a smattering of polite applause. "Ms. Mahoney, would you mind sharing just a few words about your background?"

Elaine thanked Father and looked out over the group of make-up free faces. Even a touch of lip-gloss stood out in this crowd. "I caught Father Pete's attention when he learned my master's degree is in medieval literature—heavy emphasis upon liturgy. I most recently gave up a college teaching position to follow my husband to Florida. My talk on the history of Saint Bonaventure will begin the Diocese lecture series this January. In the meantime, and to make sure I don't spend all day in your wonderful library, I will be assisting Sister Angelica. My office will be in the foyer of the rectory and my policy is always 'open door.' I look forward to meeting each of you. Thank you for welcoming me into your group."

Again a round of polite applause but Elaine thought the smiles were genuine. Sister Angelica's pursed lips didn't bode well, though. It might take all of Elaine's interpersonal skills to establish a congenial relationship, but she could understand Sister's reluctance to welcome someone with open arms—someone encroaching on her territory who was not of the Church.

The fresh fruit, croissants, and yogurt disappeared, and within forty-five minutes cliques of chatting women left the dining hall. Some, who were continuing their schooling, had two hours of study hall, several others were tasked with laundry, and three young women began to clear the table.

"I'd like to see you in my office in five minutes." With a tip of her head, Sister Angelica indicated the end of the hall.

"I'll follow you there now." Elaine fell into step beside her.

Sister shut the door behind them with a little more force than was actually needed, Elaine thought. The abrupt thud vibrated along the wall.

"Please, sit." Sister pointed to a chair in front of her desk before sinking into the swivel chair behind yet another wooden monstrosity. This desk was really a table—something a couple centuries old with gargoyle-like carvings of devilish faces at the top of each leg. The legs themselves were six inches around and carved top to floor. Sister Angelica was probably five feet, two inches tall and the desk dwarfed her. She had to be sitting on a phone book, or maybe a booster chair. Elaine fought a strong urge to peek around the corner nearest her.

"I'm sure you've been told I'm an old fuddy-duddy nun who should be turned out to pasture."

"Nothing of the kind. I think working in our later years keeps us young." Elaine thought a moment and then decided to chance it—tell Sister exactly what her priorities would be. Father Pete hadn't told her not to, and it was evident that a separate mission would help Elaine fit in. "May I share something with you and count on your discretion?"

Sister leaned forward, obviously intrigued. "Of course."

"My husband was sent to St Augustine as the chief investigator for United Life and Casualty Insurance. The Basilica's missing relics were insured with his company. There is a possibility that the murder of Sister Leah and the theft are connected. I'm an intern for UL&C, finishing a degree in criminology. It cannot be known that I'm here to snoop. I'll be talking to the women with the single intention of shedding light on Sister Leah's part in this week's incidents. Nothing more. That said, I would like to offer my assistance. For example, I'll be working some evenings, looking for anyone loitering outside the convent. Or anyone attempting to leave at an odd hour, say, after curfew. Let me lock up for you on those nights. I'm certain that we could work out a schedule that would be beneficial to each of us—no matter what the task."

Sister sank against the back of her chair. "My, my. I'm thoroughly ashamed of myself. I was allowing feelings of perceived slights to take over my otherwise sound judgment. Of course, we can work together." She smiled, stood and offered her hand across the desk. Sister was fairly beaming—from relief, Elaine thought.

"I'm sure you understand the need for utter secrecy."

"Of course. You can count on me. I'll do anything needed to help solve the brutal crime of Sister Leah's death. Where will you start?"

"I'd hoped to begin with your help. Just an interview. I need to form a profile of the young woman—her routine, likes and dislikes, background—actually anything that you might think would be helpful."

"Let's not wait. I'll have more time this morning than later on. Let's go down to the kitchen; I bet Sister Rose is still there. She'll make us a nice cup of tea. I think it will look more natural to talk in the open instead of behind closed doors." She waved a hand to include the office. "I'm sure tongues are already wagging. I wouldn't want people to think there was some kind of conspiracy."

Elaine wasn't sure about the necessity of meeting in the kitchen but she nodded, stood and followed Sister Angelica out of her office. This time the door was pulled gently shut behind them. A little truth had made all the difference.

+ + +

"This may not be as comfy as the couch in my office, but the tea will be good." Sister Angelica chuckled, "I have few vices but keeping a supply of Buckingham Palace Garden Party black tea blend on hand is one of them."

Sister Rose brought each of them a Brown Betty pot of steeping tea, white china cups and saucers and tiny pitchers of milk and cream, a small, ornate bowl of natural sugar and a narrow dish of lemon wedges. Elaine could easily have been on the set for a filming of a Miss Marple mystery.

"My mother was English. I grew up with the Brown Betty. Still brews the best tea. Something about how the water circulates."

A dollop of cream, a half-teaspoon of sugar and Elaine's tea was perfect. It was nice to have an alternative breakfast beverage—not that she could ever give up her coffee or, for that matter, talk Dan into doing it, too … still this was pleasant.

"Let's start by your sharing what you remember—what stands out about Sister Leah."

"Oh, that's easy, her boundless energy. But more than that, she was efficient—she could get things done. The younger girls adored her and the older ones tolerated her."

"Tolerated?"

"Well, you know, she did invite a bit of envy—young woman on the fast track to move up. There aren't a lot of promotions for women within the Church."

"What would her next step have been?"

"After taking her permanent vows, the United States Conference of Catholic Bishops had shown interest in promoting her to a position of authority—management of one of the charities at the national level, possibly a most coveted international spokesperson position—something of that nature. She had an awe-inspiring knowledge of language—spoke quite perfect Mandarin, I'm told. I know for a fact she was being groomed for something larger than the diocese of St. Augustine."

"That would have been quite a big step. She had been with you for two years?"

"A little over. She was just completing her two years of service after having taken her vows. There wasn't a question but that she was doing her life's work—entering the sisterhood had been her life's dream. She had almost grown up in the Church—high school in a Catholic girl's school, then prestigious schooling in Boston, a college degree from Boston College in theology. Yes, I know it's a Jesuit school but the training offered in both scholarship and service is just outstanding. One of the last really strong academically supportive institutions of the Roman Catholic faith."

"Did you ever have problems—disciplinary issues— with Sister Leah?"

"I did have to counsel her about bringing her street people into the convent. She would help anyone and spent a part of almost every day on the streets and in the mission. She often traveled across the state holding workshops in other parishes—she even went as far as Miami. One evening I heard crying and found a young Filipino girl in her room. She had brought her in for a warm meal and a bath. The poor girl was just distraught, apparently missing her parents. I can't condemn that sort of dedication to providing for the less fortunate, but the Church provides and there are channels to follow. Sister couldn't have had a penny to her name the way she gave things away. I'm sure her living allowance was gone the minute she got it."

"That would seem an admirable trait."

"I would be the last person to malign the dead but there were reported indiscretions—more of a bending of the rules, I would say." Sister sighed, added more sugar to her tea, stirred, and took a sip. "It was reported on more than one occasion that Sister Leah would sneak out after curfew. I found that to be true the night she died."

"Any idea where she might have gone?"

"None. I'm assuming she was ministering to her poor unfortunates. Many an evening during the winter months, she would walk the streets after dinner to make certain those sleeping in the open knew that shelter was available."

"When she went out after curfew—I'm assuming you mean after ten? Was anyone else aware of this? I mean, Father, perhaps?"

"No. It was not something I would have reported to Father without first talking with Sister Leah. I am not a 'snitch' and I think the women appreciate and respect me for that. No one could question her devotion to the Church. She wasn't required but she wore the habit of our order, the coif, wimple, and veil and, of course, tunic. I remember the day she became eligible to discard the white veil of the novice and don the black—very shortly after she joined us. I remember sharing a moment of sheer happiness with her. I'm not a bad judge of people, Ms. Mahoney. Sr. Leah was sincerely devout. She wore the habit so proudly."

"Never street clothes?"

"Never. I think the habit gave her instant credibility. I do, however, suspect she kept a mobile phone. Easy to keep hidden under the loose tunic of the habit. I must admit I looked the other way, never challenged her, and never reported my suspicions. I suppose in retrospect it might have been used for non-Church activities … I just don't believe that, though."

"Do you remember when she would have graduated from Boston College?"

"Four years ago. She then spent two years in China on a Church mission and to brush up on her language skills. Supposedly after that two years, she spoke Mandarin like her first language—that must have made her mother very proud."

"Her full name was?"

"Cai Ling Tran. She took Leah as her baptismal name, I suppose, to sound more American."

"Have her parents been notified of her death?"

"I know the authorities were here to get that information, but Father Pete has already notified Boston College in order to reach her father—I understand he's a fellow in the Department of Engineering. I feel so badly for the family. I'm sure they thought their daughter was safe because of her calling. And she should have been."

"I'm sure her death will be solved." Elaine hoped she wasn't lying but felt like she should cross her fingers for luck.

Chapter Eight

The morning headlines literally blared the news: Body of Teen Washed Ashore Near Flagler Pier. Probably not that unusual, Dan thought, swimming in the ocean with ever-present rip tides was always dangerous. But this was December, not the warmest time of the year. And he didn't remember reading about a young person disappearing, being lost—no report of a search and rescue effort organized by the beach patrol. Continued reading told him why: *After extensive interviews with those in the area, and based on how the victim was dressed, it was determined that she most likely fell from a passing vessel off shore. However, authorities have received no reports of a missing person. Anyone having information concerning a missing thirteen or fourteen year old female of Asian descent, please contact the Flagler county Sheriff's office."*

Asian descent. Why did that make a bell go off? Dan poured another cup of coffee. Sister Leah was Chinese. Interesting coincidence that two Asian females met their death in Flagler County in a seventy-two hour timeframe. But not his worry. His day was going to be taken up with the first written report to UL&C accompanied by updated pictures of the stolen articles and an explanation and schedule of upcoming interviews. Elaine had gone into work at nine and hoped to be home by six. She was setting up her office but thought she'd carve out a couple hours to begin work on her presentation. So, in essence, the day was his—no interruptions!

Then right out of some bad movie, his phone rang.

"Mom ... good to hear from you." This was, of course, debatable. He loved Maggie Mahoney, but for seventy-two she could be a handful. He vaguely wondered if the call had something to do with his sister, Carolyn. His only sibling, and an on-going love/hate relationship at best.

"I've moved. I've given up the townhouse in The Villages and I've found a cottage in Dragon's Bend, Florida."

"This is kind of sudden."

"Well, actually it's not. I had been renting to buy, as you know, and my lease was up in August. I had to make a decision—did I want to stay in The Villages or not be tied down, you know, be free to pursue other interests."

Did that mean men? Dan wouldn't put it past his mother to bounce back after the Stanley debacle, but Dragon's Bend? It was an incorporated village outside DeLand, Florida, named for the twists and turns in the St. John's River that looked like the rounded neck and elongated head of a fire-spewing dragon—that is, if you had a pretty good imagination. But didn't you have to be a medium or some kind of fortuneteller to live there? Dan had heard the rumors of it being a cult. Couldn't his mother just stay out of trouble for a couple months? Was that too much to ask?

"Mom, do you know anything about Dragon's Bend? The people there."

"Of course, Dan. And I'm thrilled. I'll be studying under the absolute Master of Tarot. You know, after that summer in Taos I always swore I'd make time to finish my studies. I've already been asked to assist in a table tipping this weekend."

Dan almost let a groan escape, but he clamped his lips together before taking a deep breath and saying, "I'm happy for you. You may really like the community there." Great. He got that out without once asking what a table tipping was. He simply knew it wouldn't be something he'd sign up for. But he made a mental note to Google it.

"Oh, I know I will. It's perfect. Some of the most talented spiritual people in the world live there. And I'll only be a little over an hour away from you and Elaine. Oh dear, I almost forgot—Simon is doing so well. He's such a comfort to me. I'm hoping I can keep him with me in Dragon's Bend. I have a huge backyard, completely fenced. Would you consider that?"

"Of course. I think that's a great idea." Dan had hoped she would want to keep him. The dog was intimidating. Someone would think twice about trying to get past him.

"Do you want to say hello? Simon's sitting right here."

"That's OK. I wouldn't want to upset him." Actually, talking with a dog over the phone was in the same category as streaming videos of supposed 'doggy topics' for a pet left kenneled. "After this weekend we'll have Jason with us for the holidays. We'll carve out some time for all of us to get together."

"I can't wait. I just love the holidays. And I'll expect the two of you—sorry, I guess that's the three of you—to plan on coming this way soon. You'll love my cottage. And I'll just have to give you a reading."

There were few things that Dan would look less forward to … maybe alligator wrestling. "Sure, Mom, sounds great. Give Simon some pats for me."

The rest of the day was uneventful. Elaine passed on his offer of lunch. She felt she should join the women at the convent. She thought she needed to look dedicated. She was probably right, Dan agreed. So it was a rare roast beef on poppy seed bagel with horseradish. At home. He took a break around three and watched the local news. The girl who had been found in the ocean was still unidentified and there was the start of a reward fund. How could a person so young not have someone looking for her?

The call came after hours. Elaine was working late and Dan was enjoying a beer while he typed up his notes from the day.

"Mr. Mahoney? Liz Levine here, medical investigator. We met at the lab yesterday concerning the death of Cai Ling Tran?"

"Yes, of course, how can I help you?"

"That may be the other way around. I have some information that may have bearing on your investigation. I'd like to meet this evening if you're free."

So at six-fifteen he was fighting traffic along Route 1— holiday traffic in a tourist town was the pits. He'd texted Elaine—impromptu meeting at morgue but promised food. Somehow the one made the other unappetizing. But he could always pick up a pizza on the way home if he wasn't too late. He'd give her a call later.

The parking lot in front of the county building housing the office of the county coroner was almost empty. Maybe four cars hugged the shrubbery that lined the back-most portion of the lot. There were twenty-four medical examiners' offices across the state of Florida with one office usually shared by two or three surrounding counties. This one handled cases from Flagler, St. Johns, and Putnam Counties. Ms. Levine met him at the door and took him back to her office. He had to admit he was curious— private meeting, after hours? This had to be interesting …

"Can I get you anything? I'm afraid it's the end of the day for coffee. But I could probably scare up a soda. Or how about a bottle of water?"

"I'm fine, thanks."

"Then I'll just get to it. I'm sure you've read the papers or heard the news about the teenager found drowned off Flagler pier?" Dan nodded. "Because it's been over two days without someone coming forward to claim some knowledge of this child, I took advantage of the situation to push for DNA or even fingerprint ID. We usually have quite a wait for that type of info. Sort of a take a number and get in line situation. Real life contradicts TV here. Well, I'll cut to the chase. The girl was wearing a down vest—one of those with metal snap buttons up the front. I'm still surprised but on the top snap I found a perfect thumbprint. Because our skin is oily, and I suspect that she wasn't in the water longer than it took her to float to shore, it was preserved."

"Amazing. But wearing a down vest? That seems to support the theory that she was thrown or she jumped overboard—doesn't sound like she was dressed for wading in the surf."

"Exactly. I have a theory that she was trying to get away from something or someone. The death was the result of drowning. There were no marks on her body, no struggle, no rape—but wait until you hear the interesting part. The fingerprint belongs to a hooker, a twenty-six-year-old who had slipped off the radar the last few years. She was quite the party girl in Miami and her last arrest for solicitation occurred in South Palm Beach."

"I'm not sure I'm following you—you have no record of this prostitute working locally, but somehow I need to be interested in this?"

"Working, yes, but not as a prostitute. Mr. Mahoney, my hooker is your nun."

He hadn't heard correctly. He couldn't have. Stunned silence. "Sister Leah?"

"One and the same. I had put her fingerprints into our database yesterday. I needed to rule out fingerprints found on a rosary and missal in the pocket of her robes as belonging to her. That's how I found out her true identity. But imagine my surprise to also link our newest death with her. So, Sister Leah, Cai Ling Tran or Lila Tran, as she was known at the time of her last arrest, are all the same person."

"And the young girl was also Asian? Possibly a relative?"

"Yes, but I don't think Ms. Tran was entertaining family. It leads me to suspect human trafficking. Florida is third from the top in number of cases—right behind Texas and California. The girl would have brought top dollar—a virgin, still technically a child. Human trafficking is an extremely difficult crime to curtail. It involves lots of money and neither the perpetrators nor the recipients are going to advertise. It's unusually secretive and often involves women and families of countries outside the US. China, India, and the Philippines are fertile hunting grounds for procuring young women for sale. Families often get thousands of dollars by selling a child. In the not so distant past in China, young girls were considered a liability, a cost to their families. Offering them up for money in order to provide for others was not uncommon."

Dan took a breath. This was a lot more than he'd bargained for. But someone who would traffic in human life would not have a problem stealing. Gut level said he also knew who had taken the artifacts. Smuggling, drugs, black market items, access to an international audience … fencing would be a piece of cake. And there was proof she had handled the engraved box.

"Have you notified the Church?"

"No. By the time I had gotten all the facts, it was getting late and I called you first. I'll have my report ready to hand off by morning but I'll call Fr. Pete this evening. I plan to deliver the news personally. I'm a member of his Parish, and I imagine he's going to be more than a little upset. Someone dropped the ball when vetting Sister Leah, that's for sure."

+ + +

A quick call to Elaine and he'd be picking up a pizza on the way home. What a turn of events. Made her insider position as the convent's head snoop all the more important.

Napkins and plates were already laid out by the time he walked into the kitchen. He popped the caps off a couple

Stella Artois and pulled up a stool to the center butcher-block island. By the time he got to the part proving Sister Leah was a prostitute, Elaine was just shaking her head.

"Unbelievable."

"Think you can connect the dots?"

"If you mean can I fill in the blanks as to background and possibly stolen identity? Of course. I should be able to turn up a work and school history fairly easily. I'm suspecting there is, or was, a real Cai Ling Tran. I've got a couple hours this evening for a few searches. I can always follow up with phone calls in the morning if I need explanations. It's going to be such a shock to everyone that I'm sure they'll want as much information going forward as is available."

"There isn't a way that this won't leave egg on someone's face. Ho Nun will become the new internet meme by lunchtime."

"Dan, that's not funny—actually, it's sick, but probably true. I feel so badly for the women at the convent."

"It's just tough to believe that professionals could be duped so badly—not in this day and age of instant searches and millions of online records. Of course, the Church represents a more trusting body of professionals than the average. I'll go into work with you. I need pictures and police reports. I'm assuming fingerprints were lifted from the relic safe and combination lock. Maybe results are back. Plus, I start my interviews at ten. Don't stay up too late, but I think you're doing the right thing by getting a head start."

Nine in the evening and she wasn't the least bit tired—wired was more like it. And just in case she couldn't get another three hours work done clear-eyed, she made a latte. How could they have ever been lucky enough to rent a townhouse with a specialty coffee maker? Her favorite! She threw on a knee-length T-shirt, pulled her hair up into a ponytail and walked toward the office.

She turned down a bowl of popcorn and watched Dan settle into the sofa and bring up Amazon Prime—another perk with the rental. Wow! What an evening. Pizza and popcorn—what food group was that? She needed to get back to cooking again. She set the foamy cup next to her laptop. She still had university privileges and passwords. It would be faster to check college records through channels and not as an outsider. She hoped that would save time, at least.

So, first, did a Cai Ling Tran graduate from Boston College—Department of Theology—approximately four years ago?

She was beginning to think the name Tran was equivalent to Smith in English—the list was long. She had started in General Admission before narrowing her search to Theology. But no Cai Ling had graduated. And no Dr. Tran on the faculty. Odd, she had fully expected the father to be real. Maybe not the "real" father of Lila Tran but a living person.

Idly, she saved the lists of theology students from four years ago, got out of administration and went onto the general College website. The site was full of the usual campus happenings—awards, high-achievers singled out for accomplishments in the sciences, a musical she wasn't familiar with planned for spring, a touring a cappella group, student editorials on current issues, several sports events— rowing and La Crosse? Hmm. Times have changed … then she saw it. The newspaper had an 'In Memoriam' section.

She needed to go back several years and see if the College had possibly paid tribute to a deceased Dr. Tran.

And there it was. Four years ago last summer. Mountain climbing in his wife's native Yunnan province in Southwest China; an expedition group of three climbers set up camp outside the village base to scout out the best route to the top in preparation for a climb the following day. Due to illness, one climber stayed in camp. Two climbers never returned. There was an absolutely stunning photo of snow-capped mountains, steep gorges and a trajectory that looked almost straight up. According to the article, Dr. Tran was an experienced climber with a number of well-known, worldwide peaks to his credit. This was to be a celebratory trip, a virgin climb for his daughter, Cai Ling, who was beginning her senior year at Boston College that fall. No wonder Elaine couldn't find her name—Cai Ling never graduated.

Cai Ling was the one not on the climb that day with her father, due to altitude sickness. Of the three who started on this one-of-a-kind trip, only Cai Ling survived because she remained in the camp. Due to bad weather, mounting a rescue was futile. The climber–guide who remained with Dr. Tran was also presumed lost. He was identified as Max Walters, owner of Dare-Devil Travel, based in Boston, known for their treetop or canopy walks across the Adirondacks and forests of the Amazon. Trips that guaranteed to change the way you saw the natural world. So much for that, mused Elaine. The danger would far outweigh the thrill—for her anyway. The bodies of Dr. Tran and his guide were never recovered. Shortly after the accident the local government closed the popular mountain range to climbers.

Elaine reread the article. The last paragraph lauded Dr. Tran's exemplary scholarship at the college, his dedication to promoting new and innovative programs in both mathematics and engineering, and his generous donations to various individuals seeking visas to study in the United States—a number of colleagues added condolences and sang his praises. His wife of twenty-seven years had passed away the previous year and had been returned to her native Yunnan for interment. He was survived by his only child, Cai Ling Tran. Elaine made a copy.

Elaine couldn't help but think how easy it might have been for Cai Ling to have her identity stolen. No family member alive to really dispute an imposter's authenticity or lack thereof—especially if she was living halfway around the world. But where was the real Cai Ling? Elaine didn't have a good feeling about her still being alive. It really gave a sinister feel to stolen identity.

+ + +

A call from Fr. Pete at five a. m. summoned them to a meeting at seven in the Rectory conference room. He had talked with Liz Levine and wanted to meet before any statement was released to the press. He sounded like a man who hadn't slept, Dan thought. There was no way to whitewash the situation; the Church had been dragged into yet another scandal. It wasn't something that was going to go away overnight—not with two pending criminal cases nowhere close to being solved. Dan mentioned that Elaine had information to share, and Fr. Pete assured him she'd have a spot on the agenda.

There wasn't a spare chair at the conference table

that seated twelve. Alice, Janice, Brother Lawrence, Sr. Angelica, Fr. Al, Fr. Pete, Elaine, himself, Liz Levine, a lawyer named Tom Sutter, two deacons of the Church—also lawyers—Harold Sterns and Daniel Dekker. A packed room. Nervous fidgeting, a few banal pleasantries being passed back and forth, several reading messages on their phones, most sitting quietly looking resolute. It was going to be interesting to see what stand the group would take. Or if they would even be united on what needed to be done.

Exactly on the hour, Fr. Pete stood, encouraged brief introductions and then began. "I'm not sure I know where to start. I emailed a synopsis of Ms. Levine's report to each of you, but, in short, it attests to our being very badly used by a young women who was anything but what she purported to be. On the periphery of our discussion of that falsehood today will be the horrific topics of human trafficking and grand theft of relics. All occurring under the roof of our beloved Basilica of St. Augustine. There is a press conference slated for eleven. I want us all to be on the same page. I want us to *agree* on what we'll say and not say. Everyone okay with that?" He looked around the table acknowledging the affirmative nods. "Then for starters, let's hear from Janice. You've pulled the original paperwork. I believe Ms. Tran first contacted us through her religious advisor in Boston upon graduating from Boston College Department of Theology—seeking to join the religious order that serves this parish?"

"Yes, exactly two years ago this Christmas. She had graduated mid-term two years prior to that, had become a novitiate that spring, and then spent what the school refers to as 'mission service' sponsored by the school the following summer. She took her vows upon returning to the United States that fall. I believe the entire mission service was spent in China. The process of having a school representative reach out to us first, regarding possible vocational opportunities, is a bit unusual. As a rule we would contact the school regarding any openings we might have. But taking into consideration that facilities such as we have here are becoming rare, her explanation that the school was beginning a religious placement service, made sense. I had no reason to question it." Janice paused and looked around the table for questions.

"I have something to add if I may?" Elaine waited for Fr. Pete to nod. "I believe I've uncovered a contradiction. It would appear that Cai Ling Tran did not graduate." Elaine continued to sum up her findings and handed out copies of her research. "There is no guarantee that the original Cai Ling is alive. I'm sure you can see how very easy it might be for someone to dispose of her and steal her identity. There were no relatives—father, mother, or siblings to interfere or cry foul. Do we have proof that it really was a religious advisor at the College who called to place her in your community?"

Janice was staring at her folded hands, then looked up and responded sharply. "No, of course not. It never dawned on me to check. Aside from the call's Boston area code, I have no proof of whom I talked with." A little snippy, Dan thought. This is not a woman who likes appearing foolish.

"There is certainly no blame. Why would you have thought to check the caller's credentials? Unusual, yes, but she had a good explanation." Elaine smiled. "I don't think anyone thought Cai Ling was anyone but who she said she was—Sister Leah. And from what I've heard, she proved herself to be a helpful, caring individual—for all intent and purpose, a welcome addition to this parish. It's my understanding that she gave no reason for concern, aroused no suspicions."

"Let me remind you that just because a fingerprint on a button links Sister—I mean Ms. Tran to what authorities suspect was an incidence of human trafficking, there is no more proof than that. Flimsy, at best. What *is* true is Ms. Tran's past, which is equally troubling. Her past cannot be minimized—she spent a number of years in Miami selling physical pleasures for money. But let me remind you of the scriptures." Fr. Pete cleared his throat. "More than one fallen woman was brought to Christ and exonerated of all sin. Let us keep this in mind. We are not here to judge."

Damage control. Dan thought the biblical reference was a nice touch. The meeting quickly turned into a 'what do we want the press to know?' discussion and within an hour, Father Pete was prepared. He would be the representative to give a public statement and the others were asked to refrain from being interviewed or making statements to the press. Father would draft a letter to parishioners and get those in the mail by day's end. Between snail-mail and email, all church members or affiliates would have an explanation—more or less at the same time as the general public.

There was to be no margin for error. The Church was duped, plain and simple. Father reiterated how important it was that the Church be transparent. Any hint of an association between the Church and human trafficking must be squashed at all costs. Father Pete had informed the Bishop, and the Basilica's leader was emphatic. No scandal! Not even the whiff of one. Father reminded them that the Church was not in a strong position in this day of perceived, if not actual, misconduct—finger pointing and court cases. They didn't need any more. People seemed to expect and believe the very worst. Exchanging a child for money—selling her—would bring a condemnation that could be costly. Involvement by a member of the Basilica's leadership, the inner circle, would provide more than enough fodder for Twitter Trolls. They had to assure the public that safeguards would be in place to preclude this happening again. They would be up front and honest and to some extent play the victim. But, then again, weren't they victims?

Dan listened with interest. Two young women had lost their lives, yet the Church chose to distance itself and save its own bacon. Dan thought he probably wouldn't be the only one to draw that conclusion. There was only a brief mention of the missing artifacts and no reference as to how that might be tied to Ms. Tran. Maybe it was best to simply concentrate on one problem at a time. In some ways it was less red tape for him. Wasn't 'under the radar' the preferred way to work?

Chapter Nine

Elaine walked back to her office, leaving Dan to wait in the rectory conference room for his first interview. She caught a glimpse of cameras and a mic being set up on the front steps through her one window, which faced the street. An office at the front of the building had its drawbacks. She hoped the press conference wouldn't get too loud; she needed to talk with Admissions at Boston College. She dialed and worked her way through the prompts—then was put on hold. As always there was an overly long wait, at least five minutes, which seemed uncalled for but college campuses were often understaffed and this week started the holiday break. There would be a skeleton staff in place, at best. She should consider herself lucky that there was someone in Records to help her.

The woman who finally came on the line introduced herself as Mary Stover. She remembered what she called the Tran tragedy. She had been a career counselor in the Theology Department back then and knew Cai Ling. A young woman with so much promise, one year of studies left, only to lose both parents in just over twelve months, and her father's body never recovered. She never really had closure and Mary remembered Cai Ling as distraught, completely at loose ends and feeling she wouldn't be able to apply herself to her studies.

"If she didn't return to school, do you have any idea what she did do?"

"That was four years ago. No inquires by Ms. Tran are noted here. It was my understanding that she elected to stay in Yunnan province. I believe her mother still had family there. There was insurance money—I hope I'm not telling tales out of school—but it would have allowed her to take her time in deciding what to do. I don't think she returned to school anywhere else. There are no requests for transcripts in her file. The few times we talked after the accident, I knew she needed distance and solitude."

"And there's been no further interaction with Ms. Tran in the last four years? Maybe on a personal basis with someone in the department? A friend? Maybe a boyfriend?"

"None that I know of. She was a very quiet girl, so very bright but also religious. She had considered leaving the secular life. I've always hoped she did follow her calling and joined a religious sect. I believe her parents supported her in this. I may be the only one who kept in touch for a short period of time. I knew her father and took a somewhat parental interest in the situation. Cai Ling and I exchanged texts and emails for the first six months then we drifted apart and I lost contact all together."

"So a religious advisor from the Theology Department would not have talked with a representative of the St. Augustine convent trying to place Cai Ling?"

"No, contrary to what some might think, we're not a placement service and don't intend to become one. Inquiries would come from the party or parties hoping to enlarge their religious assembly. The request would have been handled through admissions and records with letters of recommendation, grades, honors, and test scores shared with the petitioner—only if deemed a legitimate inquiry. The prospective sponsor would have gone through rather rigorous scrutiny. As I've said, however, there was no degree granted. That part is a fib. And no one called the Basilica of St. Augustine to place someone within their community of sisters. Another fib."

Elaine thanked her for her time and help. There had been no surprises and attempting to find Cai Ling, possibly a world away, was daunting if not impossible. So, now to trace the steps of the imposter. She'd contact the Miami Police Department first but wasn't confident that her position at the convent would carry enough weight to get answers. What she really wanted was a copy of Cai Ling's mug shot and a history of arrests—with dates. She needed to drop a name, and Liz Levine seemed to have the connections needed. She had given Dan the name of someone who knew the situation and could help. Elaine dug his card out of her purse, fingers crossed he'd be willing to help.

Special Agent Eric Waller was eager to help. Miami was a hotbed of human trafficking; apprehension, let alone arrests and convictions were few. Because huge amounts of money changed hands—in the multi-billions by some estimates—between savvy leaders and a worldwide network of conspirators, it was a crime without borders. The national hotline could provide help in over two hundred languages. Elaine was stunned. She'd had no idea of the magnitude of the problem.

"I know you can hear the frustration in my voice. I don't know if you're aware that Florida has just recently become a member of the elite three states with the most criminal activity in human trafficking. The pressure's on to curtail it—as in, it should have been done yesterday, of course. I think our interaction is going to be a 'I'll scratch your back, you scratch mine' arrangement. We're nowhere close to getting a handle on the ring or cartels behind the crimes. So I'm anxious to hear your side of the Lila Tran story. I'm still trying to get my mind around her masquerading as a nun."

Elaine filled him in on the lies leading up to her joining the convent in St. Augustine briefly sharing Cai Ling Tran's background. "I don't hold out hope that the real Cai Ling is alive—it's just going to be difficult to prove. When did you last arrest Lila?"

"There was only one arrest, exactly two years ago. She was detained but her bail was met and she simply disappeared. She had been a part of the Miami Yacht Club, a group of very rich men from halfway around the world who park up to five super luxurious yachts outside the harbor in international waters about twelve miles offshore once or twice a month. They hire a high-dollar escort service to provide entertainment and then they party. Actually, they refer to the women as 'stewards.' Lila wasn't a street girl. I don't think she would have ended up in a convent if someone with a little clout wasn't pulling strings, but then to be killed … gotta be some kind of in-fighting and that part interests me. Unrest—maybe jockeying for power—can lead to people making mistakes."

"I'm assuming the Yacht Club is a drugs, gambling, money laundering enterprise?"

"Good assumption. Seems like fertile ground for a little hanky-panky, doesn't it? But that's as much suspicion as evidence. Money can buy a person's way out of a lot of things. Basically it's a bunch of good ol' boy billionaires who float around paying top dollar to have a good time. There's been an unspoken rule of keep your hands clean, don't off-load contraband—you know, dirty laundry stays on the ship—guess that's why I'm surprised. This is the first time that it appears there might be a human trafficking connection."

"It would be a great cover—access to world markets, and a ready-made escape route."

"And Lila wouldn't have been working alone. She would have needed the backing. Those kinds of connections would not have come cheap. Oh, I meant to ask, any sign she was squirreling away a little something for a rainy day? The business is unbelievably lucrative, and I bet they were making it worth her while. I would have thought she was invaluable—a lot of women who move through the system are Asian. Lila was fluent in Mandarin—maybe other dialects."

Elaine could have kicked herself. She hadn't checked for a banking account. She scribbled a note to do that the minute she hung up. Then, she briefly filled the agent in on the stolen relics and the gold foil that might tie Lila Tran to the Church robbery. She knew Dan would be interested in his feedback.

"I'm not saying that she wouldn't have had access to

the best worldwide fencing operation for that type of artifact, but these guys pretty much stick to one type of crime at a time. If she was procuring and delivering slaves, she probably wasn't spending her time chasing down buyers for antiquities. A one-time shot at a couple hundred thousand versus the steady income of being a part of a business that brings in multiple billions of dollars? You do the math; why would she run the risk of getting caught in a minor crime? I don't think of her as greedy as much as just opportunistic. Her nun gig was a good one. It got past us."

Elaine didn't mention that the theft of a 1.2 million dollar item was hardly "minor." He was right—it was in a different league than the crimes of vice he'd mentioned.

Agent Waller made sense. After an exchange of cell numbers, email addresses, and a promise to keep in touch, they said good-bye. Two minutes later she received an email with an attachment. The young Asian girl in the picture was wearing a red leather mini skirt with matching halter top, more off than on, six-inch stilettos, dragon-red nails and hair that reached beyond her waist. The first thing that came to Elaine's mind was that she looked expensive.

Now to check for bank accounts. She'd contact Fr. Pete to see if he had the authority to make inquiries. Better to keep it as inside information and not go to local authorities. She reminded Father the account would probably be under the name of Lila Tran. Maybe there was a member of the parish who would be in a position to discreetly inquire? He thought he knew just the person. Within an hour she received an email with $580,000 in the subject line, no text. Wow. But the question was, did Lila get that much from the slave trade or the selling of relics? Could Agent Waller be wrong?

She typed up a short report on the information she'd gotten from both Boston College and Special Agent Waller and emailed Janice and Father. She had just opened the file on her talk about St. Bonaventure when she heard a soft knock at the door. What was it she had said about her door always being open? Well, that was true unless she was discussing sensitive issues.

"Come in." She hoped she sounded cheery. A young woman that she had seen at breakfast tentatively stepped into the room.

"Is this a bad time?"

"No, not at all. I closed the door to keep the press conference noise to a minimum. Please, join me."

The young woman turned and shut the door behind her. "I need this to be private. Will that be okay?"

"Yes, of course." She certainly had Elaine's attention ... Elaine got up and moved a stack of books from the chair nearest her desk. "Sorry, I'm trying to do two things at once and my housekeeping standards have gone out the window. Clutter isn't usually my thing." She tried to smile reassuringly as the girl came forward and took the cleared chair.

"I'm Sister Rachel. We met at breakfast." Nervously she continued to smooth her tunic across her lap with two hands.

"Yes, I remember." A little bit of a white lie, they hadn't really met but she did remember seeing the girl toward the end of the dining table. Not that the wimple and veil didn't act as a good disguise, but the young woman's dark eyes and long, naturally thick lashes made her memorable.

"I was Sister Leah's best friend. Well, maybe just a good friend, but she could depend on me."

"I'm sure she valued your friendship." What an interesting turn of events, Elaine could sense the young woman needed to unburden herself. Suddenly her office seemed to be turning into a confessional.

"I think I did something I wasn't supposed to. But I think you'll know what to do."

Elaine watched as Sr. Rachel pulled an envelope from under her tunic. "These are pictures of the young people she helped. I wouldn't have thought anything about it but this picture?" Rachel placed a 5 X 7 glossy headshot of a very young Asian girl on the desk in front of her. "This is the girl who drowned off Flagler Pier."

Elaine pulled the picture closer. The St. Augustine *Record* had printed a picture of the young victim in hopes someone would come forward who knew her. It was the same child. "Did you ever see Sister with this girl?"

"Yes, here at the convent. She would sometimes sneak in young girls for a cup of hot chocolate in the winter or glass of lemonade in the summer. Most were girls living in squalid conditions who needed food and a place to spend the night. This girl was with Sister Leah the night she was killed."

"Are you certain?"

A nod.

"How do you know this?"

"I saw the girl in Sister's room but then they left together around eleven-thirty. She'd done this many times before."

"They went out at eleven-thirty at night?"

Another nod.

"But where was Sister Angelica? Was this acceptable? To bring people into the dormitory? And then sneak out?"

"No, it had to be done in secret. Sister Angelica is elderly. She misses a lot."

"Did other women in the convent know this was going on?"

"I'm sure they did but kept quiet. We have quite the honor system." A rueful smile, "It's usually not tested."

"Were all of the people who stayed in the convent at Sister Leah's invitation women or young girls?"

"Yes. Every one, and most spoke English as a second language, if at all."

"Where do you think Sister took this young girl at eleven-thirty?"

"I used to follow her to see—just curious. That night like so many others, a really big, black car pulled up outside. There was a driver and he got out and opened the back doors for them to get in. Then they drove away. It was rather grand. Like they were movie stars or something."

"I see." Elaine was dumbfounded; this was more than finding a single thumbprint on a vest's snap closing and totally corroborated the possibility of Sister's involvement in the slave trade. "Where did you get this photo?"

"In Sister Leah's locker. There are others." Rachel opened the folder and spread five like-sized glossies across Elaine's desk. "This girl and this girl have already gone." Sister Rachel pointed to one, maybe eighteen-year-old, who looked a little worldly probably because of her enhanced lips and pouty pose, then to another somewhat nondescript young woman of indeterminate age, and finally to the one who had drowned. This last girl was obviously very young, thin, flat chested, holding a doll.

"Did you actually see these young women in Sister Leah's room?"

"Yes, some spent the night on the floor in Sister's room, but all left around midnight in the same way—a big car and all." Suddenly she burst into tears. "I can't believe Sister Leah would have been involved in human trafficking. But that's why I brought you these. I know it was wrong to take things."

"Was there anything else in her locker?"

A nod. Elaine waited while Sr. Rachel stalled by blowing her nose and tucking a limp hanky back in a pocket under her surplice before taking a much dog-eared American passport from the envelope and placing it on the desk.

Elaine opened the document and stared at Cai Ling Tran. She knew in an instant that this was the real Cai Ling—not Lila, not Sister Leah—but the woman whose identity had first been stolen. The hair was short with bangs that swept across her forehead obscuring her eyebrows and almost touching her lashes. A wig and street clothes and Lila Tran could easily have become Cai Ling. The document was five years old, possibly ordered before that fateful mountain climbing trip to Yunnan.

"You know, I need to turn this over to authorities, along with the photos."

"I know. I brought them to you because you'd know what to do."

"Thanks for the vote of confidence. I appreciate that." Elaine paused. "I don't want you to be upset. Sister Leah wasn't who she said she was. I know it's difficult to believe, but she wasn't a woman of the Church. She had survived by being an escort in the Miami area. Take a look. This is a photo of Sister Leah taken two or three years ago. I think we can say these were her work clothes." Elaine turned the laptop so that Sr. Rachel could see the woman in red leather. The sharp intake of air, a hand to her mouth, then a push to turn the laptop away said it all. It was shocking.

"Sister Elizabeth says we shouldn't dwell on the salacious. This is a House of God and we are the Handmaidens, the pure and innocent. When there's a bad apple in the barrel, God sees to it that it's thrown away. I liked Sr. Leah but Sr. Elizabeth had warned me against her before. She said Jesus had come to her in a dream with a warning." Rachel stood. "Thank you for helping me with the pictures and passport. I better go now." The girl was shaking.

"Are you sure you'll be all right?"

"It's just the shock. I'm okay."

"Thank you again. I'm glad you trusted me." Elaine watched Sr. Rachel leave then walked out into the hallway to see if the conference door was open. Closed tight, Dan must still be in an interview. She couldn't wait to share her morning.

"Ms. Mahoney, a minute, please." A tall, rather imposing nun stepped out of Janice's office and walked to where Elaine was standing with the stride of the officious. "I'm Sr. Elizabeth and I must ask you to show compassion when talking to the women here. I couldn't help but notice Sr. Rachel was quite obviously upset. This is a very great shock for all of us—on so many levels—and an outsider coming in, bombarding the innocent with questions … well, I would hope you see that your approach is injurious, not what our community needs right now in order to heal."

"My sympathies, Sr. Elizabeth. I'm afraid the severity of the situation and need for closure—if not the need to clear the Diocese of any perceived involvement—overrides what I hope is the temporary discomfort of coming forward." Elaine smiled and held eye-contact. She had worked for women like this before; academe was not a stranger to political posturing and faculty bullying. She was a veteran of in-fighting; she would not be pushed around. The twitch under Sr. Elizabeth's left eye said Elaine had struck a nerve—literally.

"I just hope you don't come to regret this." With that, Sr. Elizabeth turned and walked back to Janice's office.

Elaine wasn't certain what the 'this' was but she had more to do than stand around wondering about it.

Chapter Ten

To his way of thinking, access to the relics safe should have been one, at the most two people—Dan checked his list again: the man who built it and had made repairs here and there and the man who traveled with the antiquity, actually those made sense. They would have to have access. But the housekeepers, in this case both Sr. Angelica and Ms. Tran, Fr. Pete, and under supervision the two deacons he'd met earlier that morning. That became a few more than Dan would have liked. Deacons seemed an odd choice but apparently it was not unusual for the deacons to stand in for Fr. Pete and present the relics to the congregation after service. And supposedly with Fr. Pete always standing by.

Maybe Dan just had to look at things differently. A church wasn't an art gallery or a museum; it had entirely different needs and ways of handling security. It was a large organization that answered to a higher Master. These were not new rules and in the history of the Basilica, there had never been another theft of this magnitude. Dan checked his list. Oh yeah, one more—Fr. Pete had added the groundskeeper and head custodian. That seemed over the top to Dan, but a quick call to Father explained it.

Fire and disaster safety protocol as required by the county and adopted by the church specified one individual to have access to all locked portions of the edifice—whether it be restrooms, confessionals, meeting rooms or the relics safe. Church rules further specified that this individual be bonded and have special evacuation training in moving large groups in the least amount of time. A good precaution, Dan thought. He couldn't argue. There had been dangerous flooding after a recent hurricane. So, a man who locked up and opened up made him an important interviewee—and that's where he would start. Dan was meeting with him first, a Willis Johnson.

The man who poked his head in the door was probably fifty and a smoker. He had that wrinkled, aged-too-soon look of someone who had worked outside all his life. Baseball-cap over thinning hair, jeans a size too large, cuffs dragging on the floor and enough dirt underneath his fingernails to grow potatoes.

"Sorry to keep you waiting. Got some guys putting down asphalt where that back row of parking spaces meets the alley. Concrete was just disintegrating. You know what they say, if you want a job done right, do it yourself. I feel I need to keep an eye on 'em but I got a few minutes."

"I'll try to make this short, then. In general, I need to know if you saw or heard anything unusual the day the theft took place. For starters, do you remember what time you left that night?"

"Yeah, it was a Monday. That's a prayer night for one of the women's auxiliaries. Unless I hand off the duty, I'm the one who closes up. They usually meet in the sanctuary for prayer, then have their actual meeting in one of the classrooms. So, I would have been here until ten."

"And at that time the church is locked?"

"Tight as a drum."

"Nothing unusual that night?"

"Just more of the usual. Had to chase some vagrants out—you know, down-and-outers looking for warmth."

"Street people?"

"Yeah. I feel sorry for 'em. Most of the time I look the other way. You know, just trying to put the Christ in Christmas."

"Did you check the relic case before you left?"

"Not up close. I looked at it from the back of the church by the font. I could tell it hadn't been bothered."

"Were you the one who discovered the theft?"

"Nope. The cook, the next morning. She was running around trying to find Father and realized the door to the case was wide open."

"What time was this?"

"Early. Five-thirty or thereabouts."

"Where were you at this time?"

"Oh, I wasn't even here yet. Late night means a late morning for me unless I'm working a project."

"So someone told you what happened?"

"Yeah, this place is great for gossip. Sister Angelica had collapsed that morning when the police contacted her. You know, about the dead nun."

"Did you know Sister Leah?"

"Yeah, I knew who she was. Always thought it was funny to see a Chink nun down here in Florida. Pretty little thing, too."

Dan ignored the ethnic slur and assessment of comeliness. Neither seemed appropriate, but it probably went with the territory where this man was concerned.

"So when you locked up, nothing stands out about that night? Nothing unusual happened?" Never hurt to ask the same question twice; Willis was being just a little too glib, maybe rehearsed was the better word.

Willis suddenly looked at the floor and bit his lower lip before looking up.

"Damn. Monday, right? Come to think of it, that was a strange night—not the usual, that's for sure."

"What made it different?" Why had this suddenly become like pulling teeth?

"Normally I don't like talking about others, especially those who aren't as fortunate. But I guess you have a reason for needing to know." He'd been looking at the floor but now caught Dan's eye. "One of the street people was drunk. Weaving around, couldn't stand up straight. I was just getting ready to call someone to help me drag him outside when he barfed all over the back pew."

"Wow. Bummer. I can't imagine that's on your list of usual duties. What did you do?"

"I would have been shit out of luck if it hadn't been for Sister Elizabeth. She heard the commotion and came over to help. By this time there was a good-sized crowd. A fellow in trouble brings out the best of the group. I know most of 'em, but this guy was new. Hadn't seen him around town before."

"Can you describe him?" Dan didn't know why, but intuition was nudging him—could be just something unusual on an already unusual night. Still …

Willis sat for a minute, again looking at the floor. Dan could tell he'd caught him off guard—not a question he'd anticipated. "White guy … but not that old. Looked like he could have put in a good day's work if he'd wanted. He hadn't missed many meals, but he wasn't fat or nothin'. He couldn't a been more than thirty-something, maybe in his forties. I remember thinking, he sure is wasting his life. Guy like that could be a CEO or something, not living on the streets. He just had that look—not the usual down-an-outer. Most of the guys on the streets are older. Fifties, sixties—let go from lifetime jobs some of them. There's even some families—wife, children turned out 'cause the rent got too high or there was an illness."

"Anything else about this guy? Clothing? Shoes or boots? Hair color?"

Willis sighed. He was acting like this wasn't in his job description, but he offered the basics. "Dark hair, stringy and tied back. A baseball cap. I noticed his boots 'cause they were good ones. Musta lifted them off someone. T-shirt and jeans."

Dan realized he needed to stay in control or at least direct the guy's recall. Willis wasn't going to offer anything on his own. "Any markings on the hat or t-shirt?"

"Hat was something a tourist would wear—said Mazatlán or some Mexico thing. Don't remember anything on the shirt; it was just black. Funny, I hadn't thought about it, but I haven't seen him again. The group's been back, but without him. Course he coulda just moved on down the coast; it can get a little nippy up this way in the winter.

And facilities around here can get crowded. Like you gotta make it to the soup kitchen early or you'll miss out. Same at bedtime. The armory don't take you after eight-thirty."

"You didn't happen to hear a name for this guy, did you?"

"A woman in the group called him Max."

"What time was it after this mess was cleaned up and you could lock up and go home?"

"It was probably a shade after eleven. Don't know for certain." That was late—a good hour past the usual close-up.

"Anyone keeping an eye on the front part of the Church while the cleanup was going on?"

"Don't think so. Sister Elizabeth went to bring buckets of water and brushes and rags from the kitchen area. I think she was gonna ask one of the street women to help her clean up the mess."

"But you don't know?"

"Mr. Mahoney, I'm just gonna level with you here. I'm not good in that kind of situation. You barf, I barf. Smell of it makes me sick. Sister told me to go home." A chuckle, "I think I turned green."

"So, you left *before* any cleanup was done?"

"Yep."

"I take it you did the prep for locking up—did a walk through to make sure you weren't locking anyone inside before you left? But you *didn't* actually lock the building that night?" The guy was frustrating. Dan knew his exasperation was showing..

"Nope, I didn't. Sister said not to worry, she'd take care of it. I just got out of there thankful I hadn't given them anything more to clean up."

Willis didn't seem to have anything more to add. Dan sighed and thanked him, and made a note to add Sister Elizabeth to his list of interviews. Others he called in were mostly dead-ends. Weren't there on that date, on vacation, only came in for services on weekends … He attempted to reach Sr. Elizabeth but she was in class until five. He'd start with her in the morning. He'd been given the name of the kitchen aide, a young woman from outside the convent who helped part-time, apparently coming in to serve a meal and staying after hours to clean. If she was available, he'd make her his last interview of the day. He dialed the kitchen's extension.

He'd been told that Mary Andrews came to work every day at four. Once a week this included washing and waxing the floors of the dining room, which was usually done on a Saturday. She was also in charge of compiling a grocery and products list on a weekly basis, based upon the cook's menus and input as to what needed to be replenished. It was then her responsibility to call in the order, receive it, and put everything away. A lot for a college student of nineteen, Dan thought. But the young girl in front of him had a no-nonsense demeanor that instilled confidence. And she was pretty, even with a hairnet covering the pile of pale gold hair twisted into a messy bun on top of her head.

"How long have you worked at the Basilica?"

"Two years. I started here the year I started college."

"Have you always worked in the kitchen?"

"No. I supported housekeeping at first but only for six months. I was really needed more in the kitchen."

"What are your hours?"

"I work four 'til nine weekdays and two 'til ten on Saturdays."

"Were you given the combination to the lock on the safe that housed any traveling relics?"

"Originally it just had a padlock and I did have a key. The combination lock was only added last year. I never had the combination because I was working in the kitchen by then."

"With the kitchen at the back of the building have you ever seen loiterers? Street people maybe sleeping in the alley or begging for food?"

"I only go out back to throw out garbage."

Interesting, Dan thought. Not directly answering the question and averting her eyes.

"Just walking in from the parking lot, I've noticed people near the back doors on several occasions. I just assumed they were expecting handouts."

"Yes, well, it's a free country."

"Have you ever offered anyone food? Or talked with them?"

"Look, Mr. Mahoney, I need this job. I live with my mother. She's disabled—"

"I would think if you offered comfort by talking with someone or offering food, that would be viewed as a charitable act and no one would think less of you."

"I never thought I was doing something I wasn't supposed to."

Dan waited, then gently prodded, "What was it that you did?"

"Sister Leah often asked me to fix a sack lunch for one of her … friends. Some were children really. I'd come up with a PB&J and a piece of fruit. Sometimes I'd add Fritos but that was out of my own pocket—the nuns aren't into chips."

"Did this happen often?"

"Maybe once or twice a month. I wasn't supposed to tell anyone. But how could I have known what she was doing like they said in the paper ... selling these children into slavery? "

"I know it's shocking but you had no way of knowing."

"Mr. Mahoney, I did something else I shouldn't have." Again, he waited. "That night Sister Elizabeth called me to come back in and clean up after someone got sick in the church."

"It was my understanding that she did the work with the help of someone from the street."

"Puh-leeze. Sister Elizabeth? She's not one to get her hands dirty, and a little vomit clean-up is not on her list of church duties. She went back to bed and left everything to me."

Dan made a few quick notes. "By then it must have been ten or after."

"Yeah, closer to eleven and no one around here has ever heard of paying overtime."

"Do you remember if Sister checked to make certain everyone was out of the church when she left?"

"She just took off. I have no idea what she would have done if I couldn't have come in."

"Did you see anyone in the church? Someone who might have stayed behind?"

"Not then. But later, I was out back and this big, black car pulls up and the driver says a friend of his left his bedroll in the church—the guy seemed to know about the situation. I'd put the bedroll over to the side so I knew it was still there. Anyway, he wants to run in and get it. And, I let him."

"Were you in the church during the time he was there?"

"No. I was cleaning the brushes and mops out back."

"Was he in there a long time?"

"I don't know. The bedroll was way in the back—he couldn't just run in and pick it up real quick."

"Do you remember what time this was?"

"Must have been around eleven-thirty. Mr. Mahoney, I saw Sr. Leah sitting in the back of the car and that girl was with her—the young one who drowned. I didn't do anything. I didn't tell anyone."

"You did nothing wrong. There was no way that you could have known there was anything suspicious going on."

"But she shouldn't have been out. I could have called someone."

"And tattled … on a nun?"

"I guess not when you put it that way."

"Did you go back in the church after the driver picked up the bedroll?"

"No, I was finished cleaning. I put away the mops and buckets, locked up and went home."

Dan thanked her profusely for sharing the information and assured her once again that she wasn't in trouble. He collected his notes, made some notations of times, and called it a day. His stomach was telling him it was a little past his dinnertime.

Chapter Eleven

O. C. White's and a plate of shrimp and grits. Life didn't get much better than that, Dan decided. He was anxious to share his information and hear about Elaine's day but food came first. The restaurant was easily within walking distance of the Basilica, and dessert would probably be a walk together along the St. John's River—after a slice of Key Lime Pie.

Elaine had grabbed iPhone captures of the five young people's pictures and each page of the passport Sr. Rachel had brought her before giving the materials to Father. She handed her phone to Dan. It was tough to get his mind around what was in front of him, Was he looking at five unfortunates, one known dead, four, perhaps, already slaves? The faces of the young girls were haunting. Had the photos been mug shots taken to be used as selling tools? All but one had that winsome blush of youth. Only one wore make-up and posed with a little bit of attitude. Older than the others, more mature. Still worth a pretty penny— she would appeal to a different clientele.

Dan couldn't help but think of Mary Andrews's sack lunches—PB&Js with an apple and a sack of Fritos. These must be some of the recipients. There was something so incredibly sad about the girls he was looking at.

Elaine reached for the phone and dropped it back into her purse. "So many questions."

"Yeah. I guess I'd have to agree with Special Agent Waller. The pictures? A couple are very young girls—I was looking at the potential for a lot more money than the relics would bring—and seemingly less danger of discovery. The relics would have been a one-time shot. A grab and run doesn't have the job security of trafficking."

"I hate the way you put it, but it's like I've been living on another planet. I had no idea that human trafficking was so prevalent and so very lucrative—and such a big problem in Florida."

"And to infiltrate a convent? Pure genius—think of where Sister Leah could go and never be questioned. You don't have to be Catholic to just know that nuns and priests are a cut above. A fraternity for a chosen few."

"Or supposed to be. It would seem that she would have been valuable to the organization. So, why did someone kill her?"

"I think we're both assuming it had something to do with the trafficking. There's no guarantee that it was; it could have been something else. Stolen identity, falsifying a degree—maybe someone had found out her duplicity and was going to blow her cover, and they needed to take her out of the picture."

"True, but a half a million in the bank might mean there was a little jealousy— a lot of people would want in on that kind of action."

"I'm not ruling out vying for power—some internal money or position grab—but it could be some kind of double-cross. Loyalty is a trait that can mean life or death. Lines you can't cross. Especially when playing for high stakes. Think mafia. Maybe it was a case of cold feet. She wanted out but knew too much."

"I can't think a prostitute didn't know what she was getting into. What's your next move?"

"More interviews." Dan quickly filled Elaine in on the barf incident the night of the heist. And how the church was left unattended and an aide let the driver come into the church.

"Do you believe this girl who works in the kitchen— Mary Andrews? Or maybe I should ask do you think it was the driver of the limo who could have taken the relics?"

"Yes, I believe her and her testimony nails the fact that Sister Leah had the girl with her and that this wasn't the first time. And it puts the limo driver in a prime position to have the church all to himself and somehow open the safe, lift the relics, wrap them in an already planted bedroll and leave. It's the closest we've come to a person of interest."

"Do you think you can find this guy?"

"I'm going to try. But Sr. Elizabeth is next on my list. She was conveniently out and about that night around ten. I don't know if this is normal and she helps Sr. Angelica lock up or something else. Guess I'll find out. I'll pick up with interviews again on Monday morning."

"I'll be interested in hearing your take on the righteous Sr. Elizabeth."

"Ah, that doesn't sound good? You two lock horns over something?"

"Sort of. Let's just say I'm not a pal."

Dan took a forkful of Key Lime. "I don't want to waste the evening. Last bite's yours. Let's go take a look at that river."

Chapter Twelve

Jason pulled into the townhouse drive at eight-thirty Sunday evening. She had seen him just three and a half weeks ago, but the prospect of spending almost a month together was exciting—and over the holidays, at that. She helped him carry things in from his car—more electronics than clothing—showed him to his room and threw a pizza in the oven because, per usual, he was starving. Six foot one inch, dark hair shaved close on the sides—not a style she really liked but at almost twenty-one, this kid could go bald and look great. Okay, she was prejudiced, but he *was* handsome. She stifled the thought of 'like his father'. That was a long time ago and her feelings were very much over.

Dan was on a conference call. It always amazed her that the investigative insurance business was on a 24/7 schedule and weekends meant nothing. She cracked the office door open, stuck her head in and mouthed, "pizza?" He nodded, picked up an empty Sam Adams, and wiggled it toward her with an expectant look on his face. Okay, she'd bring him a beer. This man was her life. A little step 'n fetch it wouldn't hurt.

Jason loved his bedroom. Actually that didn't fool her—he loved being so close to a private back entrance/ exit. He had quickly changed into shorts and was already at the table when she returned from delivering the beer.

"This place is great."

"I agree. We were lucky." Elaine pulled a crisp-edged Italian Flag pizza from the oven. Red, white and green—or mozzarella, tomatoes, and fresh basil to the uneducated. Her favorite and she figured as long as it was pizza, Jason wouldn't be particular. He could live without pepperoni this one time. She loaded a plate with two slices, grabbed napkins and headed back to the office. "Won't be a minute."

She put the plate next to the computer and watched Dan fold a slice in half and continue to talk around a generous bite. She smiled, tucked a napkin under his chin, gave him a kiss on top of the head, and pulled the door shut behind her.

Then it was just the two of them. Mother and son. Each on a stool pulled up to the butcher block kitchen island. "So, what do you want to do over your vacation?"

"Maybe spend time on the beach, swim, spend more time on the beach … did I mention spend time on the beach?"

Elaine laughed. "I kinda get the idea that's the priority."

"To be honest, I need to spend some time in a library. I have a paper due the week after I get back and I need to support my online research with a little on-ground work. I assume Flagler College has a pretty good library?"

"I would think so. You've had the same major for two years now. Looks like you won't be making changes."

"Not this time around. International economics. I've ended up liking it more than I thought I would. Oh yeah, the department is suggesting everyone do a minor in a language—Chinese preferred."

"You're studying Chinese?"

"Have been for the last six months. It's tough. Hard to go from a romance language to a tonal one. I was hoping I might find a local tutor."

"Maybe in Jacksonville—a little bigger population but less than an hour away."

"I thought I'd put a flyer up on the bulletin board here just in case—I'm sure they'll post job possibilities online, too. I'll cover both bases. Do you mind if I bring someone here? I could use the school library if you have a problem."

"No, of course it would be fine to bring someone here. Lots more comfortable. I don't think I told you that Dan's mother has moved to a little town about an hour from here. We need to find time to all get together. She'd like to see you again."

"I like Maggie. Do you think she needs help with her new place?"

"Ask her. Here's her number." Elaine opened her phone, scrolled through her contacts, paused on the screen of Maggie Mahoney, a couple clicks and she'd sent Maggie's info to Jason as a text.

"Thanks. I'll give her a call in the morning."

+ + +

Elaine looked over at her driver. Riding to work with her husband was fun. Portent of things to come? Elaine thought so. She had to admit this was a great way to start the day. Lunch was probably not possible, conflicting schedules, but a drink at five on the outdoor balcony of the Casa Monica was something to look forward to.

Dan was meeting first thing with Fr. Pete so they both headed toward the rectory. Her office didn't lock—the only thing of value was her laptop and she took that home with her at night. So, when she pushed open the door to discover books having been pulled from the shelves, filing cabinet drawers pulled open, and papers scattered across the floor, she simply pulled the door closed and walked across the foyer to Janice's office.

Janice was incensed. "Damn it. I'd like to think I'm as Christian as the next person but when it comes to street people simply walking in and ransacking the place just to find money for drugs, I draw the line. Something has to be done."

"But the outside door is locked, or, at least, I can't imagine it not being."

A roll of the eyes. "Sr. Angelica makes the rounds at night—checking doors, windows that face the street. Any entry on the first floor, front or back, has to be locked up tight. Ten o'clock lock up; ten-thirty check."

"You're saying you found an outside door unlocked this morning?"

A nod. "Side door leads to the parking lot. I suppose easy to overlook in that we don't use that entrance off the alley. Plus, it's private, and offers a protected getaway; so, it would have appeal. This can't go on. Father has to replace her. Has to. It isn't that I don't like her, I do. She's served the Church well, but she's eighty-seven. She could have dozed off watching TV last night and thought she'd already checked the doors over here."

"I thought Father had someone in mind—someone who would be joining us after the holidays."

"That fell through. I thought he'd told you."

Elaine shook her head. "Isn't there someone here— someone among the Sisters—who could step in as housemother?"

"I know who wants the job. Sr. Elizabeth. She's in her thirties, no nonsense, held positions of authority before she came here … I know, for a fact, that Father is considering her."

"In the meantime I'll work out a schedule with Sr. Angelica—I don't mind coming back down here later in the evening to check locks. Not necessarily every night but we could trade off. You have a lock on your office, maybe I should ask Father to put a lock on mine."

"I think that's an excellent idea for starters."

Elaine walked back to her office. What a way to start a Monday. Janice sounded so positive that it was street people looking for money, but shouldn't she call someone? Were there cameras? She had seen some out front. But who monitored them? She supposed it would be the groundskeeper. She checked the list of internal extensions and dialed Willis Johnson.

"Way ahead of you. Janice called over and suggested I look at last night's tape from the side entrance. Hate to disappoint, but no street people—in fact, no one used that entrance the entire evening. First time someone comes in that way is a delivery this morning. Was anything taken?"

"No. Not that I can tell. Nothing of mine, anyway.

Thanks for your time— Oh, Mr. Johnson? Would it be possible to get a lock on my door?"

"Don't see why not. Got to run it by Father and get back. You let me know if there's anything else that you need."

"Thanks." Oh yeah, right, so that you can run it by Father? That rankled. She really had to laugh. It was good for her not to be in control for a change. She looked around the office. Well, she might as well get the mess cleaned up. But she couldn't stop a niggling suspicion from pushing to the front of her brain—this was an inside job. Hadn't she suspected it before she even talked to Mr. Johnson? Hadn't she just known? And didn't it support her even crazier thought that someone in the Church knew far more than they were saying—probably about a lot of things.

Suddenly she needed to get out—stop sitting around playing 'whodunit' games with herself. She'd find Sr. Angelica and see if they couldn't work on a schedule. Even though no one came in that way, the side door was still found unlocked.

No Sr. Angelica in her office. A sister sweeping the front steps of the convent suggested she look in the laundry room. Apparently an errant Maytag was demanding the attention of the housemother and a repairman. Elaine walked to the back of the complex.

The laundry room was steamy. But the day was coolish and the sticky warmth felt good. Sister was standing over a man who was half inside a front-loader and half out. Elaine felt sure he didn't need the supervision.

"These machines are relics!" Sr. Angelica laughed, "Guess you could say the same about me, no? Some of my moving parts should be replaced. Let's sit over there." She pointed to a folding table and chairs in the corner. "I heard your office was broken into last night."

"News travels quickly."

"Mr. Johnson mentioned it when he brought the repairman over. He, of course, thinks it was a street person. We walk a tightrope—lauded as humane when we let them in, feed and clothe them, but reviled if we try to punish them for vandalism or theft. Drugs make monsters out of people. And temperate climates mean our problem is constant, not just seasonal."

"The question is, how did someone off the street get in?" Would Sister own up to an oversight? Elaine was curious.

"I understand the side door was found unlocked this morning."

Elaine nodded. "Yes, that's what Mr. Johnson said."

"Ms. Mahoney, let me show you something." Sister reached into her pocket and brought out a small pocket-sized spiral notebook laying it on the table. "This is my conscience, so to speak. See? Here under yesterday's date there's a checkmark and a time jotted down—right next to 'left side entrance from alley'. December fifteen—time: ten-twenty p.m. I don't trust my memory any more—not for something so important as locking up. Every night I make notations the minute I've checked or locked a door." Sister fanned the pages of the notebook—all contained line after line of methodically kept lists of times and dates of duty completed.

"Mr. Johnson checked the surveillance tapes from the area and no one is seen entering. Could someone have hidden in the Church? Been locked in and left, leaving the side door or even another unlocked? Somehow getting past a surveillance camera?"

"I suppose anything is possible but I check the pews, the bathrooms—the office entrances off the foyer. It's just highly unlikely. It takes an hour of my time every evening." Sister paused, the fingers of her right hand lightly drumming on the table. "Ms. Mahoney, can I trust you with something? It's just an observation and, yes, maybe more of a sixth sense, but someone is trying to implicate me—prove I'm beyond my usefulness."

"Who would have something to gain by doing that?"

"Someone who wants my job." A sigh, then, "I've decided to accept Father's suggestion that I join my Sisters in Colorado Springs. The retirement facilities offer care from assisted living to hospitalization and rehab. I have a nursing degree. I can still be of use to the community. My time is finished here."

"I hope this isn't a sudden decision that you might regret."

"No, though I have to say the debacle with Sr. Leah hastened it. I liked her, appreciated her good heart, trusted her to be a good example for the younger women in our order. Well, I could not have been more wrong, could I? I think I've lost all my people skills—certainly my ability to read them. It's this younger generation—they simply don't value what I value—honesty? Integrity? Empty words."

"Sometimes people are just difficult to read—impossible actually. I would put Lila Tran in that category. Remember the good things she did. Try not to dwell on how she misrepresented herself. Money obviously blinded her to being truthful. Greed is an amazing sin—but I'm preaching to the choir here, aren't I?"

"It certainly knows no boundaries."

"Is there someone here, in the convent, who might be interested in being housemother?"

Sr. Angelica put an index finger to her lips in a shushing gesture, looked right, then left, removed it, and whispered, "Sister Elizabeth."

Of course, Elaine could have guessed that. But was she setting Sr. Angelica up to fail? Probably. "I think you've made the right decision to join the Sisters in Colorado Springs. You would be an asset to their community. When would you leave?"

"Within the week." A laugh as she noted Elaine's startled look. "I travel light—three habits and some under things. Well, maybe not quite so Spartan. But not so much that I can't go by air with two bags and send a couple keepsakes via UPS. I have two large porcelain crosses from Portugal that have been in my family for over a hundred years—they need special care. But that's it. I'm accustomed to finding my riches in the service of God. I've contacted the community director and everything is in place. If you want to know the truth, I'm looking forward to joining them."

"You will be missed here."

"By some."

"Don't be hard on yourself. You've given this parish many years of service. People speak well of you."

"And then there's a time to move on—the trick is in recognizing that moment." With a shrug Sr. Angelica walked back to check on the Maytag, which was now in pieces scattered across the floor.

+ + +

Change. Usually something she welcomed. But Elaine didn't have a good feeling about a new housemother. She had enjoyed Sr. Angelica's caring and ability to be introspective and honest, but it also was probably a good time for her to move on. The opportunity was there and if she stayed, things might only get worse. A knock on the office door interrupted any further reverie.

"Come in."

"Glad I caught you. I don't want to put this off." The nun pushed the door wide open and swept into the room—'swept' was a perfect antebellum concept but captured her entrance, Elaine thought. In this case, 'swept' was code for pretentious.

"Sister Elizabeth, please, join me." Elaine pointed to a chair in front of her desk.

A shake of her head. "No, thank you, this won't take long."

No smile. The epitome of no nonsense. Elaine idly wondered how many bruised knuckles students had to show for errant behavior. Did she carry a ruler hidden in her habit? This nun was old school. If she remembered correctly, Sister Elizabeth taught in the church's elementary school. Well, she guessed that type of punishment didn't occur any more. But no-nonsense parochial schools were being sought out by parents who still believed in "spare the rod, spoil the child."

"I'll get right to the point. I've talked with Father and he agrees that your services are no longer needed. We both feel the more the women are reminded of the duplicity, no, let's call it what it is—an outright travesty of human behavior, and that includes Sister Leah's lying on so many fronts—well, the quicker that is behind us and we can concentrate as a religious community, on doing God's work through Jesus, the better."

"I see." She was getting fired her first week on the job.

"You are a constant reminder that they were taken in by a charlatan—duped by a pretender of the faith, no less. We had a snake in our midst. But we have to get past this—clear our consciences of blaming ourselves for not seeing what was happening under our noses. We can not let ourselves be branded by this horrific act." She swallowed, then added, "I'm leaving my post as principal of All Saints Catholic Academy. I will be taking over the duties of Sister Angelica as housemother and spiritual guide for the young women living here. Sister will be moving to join her Franciscan order in Colorado Springs."

"Yes, she shared that with me this morning."

"Well, good then. Friday will be her last day. There will be a reception in the rectory conference room at three on Monday. You, of course, are invited. I'm assuming you have no questions?"

"None." Elaine's answer brought a smile. Smug or just relieved?

"Fine. I'm glad we understand each other. I'll expect you to vacate this office by lunchtime." A curt nod, a brisk turn, and she was out the door.

The rebellious kid in Elaine wished she hadn't wasted an hour picking up and putting away the mess someone had left after the supposed break in. They'd save some money by not having to put a lock on the door. She sat thinking about Sister Elizabeth. The woman was somewhere in her mid to latter thirties. Not old, but she somehow looked and acted it. Dishwater blond hair peeked out from the edges of the wimple, unadorned frameless glasses perched a little too high on a prominent bony nose, pale skin dotted with a smattering of freckles across high cheekbones. Truly someone that filling in the eyebrows and adding a touch of makeup would improve her looks immensely—Elaine chided herself, why was she contemplating a makeover for a nun? Perhaps, more importantly, it didn't take much imagination to think of Sr. Elizabeth trashing her office. The unexpected vandalism certainly got the nun what she wanted.

She gathered the few articles from the desk that were hers—a lined yellow tablet, three pens, her computer, two books on St. Bonaventure, her special coffee cup with the saying, "After Monday and Tuesday, Even the Calendar Says WTF!" A favorite student had given her that in what now seemed like a lifetime ago. Getting sacked actually had its benefits—she could spend more time with Jason, visit Maggie, even help her get settled, and maybe most importantly she could act like she was on her honeymoon! She owed Dan some one-on-one time.

Chapter Thirteen

Elaine opened the front door of the townhouse to find Jason eating lunch at the kitchen island. Beside him, sharing his lunch, was the most exquisitely beautiful young Asian woman she'd ever seen. Black hair twisted and secured at the nape of her neck in a perfectly neat bun, long tendrils escaped being tucked behind her ears to fall forward and line her face, feathery eyelashes thick and black looked to be her own, and that perfect rosebud mouth, tinted a coral-pink to stand out against pale, flawless skin. Was the young woman a model?

"Mom, I didn't know you were coming home for lunch. Here, have some of my sushi and come meet Jia Han."

The young woman jumped off the high kitchen stool and came forward. "Ms. Mahoney, so good to meet you."

She was Elaine's height, maybe an inch taller at five nine, and the handshake was firm. "I'm finishing up a degree in art history at Flagler College and I've just been hired as a tutor." She pointed over her shoulder, "My boss," and laughed with Jason. "He was tacking up a notice on the bulletin board, and I was right behind him to take it down. I was beginning to think I'd end up flipping burgers over the break."

"That's great. I assume I'm going to be hearing some Mandarin?"

"Yes. Jason actually has a good grasp already. He just needs practice in conversation. In those future board meetings in Beijing, we want him to be able to politely excuse himself to go to the bathroom or order coffee instead of tea." More laughter, but Jason was ruefully nodding. "I was born in the States—California—but my family made sure I learned the language and the traditions of their homeland."

"First tutoring session this afternoon?" Elaine turned to Jason.

"Yeah, I need to get started—if you don't mind our using the office? Maybe for an hour or two?"

"It's all yours. I'm going to make a couple sandwiches and have lunch with Dan at the Church. I need to get the car back in case Dan thinks it's been stolen. Jia, it was nice meeting you. I look forward to seeing you again. I'm glad Jason found a tutor."

"We'll probably head over to the beach later. Don't count on me for dinner."

They picked up their plates of sushi and headed toward the office. If she were being really honest, she had hoped to work at home herself for part of the afternoon. She needed to outline the St. Bonaventure presentation. But one look in the fridge and she realized grocery-shopping had just jumped to the top of her to-do list. What was it about growing young men that gave new meaning to the term bottomless pit? She'd swear there was a full, half-gallon carton of milk in the fridge just last evening.

+ + +

Dan was sorting through his notes. He still had several interviews to complete. It was interesting that after trying over half a day yesterday to reach Sister Elizabeth, she called him this morning and announced that nine-thirty was the only time she would have free. And to expect her visit. Pushy, demanding, controlling ... Then he admonished himself. She was a nun. The convent was under siege by reporters after yesterday's news release. A disgraced nun had become national news. It couldn't be pleasant going from near obscurity to notoriety overnight. She was probably busy fending off all sorts of inquiries and he'd rather see action than hand-wringing. He applauded the church's direct, no-nonsense, 'we've been duped but we're taking action' approach. It seemed to be playing well on national news. There had been a full five minute segment on the *Today* show featuring the tragedy of human trafficking— bound to garner sympathy and not finger-pointing.

He didn't have to wait for Sr. Elizabeth. She was prompt; he had to give her that. At the very second of nine-thirty, she knocked on the door of the rectory conference room, poked her head in and then came forward to shake his hand and take a seat opposite at the table.

"I don't have to tell you this place is a madhouse." The

attempted smile never made it to her eyes. Was austere something you had to practice to get right? Dan had a strange thought that he was watching someone acting a part—doing what she thought was expected of her—a student of Nun 101.

"Thank you for taking time to meet with me—I know there have been a few startling events for a small tourist town. I'm sure it's adding stress to the Christmas preparations."

A nod, a quick look at her watch, then, "How is it I can help you?"

"As you know, I'm here investigating the disappearance of the relics of St. Bonaventure. I understand the evening of the theft a number of street people entered the vestibule of the church—this was not the first time people from the street have sought warmth. However, I believe there was a commotion that evening caused by someone becoming ill?"

"This is a constant problem we have to contend with. The unfortunates need more help than the church can give them—year round. Yes, that particular evening, one of the men in the group regurgitated while attempting to put his bedroll down in the back pew. Mr. Johnson was beside himself. I was glad I could be of help."

"May I ask what you were doing away from the convent at that hour?"

"It had become apparent that the doors were not being consistently locked. In fact, it had become quite hit and miss. I had taken it upon myself to personally check. Sr. Angelica has been struggling with some of her duties for some time now. Eighty-seven is really too old for that kind of responsibility."

"What did you notice about the group that evening? Take your time. I'd like to hear from you how many there were. And did anyone use the restrooms at the back of the church or walk down front? Did anyone stand out? Was there a spokesperson, for example?"

"Well, let's see … the man who became ill was drunk. I knew a few of the people in the group, I guess there were ten total, but he was new. Earlier in the evening right after dinner, I saw this man in what appeared to be a heated discussion with Sister Leah. He was quite loud and unruly. From what I could see, she was trying to get him to leave our compound. I don't know what was said but she seemed quite rattled—unnerved is a better word. As I walked toward them, he bolted out the front gate. I asked her if I could help but she brushed me off—said everything was under control—just another vagrant seeking entry."

"This is the same man who came back later?" A nod. "And apparently drunker?" Another nod. "What time did the altercation take place?""

"Somewhere between seven and eight. I'm not sure he'd even been drinking when I first saw him then. He just seemed angry. Sometimes the unfortunates become quite belligerent—to the point of taking advantage of our good will. But this was unusual."

"So, it looked like the man was angry at being turned away?"

"Yes, he banged out the gate in a pique. As I said, Sister Leah didn't stop to talk, just hurried inside. Sister Leah. I'm still finding it difficult to accept her true identity. It's just so difficult to get my mind around. Please excuse me." She pulled a Kleenex from a pocket and dabbed at her nose.

"Of course. Take your time."

"You asked about a spokesperson? One of the women, Grace, is a regular and takes care of the others—especially those new to the group. I suppose you would say she's the spokesperson. She was the one who later begged me not to call the police or an ambulance. Looking the other way is a street person's number one coping skill."

"It was your decision not to seek medical help?"

"Mr. Mahoney, he was drunk. I'm not about to waste taxpayer money on a thousand dollar ride for someone to sleep it off between clean sheets."

"Do you remember his name?"

"Someone called him Max."

"What happened after he got sick?"

"A couple men carried him outside and the others followed."

"Did everyone leave at this time?"

"As I recall, but I had already gone next door to get a mop and pail—and disinfectant."

"You were the one who cleaned up the church?"

"Yes, I supervised the cleaning, I would say."

"Did Mr. Johnson go with you to get the cleaning equipment?"

"Yes. I couldn't find the disinfectant and I went back to ask his help."

"And he followed you out of the church and through the kitchen to the storage area off the back alley? And helped you collect buckets, a mop, towels and the like?"

"Yes."

"How long would you say you were gone—that no one from the church was in the nave?"

"We measured the disinfectant and put it into the buckets there so we wouldn't be dragging a five gallon container around. So, maybe fifteen minutes from start to our return."

"Who was left in the church when you got back?"

"Actually, no one. Everyone had gone. The nave was empty."

"Did you lock up at this time?"

"Yes, it was after ten. We certainly didn't want anyone returning."

"Were the bathrooms or confessionals checked before the church was locked?"

"I assume Mr. Johnson did that. I was busy cleaning."

"Who do you think could have stolen the relics?" He might as well be direct—catch her off guard. He could tell his question startled her.

"I have absolutely no idea. Are you asking if one of the street people could have left the group and slipped down to the front … maybe when I wasn't there? Yes, of course, that's possible but it doesn't explain knowing the combination, now does it?" She stood abruptly and pushed away from the table. "If you really want my opinion? I'd say the thief has already met her just demise. You'd do well to follow up on a lead that's under your nose. I'll thank you not to waste any more of my time." With that, she walked around the table and out the door.

Dan simply sat there. He'd just witnessed a lot of lying, if he were to believe Mary Andrews and Willis Johnson. And he did. The smug, 'I have all the answers', approach of Sr. Elizabeth just didn't ring true. Of course, she would say she felt the need to cover up a slight discrepancy. Was she thinking of the insurance money? Maybe. It wouldn't be acceptable to admit to not being there, to hand over responsibility to someone else. A noise in the hallway made him turn. Elaine was standing in the doorway with a sack that just had to be lunch.

"Wow. Office delivery. Should I tip you?" Dan suddenly realized he was famished.

"Depends on what you had in mind." Elaine winked and handed Dan the sack of roast beef sandwiches on poppy seed bagels, extra mayo and horseradish, chips, two bottles of water, and a lemon drop cookie before spreading paper towel placemats on the conference table.

"Probably couldn't do what I had in mind—you'd have to take off work."

"Not a problem. I was fired this morning."

"What?"

Elaine filled him in on her chat with Sister Elizabeth. "Actually, it's fine. I'll have time to spend with Jason and even make a few trips to Dragon's Bend to spend time with your mother. You could get spoiled with home-cooking every night. I still expect to help you—research, interviews—whatever you need. But I'm going to like not wandering around here checking doors at midnight."

"Hey, what do you say to taking off this afternoon? Not what I had in mind earlier but I need to trace this Max guy. You're free this afternoon; come with me. I want to check the soup kitchen here in town and maybe take a trip down to Bunnell and Daytona if he's moved on. The homeless follow a pretty predictable pattern of travel. I want to interview him—he was just too involved the other night. I think he might have some answers."

+ + +

One-fifteen and the soup kitchen on Riberia Street

was closing up. Dan left Elaine in the car while he walked around to the alley. He'd noticed a man cleaning vegetables over a deep sink at the side of the building. A little privacy was a good thing—especially because he was going to tell a fib. He wouldn't get anywhere if he indicated he was investigating a theft—street people protected street people. Dan presented his card and said he was trying to locate a man known as Max. He was representing the estate of what might possibly be a relative of the man concerning an insurance policy. Could he help him?

The man took Dan's card and introduced himself as Jeff, the sous-chef at the soup kitchen. He said it with a smirk and Dan assumed it was meant as a joke. He said he knew this Max but hadn't seen him for a few days. His guess was that he might have stopped in Palm Coast on his way south. He gave directions to the Winn Dixie parking lot and also thought they could check the lot behind the library at Belle Terre and Palm Coast Parkway. Those were the two most popular locations among the homeless in the area. They could leave their stuff there—tents and the like—and the cops looked the other way.

Dan really needed more information and decided to push his luck. Jeff seemed willing to help. "Has Max been a part of the group for long?"

"Naw, he comes and goes—you know, lives on the street then works a couple days, then back to the streets."

"What does he do when he works?"

"Landscaping, trash pickup—sometimes he drives."

"Drives?"

"Yeah, hires out to a limo company when they get busy or he delivers for Lowes, appliances mostly, to hear him tell it. He could drive full time; he has a CDL but says he's been there, done that. Just can't stand the loneliness of long hauls. I think the loneliness got him in trouble if you know what I mean." Dan nodded—truck stops and scantily clad females came to mind. "Says he used to have his own rig but the wife, former, that is, fleeced him good. I think even now if he makes too much money, she comes after it. He don't drink all the time but laps up any extra money before anyone can lay hands on it."

Wow. That was a new wrinkle. What were the chances that the guy who was drunk or pretended to be, had words with a pretend nun, threw up in the church, left his bedroll, came back later driving a limo with the soon-to-be-murdered same fake nun and young captive to pick it up and maybe help himself to a million-two of relics? That was a heck of a lot of coincidences or uncanny, devious planning. Now he really wanted to find this Max.

"Any idea how old he is?"

"Not too old. I'd bet still in his forties."

"Yeah, that would be the right age for the guy I'm trying to locate. Did he ever say where he was from?"

"Listen, mister, you don't know street people, do ya? We're all from somewhere and everywhere and maybe nowhere … you get my meaning?"

Dan nodded. He'd just about worn out his welcome. He was sensing a little annoyance, maybe downright irritation at being asked too many questions. Time to leave. Well, maybe *one* more question.

"Is there someone around here named Grace? She may be a friend of Max's—kinda looks after him?"

"Yeah, but she ain't here now and she's not gonna have any more info than I do."

"Why don't I leave another card? If you don't mind,

I'd like you to give it to her. If she thinks of anything, have her call."

"Will do. One more thing. In Palm Coast? Check the Winn Dixie lot first. Ask for a guy called Jerry. Just look for the biggest, baddest pit bull you've ever seen—sucker must weigh eighty-five pounds or more. Sweet as a baby but he'll scare the pee out of you. Jerry knows everyone and everything; he'll give you the heads-up on Max."

Dan thanked him for his help and walked back to the car and he couldn't stop thinking, 'what if?'

+ + +

They were just a couple blocks from the intersection of King Street and Highway 1—slower going than I-95 but it would put them closer to the west end of Palm Coast Parkway and both the library and the Winn Dixie parking lot. Sixty miles an hour, and a straight shot down the back way beat dodging eighteen-wheelers on the interstate. Wow … was he getting old? Or would he rather talk with Elaine than worry about who was trying to blow him off the road. He'd vote for the latter.

"You don't even know this Max's last name."

"I was afraid that Jeff would push me on that. If asked, I'll give a name but point out that I'm not sure he's using it. Hint at some family secret that might make him seek anonymity—some falling out that has kept him away."

"Should I worry that you seem really good at fibbing?" Elaine was laughing.

"All in the name of problem-solving … and UL&C."

"Okay, you're off the hook. Oh, I think you'll be pleased to know that Jason doesn't seem to have wasted any time finding companionship." Elaine caught him up on Jia Han, tutor extraordinaire.

"And you thought a bedroom by a back entrance wouldn't be appreciated."

"Now, I never said that. Actually, I'm really pleased that he's so school oriented. I think he's going to make good use of his vacation time."

"If she's as gorgeous as you say, hitting the books isn't going to be painful. Just look at me. I'd never thought of taking on a partner but with legs like those, how could I resist?" The playful punch landed squarely on his bicep.

"You know, I'm looking forward to visiting Palm Coast again." Elaine watched them pass the weigh station; next exit was theirs.

Elaine hadn't been in Palm Coast since she'd worked with the private investigator on the Daytona Dog Track case. As a bedroom community it had a certain sprawl that lacked focus. For example, there was no downtown. Two large shopping centers each on an opposite end of town had an anchor store like a Publix grocery or Target Superstore and a smattering of small walk-ins touting wild birdseed, craft beer, a Hobby Lobby or Michaels. Smaller malls were dotted here and there across town, again consisting of shops clustered around a bigger name store. Gas stations and fast-food restaurants seemed to be on every other corner. And in the span of a few months, traffic had to have doubled. Florida was a draw. No one seemed concerned that a part of it might be under water someday.

They had made good time. Within thirty minutes they were turning onto Parkway just a matter of blocks from their destination. The Winn Dixie lot sprawled across a couple acres of asphalt that served several stores—a Bealls, Subway, and Edible Arrangements to name a few. The shopping center was laid out in an L-shape with dry cleaners and restaurants on the opposite end, the bigger stores closer to the Parkway entrance. Several people were lounging outside the grocery store, panhandling, and no one seemed talkative when they walked up.

"Anybody here named Max?" A couple men shook their heads. "So, Max isn't around? Is he still with the group?"

"Ask Jerry." The guy pointed toward the back of the lot and sure enough, sitting in the shade was the biggest pit bull Dan had ever seen and right beside him was a bearded kid—maybe twenty-five. "Thanks, I will."

They left the car and walked to the back of the lot.

"Hi, big guy." Elaine walked straight toward the pit bull who had suddenly turned into a mass of wiggles. "I bet I could find a treat in here if your owner says it's all right." She looked at the kid beside him while she opened her purse and pulled out a baggy. "These are liver treats—all meat, no additives, made in the US." She held a couple in the palm of her hand to show him.

"Yeah, that's fine. He likes you."

"What's his name?"

"Romo."

"Oh, you're a Cowboys' fan?"

"Sometimes. But I'm more of a Bronco guy. He was going to be Peyton. But he already had his name when I got him."

"We have a Rottweiler named Simon. He's keeping my husband's mother company—she lives alone. But I miss having him with us."

"They're great watchdogs and good company."

A nudge with his head then a paw on her foot and it was pretty obvious that Romo wanted another treat. "Okay, one more." Then Elaine sat down on the curb beside him and let the big dog push against her, seeking some petting but giving out a sloppy kiss in return.

"Are you Jerry?" A nod. "Jeff in St Augustine said maybe you could help me." Dan then retold the fib he'd shared with Jeff.

"I'd like to help but not sure I can. Max left a few days ago—wasn't going far, down to Daytona and back that same night. But he never came back. His stuff is here, which is real odd that he'd leave it." Jerry pointed to a bedroll and a backpack behind him leaning against a tree. "I'm keeping an eye on his things but I'm getting worried something's happened."

"Would you feel comfortable looking through the backpack to see if there's an address or phone number, maybe the name of a contact—I don't want to see someone gypped out of what's theirs. And if he doesn't show up, maybe he'd want someone to know."

"I'm with you on that. Been wondering what to do next. Yeah, I'll look through his things."

Jerry unzipped the backpack and pulled everything out—flashlight, a small black, hard-cover notepad from the front pocket, three t-shirts, underwear, jean shorts, long jeans, leather jacket (an expensive one—something in the thousand dollar range, Dan thought), a Swiss army knife, a few packs of condiments—heavy on the ketchup—a partial roll of paper towels, a corkscrew, screwdriver and a pair of pliers all in a leather pouch and that was it. The bedroll was just that—foam mat, set of flannel sheets and a heavy canvas-like cover. No evidence it had been wrapped around a million-plus dollars' worth of artifacts. Jerry dumped everything in a pile.

"Mind?" Dan pointed at the notebook.

"No, go ahead."

Dan picked up the spiral-bound pad only to have a scrap of paper fall to the ground. "Oops. Don't want to lose anything."

"What is it?"

"Bunch of numbers. I'm guessing to a bank account. I'll take a picture and check the designation code. This could be helpful." Dan took out his cell and snapped a photo before leafing through the notepad. A few more pages of random scribbling—a hand drawn map with directions to where they were standing, a couple pages of what might have been a budget or an expense report. Expense report? Odd for a street person. There was another page of what looked like phone numbers. Notations along the side of that page indicated they were work related. These could be some leads that might be helpful. But most of the notebook was empty. He slipped the loose scrap of paper back inside.

"Anything look helpful?"

"I'm guessing these are work numbers. I'll give them a call. Maybe someone knows something." Dan flipped to page four and held it open for Jerry to see. Then, he put the pad down on the ground and took a few more photos. "Thanks. You've really been helpful. Here's my card. If Max comes back or if you think of anything else, please give me a call." He picked up the notebook, closed it, and handed it back to Jerry.

"Oh, and take the rest of the treats." Elaine gave Jerry

the remaining treats emptying the bag onto a paper towel. "Can I help you get his stuff back together?" She'd started picking things off the pile and putting them back in the backpack.

"Thanks, but I've got it."

She leaned down and hugged Romo. Apparently Romo hadn't read the latest list of doggy preferences—hugs were a number one no-no. But in this case, a prolonged hug seemed to be pleasing the big pit bull no end, if one could trust his hopping up and down on hind legs to be a happy dance. Romo had to be restrained when they walked back to the car. Dan laughed. He felt the same way—he'd follow Elaine anywhere. That dog had taste.

Dan maneuvered the car out of the parking lot, turning right before turning left to cross the grassy division separating east and west directions of Palm Coast Parkway and retrace their steps out of town.

"I have a confession to make."

Normally Dan loved to hear those words but a glance at Elaine and he wasn't so sure. She looked truly chagrined and had a tough time making eye contact. "What'd you do?" He was heading back up Highway 1 but based on her tone, he was tempted to pull over to the side of the road.

"It would be nice to have a last name. I know you consider this Max key to your investigation, so in case his fingerprints might help you—I pilfered the Swiss army knife." She gave him a tentative side-long glance, then pulled the item from her purse already safeguarded in the empty treat baggy. "Please don't be upset."

"You're kidding; that's brilliant! Did anyone ever tell you you'd make a great P.I.?" By way of underscoring his glee, he struck his palm against the steering wheel. "And I never even saw you. How the hell? You're good, lady."

"So, in the interest of justice, theft can be excused?"

"Um. The word 'pilfer' worked earlier. Let's put the right spin on this—we're not talking about evidence that needs to be presented at trial. This is an identity check of a person of interest. Heck, he may not even come back for his bedroll and backpack." But that was hard to believe remembering the leather jacket.

"You make it sound perfectly all right—expected, even."

"Well, let's just wrap it in the guise of being helpful— really helpful."

Dan couldn't stop grinning. His partner-to-be was sharp—intuitively right on the money. He was going to like this work-sharing thing—Mr. and Mrs. Daniel Mahoney, Investigators, Insurance Specialists. Yeah, had a nice sound to it.

Chapter Fourteen

Maggie, of course, I'd love to help. I'll be there at nine but get me a ticket for the table tipping in the afternoon. That sounds like fun."

Elaine tapped to disconnect and put her phone on the table next to Dan. A quiet evening at home—just the two of them—even Jason had called to say he was eating out and then heading to a movie. He didn't explicitly say someone was with him but it was implied—he used the word, 'we'. She was glad he was enjoying his break.

"So, how's Mom?"

"Stressed. The movers left a mess—stacked boxes marked 'kitchen' in the bedroom, others for the 'garage' in the guest bathroom—you know, that sort of thing. She lost Simon's dog food but found it in the tool shed. She's pulling her hair out. She still can't find her coffee maker."

"Oh, wow, why didn't you say that first? She's only a half-step from a full blown breakdown. No coffee? You might want to take some and an IV setup."

"Dan, it's really not funny—she sounds frazzled. I think she's been living out of boxes for some time now. And I think the community has expected her to be ready to work. So she's left a mess in order to accommodate them."

"I'm still not sure what she's supposed to be doing."

"Nor am I, but I'll find out."

"What are my chances of talking you into making it an early night?" A Groucho Marx wiggle to the eyebrows got the laugh he wanted. "Or I could try out a few of my sofa moves."

Now, Elaine was really laughing—"Sofa moves?"

"Yeah, you scoot over this way and we start with snuggling then we get rid of some of this clothing and—"

"Okay, I get the picture." Elaine was already sliding toward him.

+ + +

Morning. Six a. m.—she slipped out of bed, grabbed underwear, a pair of jeans and a jean shirt, then reset the alarm for seven before tiptoeing out of the room. Jason's door was closed and, yes, curiosity was almost more than she could bear but there was no reason to go barging into his room just to check the number of occupants. The idea of a mock fire drill did cross her mind. She gave herself an imaginary pat on the back for showing restraint. He was a young adult; he deserved to be treated like one.

Coffee was the first to-do item, then find a thermos and put a banana and a power bar in a bag before showering and getting dressed. Finally she was out of there. Hair tied back with a navy and gold paisley scarf and a fringed denim vest completed the 'I'm on holiday' look. She wasn't planning on dressing up to unpack boxes. And she wasn't at all certain what the dress code was for table tipping. But Florida, like New Mexico, was casual—maybe even more so if you considered most of the state's residents sported sandals nine months out of the year.

She entered the address into her GPS, put an extra bottle of water in the console and backed out of the driveway. Seventy-six miles, an easy drive. An hour and twenty minutes and she was in the rolling greenery outside Dragon's Bend and one mile from Maggie's bungalow.

If she hadn't known the little house was a rental, she would have sworn Maggie had designed and built it. Painted a blue-gray with navy gingerbread trim including the wrap-around porch, the exterior was set off by a three-foot deep continuous bed of purple Mexican Petunias on tall deep green stems. Breathtaking and still blooming in the warmish mid-December sunlight. Elaine pulled in the drive and sat there, taking in her surroundings. Quaint? From another time? Yes, and yes, but that still didn't capture the magic. She stepped out of the car still enjoying the serenity and color.

"Elaine!" The screen door banged open and a woman with bright red hair, a white shirt, and boyfriend jeans waved enthusiastically from the doorway—but it was Simon who literally flew off the porch, clearing the three squat steps in one leap. The little yelps in greeting made her feel she'd been missed.

"I'm impressed with the welcoming committee." Elaine still had a hand on Simon as they walked up onto the porch. "I'd honestly wondered if he'd remember me."

"Remember? Just look at that. You're his long-lost best friend." Maggie held the door open as Elaine and Simon, staying wallpaper close, went into the house. "He's not going to let you get away."

"Oh, Maggie, I love this house." Elaine marveled at the large stained glass panel in the door. In blues and grays and purple, it was a beautiful study of the Blue Ridge Mountains. Inside, a blue and white color scheme was punctuated by bright spots of lime green and violet.

"There's no reason to keep a secret, I bought the house a couple months back. So much more *me* than The Villages. I'm so glad you like it. I feel like I've found a home—a home for one person. I decided to chuck the heavy old leather furniture—it was too big and too dark. Way too much for this small living space. And absolutely no more recliners. Men and recliners are both out of my life for good. It's probably an age thing, but they seem to go together."

Elaine nodded but found herself not believing her mother-in-law. Not that the episode with Stanley wasn't horrific, but she just couldn't see the flirty, cute Maggie Mahoney not on the arm of some lothario. Elaine could only hope her seventies were as healthy and fun.

"I love what you've done." A bank of old-fashioned windows along the east wall of the dining room had transom-like borders of stained glass across the top—all three taken together represented a field of wild flowers, red poppies, multi-hued Gaillardia and Black-eyed Susans. Unique. "You've been haunting some art studios. The stained glass touches are gorgeous." The four-poster bed was just a bit big for the bedroom but the white eyelet cover and shams were perfect. An old-fashioned dressing table with ruffled curtain was a great touch.

"Now for the kitchen and a cup of coffee—or tea, if you'd rather. When I couldn't find my coffee grinder and pot, I switched to tea. I sort of liked it—it made a nice change."

"I think I'll stick with coffee if you're having some."

While waiting for the coffee-maker to finish, a tour of the rest of the house—bathroom with turn-of-the-last-century fixtures even a claw and ball footed tub, an office instead of a second bedroom, a garden room add-on, and a partial basement. In all, a cozy sixteen hundred square foot bit of living space.

"The backyard is fenced and really quite large—eighth of an acre. Simon loves it. I think Simon's enthusiasm made me grab it up. No more city living for us."

"Simon is spoiled. I saw the orthopedic memory foam dog bed in the bedroom."

"Oh, he's so good. He deserves every perk. Let's doctor our coffee and go out to the porch."

Two white Adirondack rockers with a small round wooden table separating them were sandwiched between a hanging porch swing and two heavy straight-backed chairs with wide wooden arms. Again, inviting and in keeping with the house's décor.

"Now, I want to hear about this job. Dan says it sounds like it was made for you."

"I think he's right. My interest in the supernatural dates back to my time in New Mexico. I studied for almost a year with a Tarot Master in Taos. It has always been my dream to move here or to a community like it. I'll be doing readings but mostly giving guidance based on inquiries—online requests. The Leader, you'll meet him later today, owns and operates two guidance clinics. Each is set up to first offer a basic online reading and then for a modest sum follow up with support and direction. A lot of it is automated. For example, a daily horoscope reading is offered once we have a person's birthdate."

"Do you work from home?"

"Almost entirely, if I wanted, but I like to show up at the office once a day. Didn't I say this was a dream job? Dragon's Bend is the psychic capital of the world—I'm not kidding; Check Wikipedia; that's how it's listed. I love the people here. It's not for everybody, but for believers it couldn't be a more perfect setting. Can you imagine how wonderful it is that when you say something a little out of the ordinary no one rolls their eyes or moves their chair away from you?"

"I bet there are more believers than not in the outside world—some are just uncomfortable talking about it."

"And you?"

"I keep an open mind. I don't rule anything out."

"Good, because I want to read your cards."

"I'd like that." And Elaine meant it—it was a topic that interested her. She wasn't sure Dan shared her interest, but he was supportive of his mother.

"We have a couple hours before the table tipping workshop. I'll get the cards. Help yourself to more coffee and let's do this at the dining room table."

"You know I came prepared to help you unpack but I haven't seen one box." Elaine followed Maggie back into the house.

"Doesn't mean there aren't any. Don't look in the basement, the garage, or the toolshed. I don't want to spoil our afternoon with work. Believe me, those boxes aren't going anywhere. They'll wait for another visit. I hate to admit to how long they've waited now."

Elaine topped up her coffee and moved to the dining area off the kitchen—the smallish space was dominated by a round oak table and four chairs. She took a seat facing the stained glass tableau of wild flowers. There was something so relaxing being away from Sisters Elizabeth and Angelica, not to mention stolen relics and make-believe nuns.

Maggie put a pad of paper and a pen in front of her. "I want you to jot down two or three questions that you'd like information on—they can be general or more specific. But ask open-ended questions. Steer clear of the yes or no, short-answer ones. Tarot often does a better job giving long, drawn-out answers that beg interpretation but in so doing, a complicated answer can become simple and workable. I know that sounds a little convoluted but trust me on this. Stick with questions that are personal—as much as you might like to know something about Jason or Dan, this reading is about you. Okay, so far?"

Elaine nodded, "This is helpful. I've been curious but I've never had the cards read for me."

"Then this will be fun. And enlightening. Just a couple more guidelines or explanations then we'll start. The cards encourage you to take ownership of the situation that you're curious about. Stay in the now. Questions about the future should be within the framework of what we need to do today to shape our future—not a demand to know what it holds. This is about preparedness and your involvement going forward."

"What about the past? Any illumination there? Maybe something I shouldn't have done?"

"Good questions. But no, do not dwell on things that cannot be changed—the past is done and over with; let it be. Take a few minutes and formulate your questions, write them down, then turn the page over. I don't want to see them."

Elaine nodded, paused, then jotted down: How can I best support Dan in his work? Then crossed that out and wrote, what do I need to know to best support Dan in his work? What do I need to be focusing on right now? Those questions seemed to go together. She turned the page over.

"Ready?"

"I think so."

"Then take the deck of cards and shuffle them. I use the Universal Waite deck—probably the most popular and true to the cards' origin."

Elaine took the cards and chose to side-shuffle from right hand to left. "How will I know when to quit?"

"Believe it or not, you'll just know. When you're finished, place the deck on the table in front of you. Cup both hands and cover the deck, touching it. Leave your hands in place while you think of your questions. Sometimes it's best to close your eyes. Take a few deep breaths and let me know when you're ready to continue. There's no hurry."

In about three minute's time, Elaine opened her eyes and nodded, "Ready."

"Cut the cards toward you with your left hand."

"My left hand?"

"Your left hand taps into the intuitiveness of your right brain. You can make more than two stacks—three or four, then continuing left to right to left put the deck together again and hand it to me."

Elaine lined up four—some larger, some smaller—

stacks in front of her then followed directions, combined them and handed the deck to Maggie.

"I'm going to do a 10-card basic Celtic Cross spread. In broad terms, we're going to look at the present and what, if any, obstacles you're facing followed by something that is a part of what is going on now. Then we'll move to the past to see what you've just moved through before taking a look at what you're aiming at. Then, the future—what happens next and what you need to know to prepare. Cards seven, eight, nine and ten are read bottom to top and I think you'll find them interesting. The column starts with how you see yourself, then a look at your surroundings and how others see you, moving to reaching your goal or goals, and any fears or hopes that you may have in accomplishing that, until finally, the outcome. The final card dwells on results of what leads up to it—choices made, obstacles to overcome and what rewards there might be."

"All that?"

Maggie chuckled. "And then some, most likely. Shall we get started? I'm going to lay out the entire cross before explaining each card and its position. Sometimes an overview is helpful to me—a sort of summation of parts, if you will. By the way, I suggest you take notes—use that pad and pen; there's too much to commit to memory. And take a picture of the final spread to support your notes. Trust me. You'll have questions later and struggle to remember all this."

Elaine sat quietly and watched her mother-in-law take a card off the top of the deck, and then another, methodically placing each card, and pausing to reflect before moving on. The first card was crossed by a second card placed horizontally on top. The present with what might be causing friction? She reached for the pad and pen and jotted down the arrangement of the ten cards and the inscription on each.

5. Fool   10. Judgment

4. Wheel of Fortune 1. High Priestess 6. Justice 9.VI Cups

2. Hanged Man

8. IX Cups

3. II Swords

7. The Lovers

Maggie studied the cards, picked up the Hanged Man, then replaced it. "I'm glad we're doing this. There are some messages here—some things I want you to consider, take seriously. I think the Universe is giving you a warning."

Elaine couldn't help it, goose-bumps prickled across her forearms.

"Why don't we trade places so that the cards are facing you?"

Elaine moved to the opposite side of the table, took out her phone and snapped several pictures of the spread.

"Of course, you know I'm going to say there is no such thing as coincidence?"

Elaine nodded; maybe she sort of believed the same thing.

"So, when the card representing you came up as the High Priestess, no surprise. This is a woman highly intuitive, steeped in knowledge, very spiritual and wise—someone you can trust to get to the bottom of things, solve sticky problems that won't be apparent to others. This is the card a female P.I. wants." Maggie smiled, "I think you're so on the right track teaming up with my son—I have such a good feeling about your partnership.

"Card number two is placed horizontally across Card number one because it acts as a 'heads up' … what can deter your natural instincts, inclinations to action in your case. It could indicate that you need to rethink how you normally approach something. Think outside the box. Suspend disbelief. But don't give in to suspended action. Get to the bottom of things. The hanged man is upside down and hanging by a thread. There may be serious things coming your way—don't hold back and don't be judgmental.

"Card number three is the Two of Swords. In that position it is literally what is below you—what you're moving through. But it indicates you're not seeing things clearly. Notice that the figure on the card is blindfolded. There's uncertainty, conflicting

perceptions. Could you have been hoodwinked by someone?

"The fourth card indicates the past—what has been completed. The wheel suggests something has come full circle. Moving, changing jobs, changes in fortune—cycles and turning points in our life define our karma and enrich our existence. I sincerely interpret this as your marriage to Dan. The Wheel of Fortune brings you new resources, money, people, and, best of all, luck.

"Card Five is the Seven of Swords—see the figure walking away with an armload of swords? Just as the artwork depicts, someone is getting away with something—literally. Are you being duped? Is someone putting something over on you? This card represents what is above you—what is happening now or about to happen. It closely corresponds to the number three card below you in the spread. There is duplicity in your life—in your surroundings. I don't see imminent danger just a need to be aware.

"Finally, we come to the Future, card six, and here we find Justice. A fitting card following all the warnings, I think. Now we face decisions. Maybe deliberations on a course of action. But rightness will prevail, harmony and balance will return to the world. This is the summation of the law of cause and effect. It could even indicate legal action of some type—with an outcome you agree with.

"I think you'll find the last four cards fascinating and very appropriately a culmination of what has gone before from your personal perspective. Position seven in this spread is how you see yourself, how you would describe your life at this moment. The Lovers indicate a partnership, reaching a decision with someone else based on shared, conscious cooperation. You see yourself as mirrored through the eyes of your partner. Through him you validate your own sense of worth. There's a wonderful harmony emanating from this card—free of guilt, inhibition, and a deep sense and acceptance of duality. You've grown to realize that love can only exist in an atmosphere that is restriction-free. You have that kind of environment with Dan."

"And, the Nine of Cups suggests the world sees how you feel. You're perceived as having your ducks—in this case, cups—in a row. Almost to the point of being smug about it. This card is good health, and wishes fulfilled, but suggests you be aware of complacency.

"The Six of Cups suggests new knowledge based upon the past. A renewal of friendships or beliefs, an explanation of what has gone before. It prepares you for the final card, Judgment.

"Card ten is a summation of questions put forth in the other nine, any problems that need solving, now reach a conclusion. I think you can see very plainly that this is the case here. Judgment indicates you've realized something you haven't considered before—new perceptions, a sense of purpose, a way of solving problems—it's an awakening, actually. This is the true epiphany card. You are in a position to question and research motives, to draw unbiased conclusions, and to base your actions on fact. It is also the card of family—of appreciation of parenthood and partners."

Maggie sat back, "I know this is a lot of information. Do you have any questions?"

"Wow. You're right, it's a lot to think about."

"If I were asked to synthesize, I'd say currently things aren't as they seem. I don't think you realize this is happening. You're being duped. But you're also being set up to solve the problem. Whatever it is, the outcome is good."

"Actually, this does sum up the situation we were in recently." Elaine filled Maggie in on the nun who wasn't a nun but actually a hooker, who was also up to her neck in human trafficking, but then was murdered and found with flecks of gold from the stolen relics under her fingernails. It sounded a little fantastic even knowing it was true.

"I agree that the cards have picked up the most recent past but there's also a warning here—don't trust appearances now, either. I feel you're being lied to. Please, be careful. Now, we've got about thirty minutes to get to the table tipping workshop. It's only three miles from here so we'll have time to browse the gift shop. They carry a book I'd like you to take a look at."

+ + +

The Dragon's Bend Spiritual Camp Bookstore was on

the corner of Stevens Street and Dragon's Bend Road. A sprawling older building with surrounding porch had been added on to and now held the bookstore, gift shop, and a conference room in the back. Parking was in a back lot or on a side street and the immediate area already held a dozen or so cars. Elaine wasn't sure what she'd expected but there appeared to be a bustling business in spirituality—mid-afternoon on a weekday!

The bookstore had a little of everything. Maggie suggested a workbook, *Tarot and Personal Transformation,* and Elaine bought that and a deck of Tarot cards. Yes, she knew she was in for some ribbing from Dan, but she was eager to follow up Maggie's reading with her own research. Dan would be referring to her as a convert, but she wasn't sure she hadn't always been a believer. She'd always been comfortable with being intuitive and at some level isn't that what Tarot tapped into? That deeper consciousness?

"Let's go in. They limit participants to twelve, and four at a time on the table. They discourage onlookers."

In the center of the room was a smallish table with the pedestal sporting three carved legs on casters. It didn't look special. Something her grandmother might have had in a hallway. It appeared that participants would stand in a circle around the table.

Did the table really move? Or did it stay in one place and 'tap' out answers using the alphabet? She knew she was in for an old-fashioned séance—popular in the late 1800s along with the Ouija Board. Parlor game or something a lot more serious? Elaine guessed she'd find out exactly what the table did. The top was barely three feet in diameter. Maggie shared that the Leader and his assistant would be on opposite sides and the participants in between—six all together. It would be crowded.

She was leafing through her newly purchased workbook when Maggie whispered, "There he is—the Leader."

Elaine looked up to see a man in the doorway. With the light of the adjoining room behind him, he appeared to have an aura. At least six-four, dressed in black tunic and slacks, a gold chain reaching halfway down his chest with what looked like an ice cube dangling from the center. A large sparkling sample of clear quartz, Elaine thought. His graying hair and beard matched exactly, both wavy and thick, eyes dark and penetrating as he searched the room. Sizing up the participants? Maybe. He was probably somewhere in his sixties, big but muscular and tan—she expected him to suddenly lean forward with a Dos Equis in his hand to share what he did when thirsty.

He continued into the room—this man who took up space but moved with the grace of a cat. Elaine's reaction was visceral. If she'd been a housecat, she would have arched her back, hissed and run for cover. She couldn't even remember when she'd had such a strong reaction to someone. Could she be overreacting? Letting her Tarot-fueled imagination run away with her? In fact, she had a strong urge to look at the Devil card in her new Tarot deck at that very moment.

Maggie leaned close, "He's one of the most powerful people I've ever met. If you get the chance, go to him for a reading. He's spellbinding. I want you to meet him."

As if that thought had zipped telekinetically to him, the Leader acknowledged Maggie and walked to where they were sitting.

"This is my daughter-in-law, Elaine Mahoney."

"Elaine, so good to have you with us today." He bowed slightly, took her hand in the two of his while ever so lightly caressing her palm with his thumb. "Is this your first time?" The words seemed to slide over her. With his deep, baritone voice and skin-to-skin contact, he could have been discussing losing her virginity as easily as table tipping.

"Yes. I admit I'm new to table tipping but very eager to experience it."

"I think you'll enjoy. I'm glad you came today. We're so fortunate to have Margaret with us." Then, a slight lowering of his head, conspiratorially leaning forward, "I hope to see you again." A smile, sly and at the same time, at some level intimate and knowing. All before releasing her hand. Elaine looked away and hoped the flush she felt creeping up her neck couldn't be seen from the outside. In the light of day and in a crowded room, she felt like she'd just been reduced to wearing nothing but her underwear.

Even the little attention he'd given her seemed to rankle several women in the room—if looks could kill. Something told her this could pass as a cult following—charismatic leader, many more women than men, a community already steeped in the occult. Would Maggie be safe? She made a mental note to check on her more often.

She watched the Leader walk to the center of the room. "I think we're all here. Most of you know Nancy, my assistant." A strikingly beautiful woman smiled and sort of half-waved to the group. Gray hair brushing her shoulders and streaked with white-blond and mottled brown gave her that wolf in summer coat look. And no make-up; absolutely none—even from across the room, Elaine would bet her life on it. And how could anyone look that good in a tie-dyed ankle-length skirt and t-shirt?

"Margaret, Elaine … why don't you take positions to my right. Edie and Jean? Here, on my left and, of course,

Nancy will be directly across from me. Margaret will be acting as an observer and not an active participant—this is part of her community training. "

Those singled out walked to the table. "Now, I want everyone to lightly place their fingertips on the table top. Like this." He demonstrated, complimenting the woman named Jean whose arching fingers suggested a lifetime of playing the piano. "I hope each of you has come with the name of the person with whom they would like to make contact. I will say a brief prayer to the Spirits and summon those who would like to speak with us. I'll request that the spirits spell out their names—the number of taps will correspond with that letter's numerical place in the alphabet—from one to twenty-six. Yes/no questions will be answered with a single table tap for yes, and two taps for no. Questions? No? Let us begin."

Elaine had absolutely no idea of someone she'd like to speak with. She felt like she'd just forgotten to bring her homework to school. She sneaked a peek at Maggie but her eyes were closed. Suddenly, the table shifted, a slight rise and a turn. Eerie. She had a wild impulse to run out of the room, out the door and peek under the house, fully expecting to find rope and cables attached to giant magnets—how stupid. She needed to rein in her imagination and live in the moment, suspending disbelief.

"Is there someone who wants to speak to us?" The Leader's melodious tones seemed to flow across the table just barely before the table rose, then lowered in a distinct tap.

"Yes? Can you give us your name?"

Twelve taps, a five second rest, nine taps, another five seconds of quiet, another twelve taps, silence, and then a single tap. The Leader paused, fingertips suspended waiting for movement before asking if that was all; he was rewarded with a single tap. "It looks like we have L-I-L-A. Does this name mean something to someone at this table? Elaine kept her eyes lowered. Lila was the real name of the pretend nun but that was just too far-fetched. Suddenly the table was spelling out another name only this time she counted—1-22-5-14-7-5 ... A-V-E-N-G-E—not a name but a single word. She felt her breathing quicken. It would make sense; Lila wanted her murder avenged. Then she chided herself—how easily one could get caught up in this world of the beyond. This was not the place for an overactive imagination.

Suddenly the woman, Edie, called out, "Grammy? Is that you?" Then with voice lowered, she addressed the group at the table. "I'd totally forgotten that was my grandmother's given name—we all called her Chiquita for little one. She was only four foot eleven."

"Does the word 'avenge' mean anything to you?" The Leader asked in a whisper.

"Her husband mistreated her. It was awful. The family secret that wasn't a secret—if you know what I mean. Do you think that's who she means?"

"Ask her."

"Grammy, it's Edie, do you want us to avenge something that happened to you? Something by a member of your family?"

Elaine could swear that everyone at the table was holding his or her breath—waiting for the tap or taps. But they never came. Lila seemed to have disappeared and Elaine couldn't help but think that she had been right. Lila, the spirit, was Lila the pretend nun and it was her death that

Elaine had been instructed to avenge. But that was absurd. She couldn't believe she was even considering this—one trip to Dragon's Bend, a tarot reading, a table tipping with supposed spirits and she was a follower? Where were the vats of Kool-Aid? She might as well drink up now.

Two distinctly different spirits made contact with women at the table. A young boy needing to say he was sorry for not saving his sister from drowning. And the recently passed husband who assured his wife he would be waiting for her when they met again. Elaine couldn't shake the feeling of being privy to real communication. And try as she might, she could not see that the Leader and his assistant were the ones tipping the table. She and Maggie stayed to watch the other two groups take their turns with much the same results. Two women who had contacted their mothers broke down in tears and needed a brief time-out to compose themselves. What she was watching was exceptionally powerful. And if misused could be dangerous. It would be easy to set up the unsuspecting to give money or worse if directed by false spirits—those who posed as the departed. She needed to keep reminding herself to have an open mind.

"So? What'd you think?" Maggie was expertly maneuvering her BMW convertible between rows of parked cars and turning onto Dragon's Bend Road.

"Lila was the name of the pretend nun who was so brutally murdered."

"Oh my God! I just knew we weren't meeting little Chiquita. The message *was* meant for you. I could feel it."

"I don't know. It seems like way too much coincidence."

"No—there is no coincidence—this was an honest cry for help. You must stay in touch with her."

"How would I do that?"

"The cards, of course. I see you purchased a deck. You wouldn't have done that if you hadn't felt the need to communicate or just delve deeper into this science—yes, I consider it a science. For starters, you need to purify your house. I have several sticks of white sage that I'll give you. Go online and find out how to best purify the townhouse where you live."

Elaine wasn't sure this was something she wanted to pursue … but what could it hurt? Was she saying that she didn't believe? Sort of. Still, it was difficult to explain what had happened this afternoon.

When they got back to the bungalow, Maggie fixed a care-package of sage sticks, candles, and copies of several articles of directions on purification—of home and self. A few pats for Simon and Elaine was back on the road heading to St. Augustine.

Chapter Fifteen

The morning was dragging. A meeting with Fr. Pete, more photos of the safe with the display case that had housed the relics, a call to the company to have its specifications sent, and sitting around waiting on three interviewees—all three of which didn't show up—one forgot and the other was out ill and he couldn't reach the third. He was going a little stir crazy. He had especially hoped to talk with the cook but she was fighting off a sinus infection. Working that closely to the back alley, he hoped she might have seen something before the theft. If it wasn't the driver in the black limo, someone might have been casing the place a day or so ahead of time … or maybe he needed to return to the idea of it being an inside job. He was just about ready to take a lunch break when his phone vibrated.

"Dan? I'm assuming I can call you Dan? This is Liz Levine, OMI."

"Of course, I'm hoping you're going to tell me that Swiss Army Knife was just loaded with prints and you have a name for me."

"Better than that. Did I catch you at a bad time? I'm hoping I can lure you out to the lab over lunch. I'm good for something from the food truck as long as you like Mexican."

"Sure. If you can spring for some pork tacos, I'll reimburse."

+ + +

He wasn't sure what this meant—it was odd that the information seemed to require a meeting. Liz didn't seem prone to theatrics. But she sure had a way of getting his attention. Frankly, it would seem they had found more than prints—or maybe prints from more than one person. Finding out the identity of this Max could be a real breakthrough. He'd left messages at a couple of the possible work places listed in Max's notebook but no one had called him back. The transiency of street people was its own kind of camouflage.

Per usual, he parked along the side of the L-shaped building toward the back and walked to the front. He was beginning to feel at home. Liz met him at the door and immediately apologized.

"We have company. I know I should have given you a heads up but he was in the room when I called." She turned and walked down the short hallway.

Before Dan could question her, they were at her office. The man who stood up when they entered was the local police chief, easy to recognize by the number of times he was highlighted in the local paper. He'd recently been part of a ribbon-cutting for an addition to a county building housing road maintenance equipment. The photo showing him with his arm around the shoulder of the county sheriff was only a day after he had been photographed presenting safety tips to a group in an assisted living complex. Dan hoped his celebrity status didn't preclude good police work.

"Dan, this is Chief Rob Mitchell." After a perfunctory shaking of hands, each took a seat across the desk from Liz.

"Chief, I'll let you start this meeting off." Clearly this wasn't Liz's show. Interesting. For whatever reason, another dimension had been added.

He turned toward Dan. "For starters, I will be recording this session. It will be acceptable as a deposition with your signature here and here." He placed the legal-looking disclaimer on the edge of the desk and offered a pen. Dan signed and dated the document. There was little doubt now that his curiosity was running wild. Either this was some cautionary internal regulation or he needed a lawyer.

"Now, tell me how the Swiss Army Knife came into your possession."

Dan handed the Chief his card, gave a synopsis of background information and reiterated why he was trying to find the transient called Max—how the search had led him to a quasi-camp of street people in Palm Coast. The person called Max had seemingly disappeared, leaving his possessions behind. Hoping fingerprints might lead him to finding him, Dan had 'borrowed' the knife so that he could have it checked. A little bit of a fib but he was protecting the innocent. Or, at least, his wife. The Chief listened intently but didn't seem to have questions.

"Were you able to lift prints?" Dan turned to Liz.

"I'd say better than that—you've come up with the murder weapon. This is what killed Lila Tran. And, yes, there were prints."

Dan was speechless.

Liz slipped three, eight-by-ten, glossy photos from an envelope on her desk. "I know how old fashioned this makes me look but not everything has to be electronically transmitted. And I'll be attaching these to my written reports." She picked up the top photo. "There are seven puncture wounds. The killer was this one." She pointed to what looked like a direct hit to the carotid artery on the right side of Lila's neck. "There were signs of blood halfway up the knife's casing. The knife had been wiped off but not cleaned. This color photo of the weapon shows the rust-colored wash that was found on the blade and part of the handle. Most of the residue was inside the knife's casing."

The Chief leaned forward. "Let me just interject here that answers for one crime can sometimes open up questions about another. I'm sure I'm preaching to the choir, but INTERPOL is now involved. The prints belong to a Maxim Smirnov, best known internationally as a bit of a jack-of-all-trades. This may or may not be his birth name—he's used several aliases and passed himself off as American, Russian, Mexican and Lithuanian with corresponding addresses and identities in each country. We know he speaks several languages and is able to move transparently in international circles."

"So either the missing relics or human trafficking would be possibilities—something he might be involved with?" Dan asked.

"I'd say both. He doesn't lack for contacts. And history

shows he's always quick to make a buck. He was on our radar about two years ago—suspicion of drug trafficking out of Miami before we lost him. But he's stayed off our radar—nothing before or since up this way."

"Any reason for the killing? What's your best guess? Was he a hit man, or maybe it was personal?"

"My instinct says hit man. But, as I'm sure you've figured out, I don't think we're going to find him. He's a pro at disappearing—with help, of course; his benefactors are well-heeled. I'll need the addresses and contact people of anyone you spoke with concerning his whereabouts."

Dan nodded, "Not a problem but, just out of curiosity, what was his name when he posed as an American? And did he have a job in this country?"

"He was Max Walters, owner of a rather successful travel agency in Boston. Ring any bells?"

"No. Never heard either name—Smirnov or Walters."

"What will your company want you to do next? My guess is the relics are long gone and not traceable."

"I still have the legwork left. I need to follow leads—establish a fairly irrefutable case that he, in fact, did take the relics, and see if I can get closer to this Max. Exhaust every possibility that he might be found. I'd love to stumble onto a paper trail but I know I'm not going to be that lucky. I'm interviewing several more employees of the Basilica. At best, I think someone saw something and maybe they don't realize its importance. The theft was not the result of breaking into the container where the relics were kept but of someone knowing the combination to the safe. Only a few within the church had access."

"I wish you luck. Let me know if there's anything I can help with." Chief Mitchell gave him his card.

+ + +

Dan sat in the parking lot, letting the information sink in. What were the chances the Swiss Army Knife in an abandoned backpack would turn out to be a murder weapon? He doubted this Max was coming back for his belongings. He must have known that fairly quickly everything would be divvied up among his street buddies if he wasn't watching. What a great way to get rid of something. No need to destroy it yourself; it would simply be lost in someone else's pocket—never to be found and never to be traced back to you. Who would have thought a devious, soon-to-be PI would sneak it out of your bedroll found in the back of a parking lot of a Winn Dixie in a town nobody has heard of … Elaine would be astounded.

And, Dan now had a name. Not that it meant too much, but a name could get them closer to the truth. He held little hope that the infamous Max was still around; yet, *if* Dan could find him, the man might have answers or could lead Dan to them. However, if his connections were as good as the Chief said they were, he was physically long gone. Hit men usually had protection—ironclad protection if they were good at what they did. A lot of conflicting thoughts—still, Dan wasn't ready to give up.

So … back to his tracking skills. Dan picked up his phone and dialed the number of the landscaping business listed in Max's notebook. Another dead end. The owner swore Max hadn't worked for him in almost nine months and hadn't left a forwarding address—even the phone on record had been disconnected. What last name did he have on file for him? Smith.

Smith? Had he heard correctly? Guess he could add one more to the list of aliases. Dan thanked him and moved to the next business on the list—a limousine service. Had to be the one that Max was driving for the night the relics went missing. Wasn't it a big black car that he'd parked in the alley when he went inside the church to find the bedroll? The boss was out but the receptionist promised he would be back in forty-five minutes—almost the exact amount of time it would take to get to Bunnell and the used car dealership, which also provided limousines for local events. Put me down for an interview, he told the receptionist— He was on his way.

+ + +

He took the SR100 exit and found the dealership across from Marvin's Gardens. The lot in front of the portable building held about fifty cars—most run-of-the-mill, nondescript three to ten year old Camrys, Sonatas, Ford Fiestas, Chevy Malibus, and a few vans and trucks. There were an assortment of signs and tethered helium balloons touting Pat's Gently Loved Vehicles to be clean and reasonable—the best bargain in the state. A man, maybe the only salesperson, was smoking a cigarette and wiping down the hood of a red Corvette. Probably his own, Dan thought. Pat was not having a blockbuster day.

Dan climbed the three metal steps to the narrow porch and went inside. A wall heating and air unit was keeping the office a little too warm for his liking and the drone of the machine was deafening. But, it appeared, one of those things one could get used to. The receptionist simply talked over the noise and asked him to wait—Mr. O'Rourke would be just a minute. Dan heard the flush of a toilet somewhere in back and a swarthy, overweight, caricature of a used car dealer walked through a rear door. Dressing the part, his plaid shirt looked slept in and was tucked into thrift store chinos frayed at the cuffs. He shook Dan's hand and looked over his shoulder out the window to see what he'd driven onto the lot. It was probably immediately apparent that Dan hadn't brought in the two year old black Land Rover SUV for a trade.

"I like your taste, young feller."

Dan bristled. Why did it bother him when men probably no more than ten years his senior put on this fake older-father-mentor act? But he was here to get information and could overlook the smarm. Maybe it sold cars.

"Thanks. Needed her in New Mexico but she's overkill for down here unless I find some mountains. Still a great general purpose car, though."

"Oh, you can't go wrong with a Land Rover—no matter where you are. Let's go in my office where it's a little quieter." He pointed at the wall unit and walked to a door next to a really ancient-looking copier. "This'll be much better." He stepped aside so that Dan could enter the cramped workspace. "Take a seat. Now, what can I do you for?"

Dan handed him a card. "Looking for information on Max Smith. I understand he drives for you?"

"Not one of our steadies—more of a fill-in."

"When did you use him last?"

"I'd have to check the books but I think it was last week. Monday."

"Do you remember the job? Where was pick up, drop off, was he required to wait, what time did he punch in coming back—that sort of thing."

"Again, I'd have to check the books."

"I'd appreciate that information."

"Frankly, I'm gonna need a little more information from you—these seem to be pretty exacting questions. He get in trouble?"

"Just trying to rule him out of a theft that I'm investigating for the insurance company, United Life and Casualty. Some highly valuable, insured items disappeared and he may have been the last to have seen them."

"So, you're some kind of cop?"

"Yes and no—just an investigator."

"Hmm, well, OK then. Marie? Bring me last week's logs."

Dan marveled that old Pat could yell above the heater's racket but the intercom system seemed to work, as Marie promptly entered carrying a large logbook. Why was Dan not surprised that the system wasn't automated?

Pat turned a few pages, found what he wanted, and then paused as he read. "Looks like this was a call-in. A Miss Chan, the personal assistant for a Mr. Frank Lee, requested Mr. Smith—and it had to be him—pick up Mr. Lee's daughter and his niece at the Casa Monica Hotel in St. Augustine at eleven-thirty in the evening. The driver would be taking them to the Daytona Airport off International Speedway. Because of the late hour—he wouldn't be returning the car before one-thirty in the morning— he insisted on paying double—a little bonus thrown in. Normally the fee would be six twenty-five—one hundred twenty-five per hour, half hours count as full hours and he'd be picking up the car around nine. Max Smith showed up here with twelve hundred and fifty cash not two hours later."

"And the car was turned back in on time?"

"Clocked in at five til two. A little late but wasn't like the car hadn't been paid for."

"How did you pay the driver?"

"He requested an envelope with cash be left in the garage, out back."

"And he picked up the envelope?"

"Wasn't here in the morning."

"What type of car did he rent?"

"Lincoln Town Car—1988—last of the luxury sedans, if you ask me. A pretty comfy ride. I got a new MKZ. Can't hold a candle to the old girl."

"Is the car he used that night here now?"

"Yeah, things are usually slow mid-week but we're booked solid Christmas through New Years. Let's go take a look."

The back yard held four Lincoln sedans, a Hummer and a stretch limo—all black, all vintage. Not a big stable but probably lucrative enough for a small operation. All looked to be well taken care of.

"Let's see, Max had the third car from the end that night. Here're the keys if you want to open her up."

Dan nodded and caught the metal ring tossed his way. He walked around the car first. No new-looking dents or scratches. Too bad the car couldn't communicate where it had been. He squatted down and ran a hand along the underside of the back bumper. Then looked closely at the license plate.

"Has the car been rented since Mr. Smith used it?"

"No. As I said we're slow leading up to the holidays— then it's gangbusters."

Gangbusters? Dan thought the truth might be stretched a bit but he reached in his pocket and pulled out a plastic bag and worked several strands of what appeared to be marsh grass from behind the tag.

"No long-leafed grasses anywhere here on your lot?" He held out the bagged specimen.

"We're pretty much asphalt all around. Nothing like that."

Dan opened the driver-side door. Sand on the floor mats but only on the driver's side. He did a cursory check of the passenger-side front and then opened the back. A little sand behind the driver's seat but not a lot. Looked pretty clean in back. He used the key to open the trunk and heard the muffled release of the latch.

"I'll just give the trunk a once-over."

The minute Dan raised the lid, he stepped back and reached for his phone. "I think you need to see this. I'm going to have to call it in. Sorry but the car is going to be impounded. You're looking at a crime scene."

Chapter Sixteen

Dan could see that Pat O'Rourke was anything but thrilled to see his vintage Lincoln limo loaded onto a flatbed and hauled away. But what a mess—deep blackened stains on the trunk's carpet, splashes of red streaking across the lid along with gouges in the foam insulation and scratches—everywhere there was evidence of a futile, but desperate attempt to escape. Dan didn't think he'd ever been as emotionally impacted by a murder scene as he was when he opened the trunk. The blood, the struggle … no one deserved to die that way—and didn't the coroner say she'd been raped? She suffered knowing what was coming and then was left to die … bleeding out. He turned away. It was difficult to digest the crushing inhumanity of it all.

The car was towed to a garage outside Jacksonville,

near the FBI headquarters. Now that a tie to international human trafficking was suspected, local law enforcement took a back seat. Dan followed the impounded vehicle in order to get the results first hand and not have to wait for the report. It was beginning to be a long day.

Armed with a cup of coffee, he sat in a glassed-in cubicle facing the garage floor. A half dozen special agents—crime experts assigned to this case—gloved and wearing protective clothing were dismantling the Lincoln. Back seats were removed and placed on sterile cloths spread out on the building's immaculate floor, then front seats. Every inch of the car was being vacuumed. Three men were working on the trunk.

Dan needed confirmation that the gold foil had come from the carpeting in the trunk and then lab proof that it was most likely from a five hundred year old wooden box.

"This mean anything to you? Found it in the trunk." The man who stuck his head in the door was holding a small clear plastic box.

Dan realized immediately that he was looking at a cabochon ruby from the exterior of the relics' container, an inset from the cross on the top of the box…

"Yeah. Let me get a couple photos of that then I'll get out of your way."

The red stone seemed to glow. Probably just the cut, Dan thought. It was big, with substantial depth. Now, he had no doubt that they would find flecks of gold foil in the trunk. But it didn't really matter, the ruby proved what happened to the container once it was taken from the church. Dan just didn't know where it ended up. Private collection, or was it up for sale on some undercover, black market circuit? Maybe it had already gone to bidding wars on the Deep Web.

But did it exonerate the woman, Lila? Or implicate her? And the same for the driver … Were Max Smith and Lila Tran in it together? Knowing the combination pretty much pointed a finger at Lila. And the young girl supposedly delivered to the airport in Daytona? Who was behind the much larger, dangerous sex slave ring? Must have been a big-ticket night for the two. So why was Lila Tran killed, apparently by a hit man doubling as a driver? She was delivering the goods. She had an almost fool-proof cover. How many Mandarin-speaking, Asian-American, pretend nuns could even an international human trafficking ring come up with? It should have meant job security.

Every time he ran through the scenario in his head, per usual in these cases, answers only led to more questions. He'd head back to St. Augustine and put in another couple hours at the rectory. At least, he'd get caught up on paperwork now that there was something concrete to report. And he couldn't wait to share all the news with Elaine. He'd give her a call but he didn't expect her back from Dragon's Bend until late that afternoon.

+ + +

Twenty-five miles south down A1A, a beer at Tortugas, and a walk on the beach. Being tutored probably didn't get any better than this. Jason spread a couple beach towels on the sand, stripped to swim trunks, and left Jia to sunbathe while he went swimming. The water was seventy plus degrees. A little nippy but it was pretty remarkable to be in the ocean at all in December. Sure beat shoveling snow or slipping around on icy roads. Flagler Beach was one of Florida's best-kept secrets—great little town with five-star restaurants, shops, galleries, a library, and not one building on the ocean side to obstruct the view. He could live this way. But that was a couple college degrees away and probably more than a little world travel.

He started back up the beach and noticed Jia had company. A young woman, a teenager maybe, was sitting cross-legged on the towel facing Jia. Spikey black hair with pink tips completed a punk look of torn jeans and slouchy, off-the-shoulder t-shirt. He caught half a dozen words in Mandarin before he reached them.

"Jason, this is Su Lin. She needs a ride to St. Augustine."

The girl hopped up, bowed slightly then met his gaze straight-on. "I'm on a school tour and missed my bus."

Perfect English but there was something edgy about her. Chip on the shoulder, I dare you to contradict me, sort of attitude. "Sure, we'll give you a ride." The school tour story didn't ring true. No chartered bus representing a school would take off without counting every student on board, but if that was her story …

They hadn't planned on staying on the beach all afternoon. He needed to put in some study time. They gathered their towels and walked up and over the dunes to the street. The ride to St. Augustine was uneventful. Their passenger sat in the back and fell asleep leaning against the window. Jason and Jia finally gave up trying to carry on a conversation in whispers and the majority of the ride was made in silence.

"I need to pick up my computer before we go to the library. Want to get a sandwich at the house?" Matanzas beach was coming up on the right so they were within ten miles of the townhouse.

"Great. Should we ask Su Lin to join us? I don't think she's in any hurry to catch up with her school bus." Jia smiled. She had also seen through the ruse.

"Sure. Looks like she could use a meal."

Coming to a halt in the drive startled their passenger awake. Crying out, she grabbed the back of the front seat. "Let me out."

Jia quickly turned around, putting her hand on Su Lin's arm.

"Su Lin. It's all right. You fell asleep but we're back in St. Augustine now. This is where Jason lives. He needs to pick up some study materials before we go into town. Plus, we're going to eat lunch. Will you join us?"

"Okay. Sorry. I had a bad dream." But she was shaking, Jason noticed. There was something unusual about her circumstances. A student tour that probably wasn't; frayed nerves that seemed to stem from fear; fingernails bitten into the quick …

He opened the garage and walked through to the back door. "Bathroom on your right."

Su Lin ducked in, closed the door and locked it.

"Odd. I wonder if she's in trouble?" Jia kept her voice to a whisper as she followed Jason to the kitchen. They worked together on the sandwiches until three plates, each holding a ham and Swiss on rye with a small bag of chips, were lined up along the counter. The drink choice was beer, soda, or lemonade.

"Su Lin?" Jia stepped into the hallway and called out, then walked to the bathroom, before returning to the kitchen. "She's not here. The back door is open and she's gone."

"Just a minute." Jason went down the hall to his room, opened the door, looked in and then closed it again. "I hate to be so suspicious but thought I better check on my laptop."

"Oh, I wasn't thinking. I should never have suggested

giving her a ride. There's just something that made me feel sorry for her. I think there's a story she's not telling."

"I'd bet on it."

Chapter Seventeen

Elaine had made good time. After leaving Dragon's Bend, the traffic had thinned out considerably. It was barely five-thirty when she got home. Dan had just called to say he'd be late. But he couldn't hide his excitement. Finding the ruby in the trunk of the limo was big—offered some partial answers, at least—and names of suspects. But the really big news was the Swiss Army Knife. She was shocked. Her little indiscretion had turned out to be huge.

Dan jokingly pointed out that he'd probably kept her out of jail and she owed him one. Ha. Not so funny. She really wasn't proud of having stolen something, even if it did prove to be a good heist—if there was such a thing. But the murder scene was just too gruesome. She was finding it difficult to get the picture out of her mind of

Lila Tran fighting for her life in the trunk of a car. Evil. She struggled to understand it. Maybe a cleansing was called for after all. Well, if she was going to smudge the house, now was the time to do it.

A note from Jason said he was at the library and wouldn't be home until after seven. So, the place was hers. She spread the smudge kit out on the butcher-block counter. First, she removed four fat, white sage bundles combined with other herbs such as lavender, cedar, and sweetgrass. All the herbs were mixed, rolled together and tied with string. The candle was in a simple glass holder and beside it was a small cardboard box of sand. She would establish a sense of ceremony—first light the candle and say a prayer and secondly, using the candle, light a single smudge stick and use the smoke to encase her own body before beginning on the house. The box of sand would be used to put out the sticks after they had burned down to an unusable length.

She was a believer in feng shui and a supporter of Native ritual. She was approaching this as more than just another way to burn aromatic incense. Incense without the thurible—but she wasn't in church. A box of kitchen matches and she was in business. She outlined her body by waving the smoldering stick above her head and then down each side—first placing the stick in her left hand and then her right, she referred to her notes. After completing the house ritual, she would cleanse her body again by starting with the soles of her feet and working upward. Maggie's directions were certainly complete and easy to follow.

When it came to the house itself, Maggie said to start at the front door and move in a clockwise direction, waving the stick above her head, moving slowly so the smoke drifted and settled, trailing out behind her—and, oh yes, don't forget the closets. Corners were stagnant pockets of energy. Corners needed to be gone over twice. Maggie warned her to stay grounded and breathe. If the smoke was seeming to clump and not spread outward, she had included a feather that could be used to disperse it. The feather looked suspiciously as if it had come from the rear end of a turkey. She had to hand it to Maggie—her kit had everything.

The smoke actually had a pleasant scent. Truthfully, Elaine was enjoying the exercise. Whether she would feel energized or gain additional stamina after she'd finished, time would tell. She finished the living room, breakfast nook, kitchen and dining room and moved to the hallway. She took extra time in their bedroom, spreading the smoke with the feather across the bed, along the sides and underneath. Going back out into the hall, she continued out the back door, down the steps into the garage and smudged every corner of the two-car garage. She opened all four doors of her BMW coupe, even popping the hood and opening the trunk to smudge both areas before coming back into the house by the door closest to Jason's room.

She had made it a rule to never invade his privacy. His room had always been off-limits. She had worked past caring that his bed wouldn't be made, that there would be an empty pizza box or two and books and papers everywhere ... actually, she was really proud of herself that she could overlook a mess. Should she wait and tell him first what she needed to do? Or, not wishing to break the clockwise trajectory of her work so far, simply continue?

She needed to finish. She would break one of her rules

this time. She turned the knob and pushed the door open. The room was absolutely pitch black. Perfect if a person worked at night and slept during the day. Or if you were a bat. She stood in the doorway and felt along the wall to her right for a switch. Nothing. Must be on the other side.

The natural light from the hallway behind her barely penetrated the darkness in front of her. Later she would remember seeing the closet door on her left open—noiselessly. And only an overactive imagination would see the figure dressed in white as an apparition. But this was no ghost. With head down, mostly hidden by a pillowcase or a hoody, it barreled toward her and slammed into her before she could step out of the doorway. Two arms with balled fists struck her torso with a force of a missile, then it backed up and placed a well-aimed kick to her head. A one-two punch delivered in a Nano second. Jerked backward, she struck the opposite wall in the narrow hallway—her temple slamming against the doorjamb of the linen closet. She slipped to the floor as her assailant yanked open the back door, leaped to the garage floor, and disappeared. The side door to the yard banged shut, and then there was quiet.

Breathe, she admonished herself. But the searing pain made only shallow breaths possible. Don't try to move until the dizziness passes. Something warm trickled down her face near her ear. She didn't need to wipe it away to know it was blood. Even if she had to crawl, she had to find the smudge stick. Thank God it was almost burned down to nothing—but it could still start a fire. She managed to get onto all fours and inch across to the doorway to Jason's bedroom. The butt of the smudge stick was smoldering in the shag of a brown throw rug—a rug easily replaced. She was more worried about the streaks of blood down the ecru colored hallway wall.

Carrying the smudge stick and rug, she used the wall to guide her upright, then slowly she leaned against it and worked her way to the kitchen. She ran water on what was left of the sage bundle and the wadded up shag rug leaving it all in the sink. Her head was throbbing. Ice in a zip-lock bag would offer some relief, but first a handful of wet paper towels to clean up the hallway.

She was ducking the question of stitches but knew the cut was still bleeding. And breathing was a problem—she still couldn't take a deep breath without debilitating pain that spread from her sternum across her rib cage and under her arm. Without warning, the room started to spin. She grabbed a high-backed stool at the counter but only pulled it down on top of herself as she hit the floor. She tried to reach her phone, which had clattered ahead of her when she fell, but couldn't focus through the curtain of blackness that dropped suddenly in front of her eyes.

+ + +

Dan got the call from Jason, who had come home to find his mother unconscious in a pool of blood with a gash on the head, and possibly other injuries. Jason had ridden in the ambulance with her and was at the hospital now. Could he come? Dan couldn't believe he wasn't pulled over but was pretty certain he'd managed the trip across town in record-breaking time.

The doctors were encouraging—she would mend. She'd have a two-inch scar along her left temple, facial bruising that would go away in a couple weeks. As for the two cracked ribs, they would take a bit longer and be sore but with restricted movement, those would knit perfectly and not be a problem. They were keeping her overnight as a precaution but felt they had found and fixed the worst of it. She was resting and wasn't to be disturbed. Dan looked in her room but wasn't prepared for how white she looked— head bulbous with bandages and an IV running into her arm.

"What happened?"

Dan followed Jason to a visitor's alcove two doors down. He pulled a straight-backed chair away from a table in the corner, turned the back to face Jason then straddled the seat, resting his arms across the top.

"I don't know. The police think someone followed her into the house. She had just gotten home—the garage door was still open."

"Burglary? Was anything taken or did you have time to look?"

"I don't know; the minute I saw Mom, I called 911. The house wasn't torn up, though. And I think it had just happened. I think the police are right—looks like someone followed her in the back door and attacked her in the hallway. There's blood on the wall opposite my bedroom. I wasn't planning on coming home until seven but Jia and I decided to go to a lecture at Embry Riddle College that starts then. I ran by home to change clothes about ten to six and found her."

"Thank God you did."

"Yeah, I hate to think ..." He didn't finish the thought out loud.

+ + +

Elaine came home the next afternoon, moving slowly, not taking deep breaths, and leaning on Dan going up the steps. Jason and Jia met them at the door. The hallway was scrubbed clean and repainted, with no sign of a scuffle anywhere. The shag rug was gone. The three bouquets of flowers—one of them heavy on red roses—were beautiful. It was so good to be home, the flowers could have been vases of dandelions, and her feeling of euphoria would have been just as great. It was simply good to be alive.

The police had interrogated her for an hour and a half that morning but she hadn't had a chance to speak to Jason or Dan.

"I'd love a glass of wine." She said it rather wistfully knowing that she hadn't bought any.

"How about a beer instead?" Jason was already halfway to the fridge. She nodded. "Jia? A beer?" Another nod.

"Might as well make it four." Dan got up to help Jason open bottles and grab a couple glasses.

Seated back at the table, Jia held up her glass. "Here's to good health and no more scares." A pause to clink glasses and bottles. "You know we're curious but I don't want to press you to tell us what happened if you'd rather not."

"No, it's fine. It's bizarre, actually. I'm still trying to understand it myself." Elaine told them about the cleansing—the smudge stick and how she applied the ritual to the town house. How, when she got to Jason's room, it was dark and she couldn't find the light switch. Then an apparition had jumped from the closet and attacked her before running out the back door. "I don't buy someone following me into the house. I distinctly remember locking the deadbolt, and I was in the house probably fifteen minutes, maybe more, before I even lit the smudge stick."

"Oh my God! I know—that is, *we* know what happened." Jia turned to Jason. "It was Su Lin. She didn't leave; she hid in the closet."

"Wait. Go back to the beginning—Su Lin? Su Lin who?" Dan was thoroughly confused.

Jason took the lead and reiterated how the two of them had met this girl at Flagler Beach and, although her story seemed a little bogus, they brought her here. Both thought she had left after using the bathroom.

"Hindsight always makes us brighter, but don't beat yourself up. We would have done the same. Someone in need should be helped. I know you couldn't have guessed her reaction. But why would she react *that* way?" Elaine was truly baffled. "Do you think she's mentally ill? Or just trying to get away from someone or something? I appeared to be a perceived danger—she was frightened of me— fighting to get away from me, not kill me."

"Mental illness is one explanation." Jia paused. "But there could be others. While Jason was swimming, Su Lin shared a little of her history with me. I don't know how much you know about Chinese customs. Su Lin was a 'Mei Bao' or 'beautiful baby'. Her mother came here as part of 'birth tourism'—pregnant women come to this country to give birth so that their children will be American citizens. It's expensive; they pay dearly. There are numerous sites across the country all making good money off the intentions of pregnant women to provide a better life for their babies. Su Lin was born in Queens, New York."

"Are these hospitals?" Elaine had never heard of them.

"Not really. The ones in New York can be simple storefronts, even homes—some are quite elaborate, and others are probably not even up to code. They aren't policed. The women offering services are midwives. And the services are steeped in Chinese ritual. For over a thousand years it has been the custom for the birthing mother to rest one month after they deliver a child—if they can afford to. The care of the child, the 'Mei Bao' or beautiful baby, is completely taken over by women called 'aunties'. The mothers are pampered. Everything is provided for them—meals, a room, often private. At the end of the month there's what is called a 'red egg' celebration to commemorate the survival of these babies. Only Su Lin's 'Auntie' stole her and sold her—not once but twice. She has spent her seventeen years looking over her shoulder, never knowing her real family but fearing being taken against her will again. Two years ago the family that raised her sold her for a third time—as a bride to an older man. She ran away. But she believes he is trying to find her. Her life has been nothing but deception."

"That's terrible." Elaine voiced what the others were thinking.

"I believe she thought Jason and I lived here. Maybe she needed a place to hide for awhile but was panicked when she encountered Elaine. The smudge stick probably didn't instill confidence."

Elaine laughed but quickly hugged her bandaged ribs. "It's not funny, but I can only imagine how spooky I must have looked wreathed in smoke, tapping along the wall trying to find the light but walking straight toward the closet."

"That is no excuse for what she did—hiding in the first place and then attacking you," Jason offered. "I'll call the police."

"No. I couldn't live with incarcerating someone with a

history of mistreatment, who was only acting out of abject fear. The police believe it's a thwarted robbery. Let's leave it at that. I was unable to give them a clear description of her—in fact, I think I referred to her as he."

"Are you sure you want to let this go? Maybe if we reported it, she'd get help."

"Dan, that's a little pie-in-the-sky, don't you think? I'd like to agree but I'm just not as trusting."

"Well, I think you're admirable. I don't know if I could do what you're doing—overlooking serious injury to help someone." Jia continued, "If I know her type, she's long gone. There's a black market stigma that follows those who are forced to live on the streets. They learn early how to get lost—become just another face in a big city's China Town."

"I'm surprised she opened up to you." Dan was wondering about that. On one hand the girl-child seemed almost wild, but then she shared a lot about her beginnings with a stranger.

"I told her that I was a 'Mei Bao', too. A much luckier one, but still I gained my citizenship by being part of the 'birth tourism'. Only my adoptive parents chose my birth mother in China and brought her to California. They let her go through the ritual of a Chinese birthing center because it meant less trauma. For example, her native language would be spoken, and it was a custom my real mother would have known and been comfortable with. Chinese birthing facilities in Los Angeles are much coveted. They often cost eighty thousand dollars or more for the month and almost always come with a Rodeo Drive shopping spree. It was an honor to have been chosen by my parents. At the end of thirty days, my Auntie/Nanny brought me to San Jose and the people who became my new mother and father. They took over from there. My birth mother went back to China."

"Are these places legal in California?" Elaine asked.

"On the fringes there, too, actually. Some are quite nice and licensed legitimately. Services are offered in exchange for money—a set fee. Centers in New York often accept babies in exchange for payment for the month. Flushing in Queens is well known for black market dealings—human trafficking."

"You know a lot about the clinics," Jason noted.

"My own birth has made me curious enough to do the research. Actually, I've tried to find my birth mother but even with the DNA banks today, it's difficult. Finding one's ancestors in China doesn't have the same appeal that it does here. Quite simply, Chinese people are just that, Chinese. They didn't come from some place else within recent generations. So there's a very small database of Asian DNA. I think it's getting better, more people are coming forward to register but, for now, it's difficult to trace one's ancestry. I'm not trying to run away from my heritage. I don't consider it a stigma."

"Thank you for sharing that with us. And thank you for understanding my need to not be vindictive. I'll heal; I'm not so sure about Su Lin. I hope she stays out of trouble."

Chapter Eighteen

The open house was scheduled for Sunday—all Sunday afternoon and into the evening. The Army of Spiritualists, as they liked to be called, stayed in the good graces of the greater community by once a year having a festival—free to participants. There would be book signings, card readings, two different séances, more than one table tipping, games, a nursery for children under age six, and food and desserts prepared by the congregation. It would be an introduction to the commerce of spiritualism and remind surrounding landowners what a gift to their livelihood the AOS really was. No one could deny it was a draw. It kept restaurants in the area bustling year around and property values up. There had even been a TV documentary some years back touting its uniqueness. That led to caravans of the curious.

Maggie had left a message for Dan, not realizing until he sent a text later the scare he'd just had with Elaine. Still, she texted back, wasn't that a pretty good reason to get away? New scenery, a family visit, a chance for him to see her new house … She invited Jason and Jia, even suggesting the kids drive up separately in case they wanted to leave before the adults. Kids. She needed to revamp her thinking. Jason was an adult. Still, he and Jia would have other interests.

The quick return call she got from Dan was a "yes" depending on Elaine's continued recovery. So far, the ribs were still really sore and the bandage on her head, though greatly reduced in size, still challenged a scarf to completely cover it. But he agreed that a change of scenery was called for and hoped by Sunday a car ride wouldn't be too uncomfortable. He'd stay in touch. Maggie crossed her fingers. It would mean a lot to have family celebrate with her. She was one of the new additions to the spiritual group. There would be a welcoming ceremony with an award of her angel's wings, earned by adding over three hundred new converts to the on-line rolls. Paying converts, too. For thirty-five dollars a month or, as she was trained to say, "for about a dollar a day", someone could receive customized, daily readings and an astrological chart.

She was developing quite an on-line following because she shied away from computerized answers. 'Customized' was just a sales tool by the Army of Spiritualists or the AOS as they liked to be referred to, but she took the promise personally and cast each reading individually and relayed the results via email sometimes with a personal note. That was appreciated. She appeared to be a real person—and she was! Time and again, members of her new following would write to tell her how her reading had helped them. She just wasn't certain how she could keep up if she got many more applicants. She was just about working 24/7 now. But the work was so rewarding. She had known it would be. Living in Dragon's Bend was the dream of a lifetime come true.

She put the finishing touches on her hair, slipped the off-white tunic over her head and belted it below the waist with a gold leather belt. Black tights and gold, low-heeled pumps and she was ready for the town hall meeting in the conference room. Most of the women dressed in a like manner. She didn't think of it as a uniform but she guessed it actually was. The midweek meeting was billed as a planning affair, but she knew there would be pictures taken—kind of a dry run for Sunday's celebration. The pictures would be used to update the directory. A picture, a name, and a list of that person's degrees or specialties. The general public didn't realize that Astrologers were certified. In addition, there were a number of very gifted and learned spiritualists in Dragon's Bend.

Living some three miles from the center of the community kept her isolated a bit, but she preferred it that way. She'd had it with living on top of others as in The Villages, with barely ten feet on either side between houses. She missed out on the in-fighting and gossip that's usually rampant in any close-knit group but that was great, too. She wasn't tempted to take sides and could concentrate on her work.

The Leader didn't discourage competition for his favors. There was always a scramble to please him. There were many rumors of "close" relationships and she didn't doubt a one of them. But from what she could see, Nancy was the travel companion, keeper of the calendar, and the one who sat closest to the throne. Court intrigue. In so many words that was exactly what she witnessed here. Civilization really hadn't changed much in hundreds of years.

She parked in an alleyway. Being early, she found a seat down front. The Leader was in rare form, laughing and joking, giving her shoulders a squeeze as she came in. He inquired about Elaine, saying once again he hoped to see her join them on Sunday. She assured him Elaine was looking forward to the celebration, hoping that wasn't a fib. But Maggie was also looking forward to the evening ahead of her. Twice a month everyone gathered in the conference room—usually to standing-room only. The hundred and fifty or so residents who were a part of the inner core of the Army for Spiritualism got re-invigorated from a rousing lecture by the Leader. He would often single out members with encouragement or even warnings that had been relayed to him by those who had crossed over. Through dreams or a reading of the cards, all was made apparent and it was up to him to interpret and share.

She switched off her phone and pushed her purse under the folding chair. Five til eight and a deep, resonant chanting began in the back. The lights dimmed to shadows, then went out altogether. It was so dark she couldn't see her hand in front of her face. The chanting stopped and a tomb-like quiet blanketed the group. She sat riveted, waiting for the familiar melodious tones of the Leader's welcome.

"Good evening, my fellow followers on the road to erudition."

As always he had an aura of light. It so perfectly surrounded him and moved with him as he proceeded to the front of the room that she couldn't tell where it came from. It was simply there, emanating from an ethereal source, or so it seemed. His robes were white, complete with hood and rope tie. He appeared to be some kind of angelic monk.

"Let us stand and clasp the hands of those on either side of us. Feel the life flow from one being into another. Electric, a current—do you feel it?"

Murmurs of "yes" rippled across the room. "Then show me you feel it. Look to your right. Clasp your neighbor's hands with both of your hands, tell your fellow soldier that you will not let them down on this journey."

The man on her right had probably not eaten his vegetables in years unless it meant mashed potatoes smothered in gravy. His slightly moist grip made his hand feel slimy. She hated this part of the evening but it would be over soon. The man mumbled that his name was Buster … how perfectly apt. She whispered, "Maggie," but hoped he hadn't heard her. The Leader motioned for those standing to sit.

"And now it's time to reveal the real reason you've been called here. Over this last week I have been visited by several spirit guides—guides that belong to you. Lost because they seek those who are not welcoming." A hand with a pointed index finger waved across the audience. "Many of you have dismissed these guardians or simply have never sought them out. Do not just give lip service to the joys accorded you through your beliefs in a greater world beyond—be active. You must seek out the members of that shadow world, pay homage, embrace those who promise you riches. With your support will come the answer to dreams. Oh my dear ones, you are close to realizing everything you've ever wanted. Money, stature, love ... Do not be timid. Supplicate for what is yours—for what is waiting for you.

"I have names here of those who need to get in touch. Donald and Rebecca? Call upon Iris. She's waiting to hear from you. Charles and his daughter, Hope ... Edgar expects you to contact him. Margaret Mahoney? Both Gertrude and Theodore request that you reach out."

The list went on but Maggie had tuned out. Well, Gert and Theo—new friends. She had to admit that in the nearly complete blackness of the room, with only the Leader bathed in light, it was easy to accept this alter-world of guides—the departed who have been tasked with protection? Surveillance? Interference? All under the guise of guidance for the worldly ... She wasn't even sure what to call it.

Finally the lights in the room flickered, then returned to normal strength, but by then the Leader was gone. She helped herself to a glass of lemonade and a sugar cookie before returning to her car. But she did make a mental note of giving Gert and Theo a shout out when she got home. It couldn't hurt but she wouldn't be buying a lottery ticket anytime soon. She believed in guides but made certain she didn't ask too much of them.

She fumbled in her purse for the car's fob and pressed the trunk open. She'd brought a folding chair just in case there was a call for extra seating. Now she needed to secure it for the ride home. She covered the chair with an old quilt she carried to keep it from rattling around and pulled the trunk lid closed before turning toward the driver's side of the car.

She hadn't meant to cry out, but she hadn't seen the Leader walk up.

"Margaret, I'm so sorry I've startled you. Please, accept my apologies." The Leader reached out and drew her to him in an intimate hug. "It's so dark in this parking lot; flood lights are my next project." He released her and stepped back. "I have been woefully remiss in welcoming you to the fold. I hear nothing but good things about the way you've jumped right in, taken on a lion's share of the work—believe me, that is appreciated."

"I'm loving my time here. I feel like I've come home."

A little half hug with an arm around her shoulder. "I wish we had more just like you. Nancy tells me you have family here in Florida? Fairly close by, no? I met your daughter-in-law at the table tipping. I don't think I realized that she lived in the state."

"Yes, Dan and Elaine live in St. Augustine. My son is investigating a theft at the Basilica. He works for quite a large insurance company."

"Ah, I've been following that story in the papers, along with that of the errant nun. So unfortunate about that woman—about her duplicity, that is. The Church doesn't need more bad press at this time."

"So true but I think people will realize that the fake nun was just a plant and the Church was duped."

"I hope you're right, but a theft on top of that doesn't instill confidence. Is your son closer to solving the disappearance of the relics?"

"He hasn't said, but I'm guessing not. He and his wife have just taken on a long-term rental."

"I do wish him well. Will all your family be joining you this weekend?"

"I'm hoping so."

"Again, welcome. Make sure I get to meet your son on Sunday."

With that she watched him hurry over to waylay two other 'pilgrims'. It seemed odd that the Leader would detain her for a discussion of current affairs. She had never really thought casual chatting was his MO. She was too tired to think about it more tonight. She slipped behind the steering wheel and started the Beemer.

+ + +

Sunday was clear, seventy-six degrees warm, and bright with sunshine—a perfect day for a road trip and an Open House. Dan had been a hard sell. No hocus-pocus for him; he didn't care what his mother was into. He was going along to be supportive, not to take part in activities. Jia and Jason went in Jason's rental—ostensibly to practice conversational Mandarin but Elaine wasn't certain her son wasn't developing closer ties to his tutor. Worse could happen. It certainly seemed to keep him focused on his education.

They met at Maggie's house at eleven. A tour of the bungalow left everyone impressed. The stained glass shone to perfection, casting slivers of refracted light across the floor. Much to Simon's chagrin, they didn't stay long but Dan played fetch until his arm ached and the dog finally flopped down for a nap. A few liver treats and all seemed to be forgiven. As much as a dog could be, he was probably used to long separations from his best pal. And Dan's sacrifice was for the dog's own good. A fenced-in backyard with squirrels to chase and grass to roll in beat the townhouse's lack of grounds.

Festivities were scheduled to begin with a catered noon lunch on the lawn outside the conference center; parking promised to be a challenge. Narrow streets added to the charm of the community but required special navigation. Maggie rode with Dan and Elaine; Jason and Jia followed.

"I can't tell you how pleased I am that you would take the time to come today."

"C'mon, Mom, you know me. Give me a chance to enjoy a little hocus-pocus and I'm first in line."

"Maggie, he doesn't mean that."

"Mom can take a joke." But a look in the rearview mirror and his mother's pursed lips indicated otherwise.

"Dan, I don't expect you to be a believer, but I do expect you to not belittle those who are."

"Scout's honor, I'll be good." Dan didn't need to look at Elaine; he could feel the glare.

Maggie leaned forward. "New topic. I'm absolutely blown away by Jia's beauty. And what a sweet girl. I'm assuming she and Jason are a couple?"

"I haven't figured that out yet. But if time spent together is any indication, things seem to be progressing." Elaine added, "I really think they share a lot of the same interests."

"He's as handsome as she is beautiful. And didn't you tell me she's tutoring Jason in Mandarin?"

"Yes, Jason has an International Business major, emphasis on economics with a language minor, Mandarin. Frankly, the language requirement is so smart. I think his Bachelors will really be worth something."

"I'm always reading that any degree in world trade is much sought after. What is Jia working toward?"

"She said a degree in Art History, emphasis upon ancient architecture. I just can't believe that she would come to Flagler College to pursue that area of study—not with all the really top-notch schools in California specializing in the field. Of course, she might have just needed a little separation from family."

"Kids are like that." Maggie gave the back of Dan's head a flick of her finger.

"Oh, I almost missed it. Here's your turn. We'll have better luck parking in the residential area."

Dan flipped on his blinker and turned to the right. Several houses had roped off their lawns and offered ten-dollar parking spots. Dan and Jason both opted for one of those. A quick block's walk to the conference center and they were in the thick of things. The festival was well attended and rightfully so. Probably the best smoked chicken Dan had ever eaten was being served with two sides, slaw and beans, and a butter-smothered chunk of cornbread—all from a roadside smoker pulled behind an old pickup. Tea, lemonade, or water rounded out the selections and Saran-wrapped trays of homemade cookies were the centerpiece of every table that lined the yard.

Donations were encouraged but not necessarily expected. Colorful tents dotted the periphery, offering card readings, palmistry, and plain old fortune telling. Lines were starting to form. For those not interested in the occult, games of horseshoes and darts were set up in a back parking lot. There was even a local band of what looked like high school kids—loud but definitely not Carnegie Hall quality. A bounce-house, face-painting table, and several booths that advertised opportunities to win large stuffed animals completed the carnival atmosphere and appealed to the youngest visitors. Two rows of port-a-potties lined the closest street, which had been roped off. The festival planners had anticipated a good-sized crowd.

Jason, Jia and Dan were in line for horseshoes, and Elaine and Maggie were touring the grounds when an aide breathlessly rushed up to ask Maggie to fill in at one of the card reading tents.

"Damn. I really wanted some time together. This was meant to be just a fun, relaxing day—for all of us."

"We'll catch up later. I can only imagine what a nightmare orchestrating this event must be. And, really, so far, so good from what I can see. Lunch went off without a hitch."

"Yes, kudos to the planning committee. I won't gripe about being pushed into service. Listen, I meant to mention this earlier. There's a lounge at the end of the hall behind the bookstore. If you get tired, rest there. If you don't mind my saying so, you're looking a little peaked. All this walking around can't be good for cracked ribs. The room will be quiet and offer a bit of a retreat from all this craziness. Here's my key. It'll be locked today."

Elaine returned Maggie's wave as she rounded the back of the conference center, heading toward a nearby tent. Energy—and the woman was how old? And here was Elaine hating to admit how good a rest in the lounge sounded. She got a pass because of cracked ribs but, still, she shouldn't be outdone by a woman in her seventies. But maybe just a half hour rest would give the boost she needed.

The bookstore was packed and doing a brisk business in books and posters—even the jewelry counters were three and four deep. Crystals in settings encrusted with precious stones, combined in sterling, and hanging from chains and ribbons seemed to be in high demand. Elaine walked through the crowd and opened a door marked 'employees only' that led to a short hallway.

There were four more doors, all closed, none marked, so she tried the handle of the first one on her right. She was surprised when it opened, but once she stepped across the threshold, she realized she was in someone's private office—not the lounge. Bookcases, viewing equipment, and a huge ornate desk backed by a credenza filled the room.

She was just turning to leave when she saw it. On the credenza was an eight by ten inch photo of someone very familiar to her—Lila Tran. It was the same professionally done photo of a woman in red leather mini skirt, hooker heels and exaggerated makeup that the cop from the Miami vice squad had emailed to her. She walked around the desk and leaned down. One quarter of the photo was filled with Chinese letters. She pulled her phone out and zoomed in on the vertical columns of figures and took several snapshots. And this was what her son was studying? It would be so difficult to master.

She slipped her phone back in her bag and eased around the big desk. She paused at the door and checked the hallway, but she was alone. Her action wasn't as bad as taking the Swiss Army Knife but it had the same feel. She just wasn't good at doing something sneaky. The lounge proved to be the last room on the left. She unlocked the door to enter and quickly locked it behind her once inside. It was quiet. The sounds of the crowd were muffled. A soda machine with bottles of tea and water looked inviting. She put four quarters in the machine and chose an unsweetened lemon tea before sinking into a Naugahyde-covered overstuffed chair—and took her first steady, unlabored breath in thirty minutes.

What did it mean that a photo of a pretend nun, known hooker, and suspected human trafficker—possibly specializing in young women for the slave trade—was found in an office in Dragon's Bend, a spiritual retreat? A young woman who had been raped and brutally murdered, she could add. Had Elaine been in the Leader's office? And, if so, what was his connection to all this?

An hour later Maggie came to check on her and they walked over to watch Dan and Jason win at horseshoes. Jia had scored a breath-taking pink quartz pendant surrounded by several tiny, cut amethyst stones from a jewelry vendor who had set up a table on the Center's wrap-around porch. It was a striking piece that Jia had purchased for herself. That seemed to answer the question of whether or not Jason and Jia were a couple. Or, at least, gift giving wasn't yet part of their relationship, Elaine mused. But, then again, did it mean anything? The twenty-somethings seemed to live by a different code.

Suddenly the afternoon calm was shattered by the insistent clanging of a cowbell—actually more than one.

"That's the call to gather. The Leader has a few announcements." Maggie was already walking toward the array of folding chairs in front of a makeshift stage. Elaine took a chair on the aisle and held three others for Dan, Jason and Jia. The Leader had just bounded up on stage when she saw him look sharply to his left, staring at something in the distance. He seemed fixated, even brushing off a young woman trying to speak to him. Elaine turned to see the focus of his attention and realized it was Jia.

Jia appeared to acknowledge his staring with a faint, almost indiscernible half smile before turning toward Jason and ignoring the Leader. Odd. Did they know each other? There wasn't any overt implication of that. Was it just a case of Jia's breathtaking beauty that attracted him? She certainly must be accustomed to being stared at. And there was nothing else—no wave, big smile, not even a nod. Yet, something didn't seem quite right; or was Elaine just letting her imagination run away with her? The Leader for all his pomposity seemed shaken. He grasped the lectern with his right hand—to steady himself? It certainly looked like that.

But the moment passed quickly. With a broad smile, the Leader turned back to those on stage and adjusted the microphone. He was ready to begin. By now the audience was spilling over the confines of the outdoor 'auditorium' and it was standing room only.

"Friends." His sonorous voice, deep, throaty, perfectly calm and steady floated above the crowd. "First, let me welcome you to our festival and open house. Some of you know what we have to offer; for others, this may be an initial visit. I've asked some of our residents to pass out calendars of the upcoming year's events. Save these, put them in a safe place and return to take advantage of our workshops, lectures, and individual psychic readings. It's not that we have the answers to your concerns but we can put you on the *path* of discovery—the path of finding those answers for yourself. We help you draw upon your own strength and knowledge. And now let me introduce some of the companions, the earthly guides for your journeys."

The Leader called for ten individuals to stand while he introduced them and touted their credentials. Then he turned his attention to newcomers—those just joining his faculty—and here he highlighted five others, including Maggie. These five were called up on stage to receive their angel's wings and say a few words about their calling.

Elaine stole a glance at Dan, but he was applauding his mother along with the rest of the audience. She was pleased. Even if this wasn't his thing, he was being a good sport. She could see that Maggie was thrilled at his support. After a piece of sheet cake commemorating the event in icing and more lemonade, Jason and Jia said they were taking off.

"Before you go, Jia, I'd like you to translate something for me." Elaine had cropped her phone photo of the message on Lila Tran's picture to reveal only the text. It was impossible to see what it had been taken from. She brought up the picture and handed the phone to Jia. She and Dan had left Maggie to mingle with the audience, accepting congratulations and best wishes while they walked Jia and Jason to their car.

Jia looked up. "Do I dare ask where this came from?"

"I know it's a personal message from a woman to a man."

"Yeah, that's putting it mildly." She continued to study the phone before handing it back. "In brief, she pledges all of her love, even in death. She assures the man that he is the one for her now and for always.'"

Dan was looking at Elaine. "Not sure you've told us where you got that and why or how it might be important."

"I'm fairly certain it was meant for the Leader, and I'm dead certain it was written by Lila Tran. Here's the original—the photograph with the inscription. I accidentally walked into what must be the Leader's office at the conference center and this was on the credenza. It's a piece of solid evidence tying them together." Elaine held her phone out and couldn't help but notice that Jia seemed to recoil, pull back from taking the phone for a closer look. And then without thinking, Elaine blurted out something she hadn't really paid attention to until now. "You look so much alike—you and Lila could be twins."

"Don't you *know*, all Chinese look alike to 'round eyes'? Yet, you have to compare me to a *prostitute*?"

Elaine was shocked by the instant retort, and the rancor was a slap in the face. "Please, Jia, let me apologize. I meant no disrespect. You are both breathtakingly beautiful women. It was not a comment on vocation."

The moment seemed to pass as quickly as it had arisen. Jia grabbed Elaine's hand. "I am so sorry. I'm too sensitive. You can't imagine the offers I've received, to go into the 'business'. As if there's nothing else we're good for."

"I'm sorry, too. There are a lot of insensitive people in the world. I don't want you to think I'm one of them."

Heartfelt hugs all around and Jason and Jia left to go back to St. Augustine.

"Let's find Mom and say our good-byes."

+ + +

Nothing had ever felt so good as sinking into the leather seats of the Land Rover and leaning back against the headrest. Elaine was worn out. She certainly couldn't say the day had been boring. And it had probably left her with more questions than answers. She couldn't shake the feeling there was something she was missing. Something so close she could touch it—if she only could figure out what it was. Hadn't the cards warned her she was being duped?

Something was presenting itself as truth when it was a lie?

"A penny." Dan waited for the car in front of him to pull out before following it onto the highway.

"I'm pretty sure we need to be talking a quarter here."

"I'm game. What are you thinking?"

"I'm still hung up on Lila Tran's connection to the Leader. No wonder her name came up at the table tipping."

"Am I going to have to worry about you moving to Dragon's Bend?"

Elaine laughed. "Not any time soon. But I think bringing up Lila was going to be a setup to find out what I knew about her. Chiquita's family kind of messed things up. And then I really stepped in it today when I compared Jia to Lila. I hate to appear ethnically uncool."

"I just think her beauty gets in the way of her brains. I'm sure she's hit on all the time. But it seemed to be a short-lived reaction—I'm pretty sure all is forgiven."

"I hope so. I like her. This place is fascinating; it's easy to get sucked into the hocus-pocus part—as you would say."

"Maybe it's not hocus-pocus. What if all this is for real—spirits and guides—maybe you should have the Leader read your cards."

"That's a really interesting idea—coming from you." And it was. One of those ideas that kind of sent a shiver down her spine though. She just didn't have a comfortable reaction to the man. "In fact, your mother said the same thing. Of course, she seems to think he's some sort of god."

"At least she's not running off with someone. I honestly think she's happy at Dragon's Bend. She feels useful; her life has meaning. Nothing says I have to agree with that meaning."

Chapter Nineteen

What do you get a nun as a going-away present? Elaine chose a bright red and navy, wool-blend muffler. Colorado Springs would be a far different climate than the sultry, warm Florida weather Sr. Angelica was used to. It had been a fun break to shop the outlet mall just outside St. Augustine. She was feeling better about going out in public. The stitches were out but a baseball cap was becoming an everyday staple of her wardrobe. The skin along her temple was red and puckered, but makeup was a no-no until more healing had taken place. The ribs were another story—not feeling perfect, but so much better that a deep breath didn't double her over anymore. All in all, she had been lucky—lucky she'd gotten treatment so quickly. She was mending. Life had taken on some semblance of normalcy.

The reception was scheduled for two and Fr. Pete had requested meeting at one for an update. The trail of clues seemed to indicate the elusive Max had taken the relics, now that there were fairly conclusive indications that he had been left alone in the church feigning to retrieve a bedroll. The murder rap gave him the dubious honor of being one of the FBI's Ten Most Wanted, which upped the chances he would be caught. Whether or not this was all too late for the relics to be recovered, Dan had his doubts there was going to be a happy ending.

"Come in." Fr. Pete seemed in good spirits, and Dan and Elaine took chairs in front of his desk. "I'm glad we have some time to chat before the party."

"Father, before I forget, I've wondered if the Church was able to claim the money in Sister Leah's bank account."

Fr. Pete hesitated, "I know this is part of the ongoing investigation and it's not for general knowledge, but it isn't as if the two of you aren't involved … I know you'll treat this as confidential …" Father Pete paused. "The money was withdrawn before any injunction could be finalized to freeze assets."

"Half a million dollars was taken out of the account? How could that happen? Sr. Leah—or Lila—was deceased." Elaine was dumbfounded.

"It seems there had always been two names on the account—Sister's and what was reported as a family member's. The morning I had a deacon of the church check—it was gone that same afternoon. It was wired to a bank in Lyon, France."

"France?" Dan questioned.

Father nodded. "I was not made privy to a name, only to the circumstances. Once the account became part of a murder investigation, there was no more sharing of information. That avenue was closed down quickly."

Maybe Dan knew of a connection—why the money had left the United States. He took his phone out of his pocket and pulled up his photos. "Is this number a part of the bank account code?" Max Walters—Smith, *Smirnov*—might explain the international tie, and the scrap of paper that had fallen out of the notebook found in his bedroll might help prove it.

Father took the phone, looked at the number, put the phone down, and sat back in his chair. "Where did you get this?" Dan shared finding the belongings of Max Smirnov, alias Walters, or Smith. "Well, maybe a part of our mystery is solved—this is the combination to the relics safe."

Dan didn't know whether he was pleased or not. This last piece of the puzzle seemed to prove beyond a doubt that Max had been the one opening the relic's case and helping himself. And it would seem to indicate that Sister Leah could have written the combination out for him. Should he feel good? He had the culprit. But not the goods.

+ + +

The conference room had a festive *bon voyage* feel to it—banners crisscrossed the ceiling and gifts took up almost a quarter of the big conference table. A three-tiered cake was decorated with green, cone-shaped, confection mountains, and between them was a plastic skier in a nun's habit poised for a downhill run—where in the world had someone found that? Scrolled words of best wishes and lastly, mounds of spun sugar snow completed the winter scene. It was a masterpiece and the cook was reveling in the accolades from the crowd.

Dan and Elaine stayed long enough to watch Sister open her gifts before they offered their own best wishes and started to work their way toward the door to leave. Both agreed that Sister Angelica looked relaxed, maybe relieved was the operative word, and the atmosphere was festive. Yes, there were a few tears but overall it didn't feel like the end of an era but more of a new beginning for a treasured employee. Fr. Pete offered the benediction and invited anyone wanting to speak to approach the podium. Several came forward to offer thank-yous and best wishes and share stories that proved the Mother Superior to be a caring individual true to her faith. It would be a celebration for Sr. Angelica to treasure. Elaine was so pleased that Sister was receiving the accolades she deserved.

Dan and Elaine continued to say their good-byes and had just stepped into the hallway when Sr. Rachel broke away from a group on the far side of the room and hurried toward them.

"Wait. Please, Ms. Mahoney, do you have a minute?"

The nun caught up with them, out of breath. Whatever she wanted she was certainly conveying a sense of urgency, Elaine thought. "Of course, Sister Rachel, What do you need?"

"I'd like to talk for just a minute—alone, if that's all right?"

Elaine turned to Dan, "I'll meet you at the car. Now, let's step over here." Elaine pointed to a bench in the foyer.

"I know you'll think I'm a terrible person."

"I highly doubt that. And, anyway, I don't judge. If you need me to keep a secret, I can do that."

A nod from Sister who was biting her lower lip and staring at the floor.

"I would like you not to tell anyone what I did."

"All right. You have my word."

"When I brought you the pictures I had found in Sr. Leah's locker, I didn't tell you that I had also found her phone. It's against the rules to have a phone and I didn't want there to be more evidence of her … sins … so, I didn't tell anyone. I kept it. But then I thought, what if it might help you find the person who murdered her? I needed to give it to someone who could help." She reached into her tunic, brought out a smart phone and held it out.

"This could be crucial in finding her killer. I really appreciate your trusting me to help. Do you know what's on it? Texts? Email?"

"It was dead and I didn't have a connector to charge it."

"I'm sure it's password protected."

"I have the password. Sr. Leah shared it with me because she thought it was clever—NoNunsSense at Gmail for her email account and 003100 will open the phone. She let me call my parents when I needed to and trusted me with the code."

"NoNunsSense?" Elaine repeated. It was cute. "Did anyone know she had a phone?"

"Sr. Angelica, probably, but she was so good about looking the other way. If Sr. Elizabeth found out I had a phone, let alone *her* phone, I'd be in really big trouble."

Elaine didn't doubt that. She carefully put the phone in her purse. "Again, thank you for sharing this. And your secret is safe. I think this looks like something the coroner might have found among her belongings and forgot to make available—if anyone is questioned." She gave the young woman a quick hug. "Please, don't worry—you've done the right thing."

"Ms. Mahoney? There's one other thing. Another young woman came looking for Sister Leah a few days ago. She was new to the area and didn't know about her ... death."

"Did she say what she wanted? How she knew Sister?"

"No. But she was a young Asian girl and seemed distraught when I told her what had happened to Sister. Demanded that I put her in touch with Sister's partner. Didn't believe me when I told her I had no idea who that would be. She all but said that she'd been promised something—maybe money, a new home ... something big and had traveled a long way to get it. She was so angry, but she was scared more than anything else. I felt sorry for her."

"Did you get a name?"

"Su something."

"Su Lin?" Elaine immediately thought of the girl Jason and Jia had given a ride.

"Yes, that's it. I think she was living on the street. I might have felt sorry for her but I couldn't help her—Sister Elizabeth doesn't allow any street people in the convent. The cook used to offer handouts in the back alley, but Sister Elizabeth put a stop to that when she took over. And then after it came out what Sister Leah was really doing—selling young women ... well, I think maybe this girl would have been one of Sister's victims. Then I wished I had done more. I did tell her where the soup kitchen was."

"If you see the young woman again, call me. Tell her I have information for her." There might not be a reward but Elaine bet there was probably some recompense for information. Elaine scribbled her cell number on a scrap of paper from her purse, handed it over, then quickly hugged the young nun and once again assured her that she'd done the right thing by turning over the phone.

A quick wave and Elaine walked to the parking lot and hurried over to the Rover. "You won't believe this. I think I may have just struck gold. Know whose phone this is?" She held out the phone.

"Let me guess. I have a feeling Sr. Elizabeth didn't give it to you."

She filled Dan in and used the car charger for her own phone to begin powering up the one that had belonged to Lila. She hoped she wouldn't be disappointed.

"You know we need to turn this over to Chief Mitchell. Withholding information in an active investigation … Law enforcement takes a dim view of that sort of thing—I don't think I need to remind you."

"Aren't you just the least little bit curious?"

"Of course. But I'm maybe more into playing by the rules. The locals have been good to me—kept me in the loop—I'd like to return the favor."

"Okay. I know you're right. It's just difficult. Will you have to tell anyone how you got the password?"

"I think I can fib around that. Of course, if someone were to copy the text messages and emails and had them forwarded to her own phone …"

"I love you!" Elaine leaned over and kissed him. "You just saved a cat's life. But what do you make of Su Lin? She could prove invaluable to the investigation. I can only imagine how helpful she might be—names, places—her own story might answer a lot of questions, if we can locate her."

"You know it's worth checking into. We have the time; I'm going to swing by the soup kitchen and see if Chef

Jeff knows anything."

King Street was nothing but 'slow and go' traffic—for its entire length. But the kitchen was between meals and Dan found Jeff unloading boxes of donations—everything from cake mixes to mayonnaise. The holidays brought out the giving nature in people and their generosity always meant a couple months' stores.

"Don't mean to slow you up," Dan said, when Jeff paused. "I'm looking for a girl, Asian, maybe sixteen or seventeen. She's new to the area and goes by the name of Su Lin. Someone said she'd asked about where the kitchen was located. Ring any bells?"

"Yeah. Cute kid. Scrappy. I got the idea she's been on the street awhile or maybe just bounced around the foster system for a few years."

"Is she around?

"No. Took off yesterday, to be exact. At least I didn't see her after breakfast. She lifted a couple bottled sodas and walked out of here. Someone said she got a ride—at least got into a car with some guy. Course she could have just been working—if you catch my drift."

"Yeah. If you see her—"

"I'll get in touch. I still got your card. Hope you had better luck finding Max."

"Nope. Struck out there, too."

"Sorry. Have great holidays." With that, Jeff turned back to the crates of food.

Dan wished him the same and walked back to the car.

+ + +

Home—at last. Dan had dropped the phone off

at the station on the way and got a receipt. Elaine was disappointed that Su Lin couldn't be found but admitted to feeling pretty good about possessing what would probably prove to be the most interesting, maybe incriminating, information—and knowing that it was safe on her own iPhone. She wanted to spend some time with Dan before closeting herself in the office to begin snooping. She was looking forward to a beer on the deck and a chance to put her feet up.

Dan and Elaine both agreed a quiet afternoon sounded inviting. Jason was at the library, and she assumed he had a date later. At least he said not to count on him for dinner. So, the time was all theirs. Dinner was a salad, with all the fixings in the fridge just waiting to be added to a bowl of arugula and chopped kale.

"Do I remember you saying earlier that Max Smirnov, or Smith, had also used the name Walters?"

"Apparently that was a name he used when posing as an American. Smith seems to be a later addition."

Elaine sat forward, "When I researched Cai Ling's background, the travel agency in Boston that arranged the fatal mountain climbing trip to Yunnan four years ago was owned by a Max Walters. In fact, it was Mr. Walters, acting as a guide, who *supposedly* died along with Professor Tran—neither body was ever found. I think it's more than a coincidence that Cai Ling disappeared, as well as Max Walters, only to reappear in the same place at the same time. One being impersonated by a nun and the other, a street person who was also a hit man. And, it would appear, a thief of very expensive artifacts. I'm convinced Cai Ling is dead—probably killed for nothing more valuable than her identity."

"Which in itself was worth a lot. We'll never know how many young women Lila Tran was able to add to the market. We only know about the one who drowned, but Sr. Rachel brought you pictures of four others and there was no reason to believe that they were the only ones. I think Su Lin is proof of that. "

"So why was Lila Tran killed? The organization went to a lot of trouble to set up a really fantastic cover—one that was undetected when I talked with Miami police. And the Yacht Club, or whoever is behind the operation, risked exactly what has happened—the discovery of the duplicity within the Church bringing national attention. And if that's not bad enough, the identity of this Max person with traceable ties to human trafficking and a murder—that's a lot to try to remedy. You know, internationally this has got to have been a coup for INTERPOL operatives. Lila Tran's death provided some solid ties to a worldwide ring of corruption."

"Any ideas who the family member was who withdrew the half-million dollars? I have conclusive proof that Max was involved in the theft of the relics; my guess is he could also have been on the account. Indications are that Lila gave him the combination to steal the relics. Maybe they were close."

Elaine looked skeptical. "Doesn't ring true to me. This was a woman who was pretty independent. I don't see her relying on a man in any way—certainly not with her money. No, the family angle might be true. There's no proof that Max even knew Lila. He came back from the dead after the climbing accident, killed Cai Ling and sold her identity. Lila had been a hooker in Miami and was simply the right person, in the right place, at the right time."

"Good point."

"Any idea what you'll do next? A perpetrator without the goods still leaves some work to be done."

"I need to follow up with groups that internationally police the sale of antiquities. Usually, United Life & Casualty is notified of any finds. UL&C puts out a list of losses complete with pictures and in-depth descriptions. It's only a matter of time before some billionaire turns up gifting a church with priceless *objets d'arte*."

"I can't stand it any longer. I'm going to take a quick look at the texts from Lila's phone. Think you can handle putting the salad together?"

"Sure. You can have one hour then let's eat and take a walk on the beach."

Dan was just slipping the completed salad back in the fridge when Elaine asked him to take a look at something on her laptop.

"Look at these texts. The phone numbers are no longer in use and names aren't mentioned but someone she calls M has promised to get her out of the trade—new identity, including plastic surgery, passport, a place to live. He's apparently asking 1mil. Looks like she wants to keep her savings intact but offers a more lucrative opportunity. Dan, I think she used the relics as a down payment on a new life."

"And getting out of the slave trade would be reason enough to kill her. I get the feeling she could have brought down some pretty big players. Do you think M is Max?"

"Distinct possibility."

"Maybe the police will be able to get information on whomever she was texting."

"Doubtful. I'd bet my life on the person receiving those

messages having a burner phone. A burner lets you text, send pictures, talk—but not give up a real phone number. And don't forget they're disposable—they get traded out pretty routinely."

"The bad guys always seem smarter than we are."

"Not always. Have faith. Now, any chance you'd like to have dinner?"

Chapter Twenty

Monday was always a letdown after having a very social weekend, and Maggie had purposely taken herself off the staff calendar—she just wasn't going to be available to work today. At least not go into the Center and be on call for anyone stopping by for a reading. She could work from home in the morning and then spend some time on her house in the afternoon. There were at least fifty emails from devotees waiting for answers, just from the weekend alone. She'd been remiss in answering any inquiries since Friday. It was unbelievable how quickly work could pile up.

She brought her laptop from the spare bedroom-office into the dining room. There was just something about the light in that room—light streaming in through stained glass—that warmed the room, made it inviting. A bowl of kibble and chicken entrails for Simon and an espresso with extra froth for her and she was ready to work—find out what her spiritual sisters and brothers wanted to share—and provide direction, if not answers, whenever she could.

She did a quick read-through of the first email. It was going to be representative of the rest—what she called 'the how to' syndrome. How to find love, riches, peace, etc. What did their stars, cards, numbers, etc. say? Would she help them? She could never turn away from a sincere cry for help. And the many thank-you emails attested to that. She was appreciated because she cared and people knew that.

She referred to herself as their Spiritual Sister. Others at the Center signed their correspondence as Personal Protector or Celestial Medium. That was just a little over-the-top as far as she was concerned. Only the Leader could really claim either one of those titles. No, she was comfortable with Spiritual Sister and so were her followers. She scanned the subject lines of the first ten or so messages—yep, they were all how-to's from curing a bed-wetter, to paying for a child's college tuition, to better handling a domestic dispute caused by a live-in mother-in-law. She said a quick prayer to her own guides and opened the first email.

Lonny of Aurora, Colorado wrote:

"This is just to thank you for the reading from last week. I want to tell you that everything you predicted came true! I realize now that the fear you read in my cards was what was holding me back. On Monday I asked for a raise and I got it! Thank you so much for seeing the courage and strength in my own being when I could not."

A quick congratulatory response and she filed the email in the 'completed' folder and opened the next.

Tina from Albuquerque wrote:

"If I had a real sister I would want her to be exactly like you. I think you are the only person who can help me. Can you talk with your guides and help me to decide on which man would make the best partner. I'm trying to decide between two men and like them both. My mother thinks I should get married but I don't want to make the wrong decision."

Maggie reached for her tarot deck and cast a three-card reading. It was quickly apparent that the young woman would fare best with the older of her two suitors as the dark knight came up. She wrote a note back and also filed that email under complete.

The third email didn't have a subject and the sender seemed to be some kind of gibberish but then many email addresses didn't make sense. She opened it.

"Be careful. Watch what you say. You could be in danger."

What? She couldn't suppress a shiver. It was just a joke. It had to be. Someone playing games, but who would pay thirty-five dollars to join her spiritual following just to prank her? Did someone know something that she didn't? Was it a warning—a for-real warning? She half-heartedly looked for it to be signed Gertrude and Theodore. There, that made her smile but any feeling of safety was short-lived. What if the warning really was legitimate?

She sat back and finished her coffee. She'd lost all interest in opening any more emails. Maybe it was time to catch her breath and attack a couple more of the boxes in the basement. Simon was already in the backyard trying to outwit the squirrel that was teasing him by running along the top of the fence, well out of reach, but in full sight. It was a daily game of 'catch me if you can'. If that squirrel ever accidentally fell—but then they never did. She felt a little sorry for Simon but it was great exercise for him.

She went out the back door and around the house to the basement stairs. She had had the basement windows sealed and the room thermally regulated. It was wonderful storage for metal lawn ornaments, in addition to ladders and awkward-sized items like seasonal decorations, as well as doubling as a utility room. The washer/dryer, clothes-folding table, and deep sink in the corner could only be improved upon if she had a dumb waiter connected to the upstairs bath and could just toss the laundry down a chute.

She chided herself. Whether she liked it or not, it did provide some good exercise to have to haul the laundry basket around the house and down a flight of steps. She'd even had a two-rope clothesline installed under the stairs with a circulating fan. Wasn't it better to air-dry undies and anything with lace? Or did that—like a hundred other things—just date her?

She worked at rearranging and unpacking, took a break for lunch and then returned to the task of mounting pegboard to the wall above a workbench. Both had been left by the previous owner and would really come in handy. It would be heaven to have all her tools in one place and easy to get to. She'd thought of putting each tool's name next to it—claw-hammer, needle-nose pliers, 3/8 inch Allen wrench—but for whom? Was she just being too Virgo? She certainly wouldn't even consider cohabitating with a man who didn't recognize which basic tools were which.

Yes, the era of the shade-tree mechanic was long gone, lost to computers, but still, knowing the basics was somehow important. It was a masculine thing—not macho, just manly. She was no longer drawn to any man who couldn't fix things. She'd finally thrown out the toaster that Stanley had "fixed".

But there wasn't much she couldn't do. Older, mature, girl power. She laughed. Maybe most importantly, the tools would be protected in the basement, under lock and key. The single car garage at the back of the house was partially hidden by shrubbery and didn't lock. That was an open invitation for someone up to no good to investigate. A quiet country road had its perks and its drawbacks. Thank goodness Simon had the run of the house and backyard. The basement was really a godsend. But so was Simon. And if she really was being watched, then whoever it was also knew that she had a protector—a very furry one but nonetheless imposing.

She was still puttering around emptying some large plastic containers of bedding, washing a comforter and set of sheets, when Simon pawed at the basement door. He didn't like steep stairs but loved to keep her company by sleeping outside, body snugged against the door. She certainly couldn't get away from him without being noticed. She checked her watch. Oh, good grief, it was after six-thirty. No wonder he was antsy, she always took him for a walk *before* the six-thirty national news. Well, this was as good a place as any to stop work for the day. It would all be waiting for her in the morning.

Based upon the elaborate 'dog dance' he was doing at the top of the stairs, bouncing up and down in half circles—most of the time landing on her foot—he knew a walk was next. She loved the way he always telegraphed his excitement—made her want to go for a walk too. She grabbed his leash off the back porch and the two of them walked through the house to the front. She opened the door and was just leaning down to snap the leash in place when Simon gave a low "woof" and literally went airborne.

Deer. A buck, doe and fawn stood mesmerized at the edge of the lawn. But not for long. Leaping straight up, all three took off into the woods surrounding her property with Simon in hot pursuit.

She yelled, "Simon!" But knew, of course, it would do no good. Even a treat would pale in comparison to live, on the hoof, game. Not that she worried he could catch them, it was more a case of his getting lost. He could easily wander off, and keep on going, following the scent instead of returning and then not be able to find his way home. Maybe she shouldn't sell his 'nose' short but the last thing on earth she wanted was to lose her son's dog. Plus, he'd become her best friend, too. She grabbed a sweater from a hook by the door, a flashlight from the bedroom, and took off after him.

There was a trail of sorts, if one could call broken branches and flattened grass and weeds a trail. At least it was something to follow. But then it ended. Well, didn't exactly stop but led into a stream and, due to the rocky embankment on either side, she couldn't tell where it continued. Or had they even crossed the narrow waterway? Maybe they stayed on this side? But if they did cross, did they go straight or turn? She was just about ready to turn back and get the car when she heard a bark. Not that close by but off to the left somewhere across the stream.

She waded into the water and up the bank—thank God she was wearing canvas shoes—and jogged in the general direction of the sound. She still didn't have the dog in sight when she came into a clearing. The Leader lived somewhere out this way—was his the split log house in front of her?

As if on cue, a car turned into the long drive that led up from the road. She stepped back into the thicket and turned to go around the back of the property. The last thing she needed was to be detained for chitchat—or found in the bushes staring at his house. But then something caught her attention—a voice she recognized along with the laughter floating out the open car window.

She crouched down and watched as the Leader got out and came around the car to open the passenger-side door. He literally pulled someone out and into his arms. The embrace was steamy. His two hands grabbed her buttocks before pushing her back onto the hood of the car and sliding a hand under her sweater. The woman playfully tugged him down on top of her while unbuckling the belt to his jeans. All the while their mouths sought out the other, playfully then with more ardor.

The woman kicked off her jeans before he lifted her and she wrapped her legs around his waist, their mouths never parting. With a free hand the Leader was fumbling with his own jeans—and losing the battle. Hopelessly tangled around his ankles, his pants had him pinioned to the spot. Taking advantage of his predicament, the woman wiggled free, grabbed up her jeans, and laughing, ran up on the porch. Looking like he'd just lost a two-legged, potato-sack race, the Leader finally scooped up his own clothing and hobbled after his playmate, up the steps and into the house. There was little doubt that Maggie knew where this play was headed—straight to the bedroom. The Leader was preparing to screw Jia Han.

Maggie slipped to the ground, sitting forward and hugging her knees. What had she just witnessed? She wasn't into voyeurism and the shock of what she'd seen took her breath away. Wasn't Jia an item with Jason? Maggie wasn't a prude—far from it. But this sickened her. Someone in his sixties with a twenty-something? May to December relationships usually revolved around money or power—either one a lethal aphrodisiac. Yet, it wasn't her business. The Leader's reputation was out of control. This wouldn't be the first young woman rumored to be his plaything! This was simply proof.

But Jia? She couldn't let this interfere with her friendship with the girl. She liked her. No. She couldn't dwell on this. This simply wasn't any of her business—she had to make herself believe that. She was probably reading in the duplicity she'd suffered with Stanley and simply identifying. She needed to disassociate. She waited until the front door shut before standing.

She stood silently for a moment taking deep breaths. All was quiet. No distant barking by an errant Simon. She'd walk down to the road. That would be the fastest way to go home. Simon was chipped and tagged so could be easily identified; her worry was that someone would panic at seeing a hundred and forty pound Rottweiler and do something foolish. He was a lover, not a biter. But then did she really know what the dog would do if cornered and threatened?

The mile home seemed like ten after stopping every fifty yards or so to call and listen. Her fingers were crossed that she'd find Simon sitting on the porch when she turned in her driveway, but no—no dog. It was now after eight and pitch black. The country road would only be lighted by her headlights if she decided to search by car. And walking through the brush with light limited to a flashlight beam was probably not a good idea. The thought of snakes came to mind. Florida had a nice assortment.

She walked into the house, poured a glass of wine, slipped on a sweater, and walked back out to the porch. She turned the porch light off and sat in the swing. Even in near pitch-blackness, the night was beautiful, a crescent moon and stars offered that beauty but not much illumination. She wasn't tired and couldn't imagine abandoning her post to go to bed.

When would Simon have stopped and given up? Or was giving up even in his vocabulary? She doubted it. There would be wonderful smells in the woods, as well as the surrounding open fields. This time of night there would be lots of creatures out foraging. So, if he gave up on the deer, he might just turn to another critter to chase. Oh God, what if that was a skunk? Was it vinegar that took the smell out of fur? Scrubbing a dog in the middle of the night wasn't her idea of a good time. Maybe she should just go to bed and hope for the best.

Still, she couldn't bring herself to go in. Nothing had happened in over a half hour but somehow, vigilantly sitting on the porch keeping a lookout made it seem like she was doing something. Maybe if she walked down to the edge of the road and called for him. That would really be doing something. Plus, she needed to check for mail. She had a box at the Center for work-related mail but this was the personal stuff—personal and junk. She grabbed her flashlight and walked down the drive. Her mailbox was a miniature copy of her house—painted to match. An artist in the area took orders for replicas and it was a cute addition. A Victorian cottage on a post.

But, just as she thought, the box was full of advertisements—no, she didn't need hearing aids, a hip replacement, or assisted living care. Her unpurified water was fine, the brakes still worked on her car, and her roof didn't leak. Good grief! What a waste of a tree! She wasn't a fan of email but it probably had already saved a forest, or several hundred.

She was just turning around when headlights coming toward her from town caused her to stop. It was a light-colored pickup with its brights on going too fast for the gravel road and losing traction on even the slightest curve. It passed her in a cloud of dust. She couldn't see through the dark-tinted windows but she knew it was kids. They should be home on a school night, or had Christmas vacation started already? Whatever, they should be home at this hour. She turned the flashlight toward her watch—ten 'til ten. Well, that really made her sound like a fuddy-duddy, but tearing around the countryside wasn't exactly safe. Her first thought was Simon. Her heart sank. Hopefully he'd stay off the road.

She walked in the direction the pickup travelled, calling his name, but no big black dog came running toward her. But somehow this was better than just sitting on the porch. Would snakes really be on the road at night? She could only hope not, because she decided it wouldn't hurt to continue up the road calling Simon's name. Surely by now he'd be heading back from wherever he had ended up. Fifteen minutes turned into thirty minutes, then forty-five—nothing. She turned back and struggled not to give into despair. She had to believe that he was all right, just out having a good time—sans skunks!

Long before she could hear the car, she could see the bright dots of its headlights coming up behind her. She slipped down the embankment, crouched next to a culvert and switched off the flashlight. Alone, on a seldom-traveled road, at night—it wouldn't be good to advertise her position. As the car neared she could see it was the same light colored pickup that had raced passed her earlier, going the opposite direction. It hadn't slowed and once again was fighting for traction on the corners.

Where had they been? Did they forget something? Why was it going at break-neck speed on a country road, retracing its route? It had barely been forty-five minutes since it raced past her going the opposite direction. This road seldom had traffic—not at this hour, anyway. Kids absolutely had no sense. They were immortal as teenagers. They could take chances because nothing would ever happen to them. She sighed. There were a lot of life's lessons in store for them.

She wasn't sure why but it made her feel uneasy. Did this have something to do with the email's admonishment to "be careful"? Mud obscured the license plate and most of the back of the truck, so she didn't even know if it was local—at least a Florida vehicle. Somehow there was franticness to its speed and wanton concern for safety.

She felt relieved to see her driveway up ahead. But a thousand times more thrilled to see a large black dog with rust-brown markings sitting by her mailbox. Simon ran out to meet her, and she got the idea that he thought it was her fault she wasn't home to greet him. Treats for coming home were in order. Then it was off to bed. But she couldn't stop petting that basketball-sized head that pushed against her knee. Did he have a sense that he'd worried her?

It wasn't late but she felt like she could absolutely collapse. Getting undressed sapped any remaining vigor she might have had. Worrying could use up a lot of energy and she had been half sick over losing Simon. Seeming to know that he needed to be good, he quickly curled up on his orthopedic foam dog mattress at the foot of her bed. She pulled back the covers on the king-sized four-poster, climbed in and didn't even remember turning out the light.

Six a. m. She sat up blinking at the pale sunlight seeping in around a set of wooden shutters and reached for her phone that was jangling away to "Wake Me Up Before You Go-Go." She grimaced. Note to self—change the ring tone! She slipped on her readers. It was the center's number; she swiped across the screen to answer.

"Nancy, good morning."

"Maggie, I'm so sorry to call this early. I hope I didn't wake you. The Leader was supposed to be here by now. He's the keynote speaker at the Evangelical's Breakfast of Champions for Christ. I don't know if you realize that he lives just a mile from you. I checked the schedule and you're due in at seven-thirty. Would it be a terrible imposition to ask you to run up to his house before you come in? It's the house closest to you, same side of the road. It's a split-log cabin. He's not answering his phone and he may just be outside—car trouble or something—he's famous for tinkering in the garage and leaving his phone in the house and then totally losing track of time."

"No, I'll be glad to." It wasn't as if she didn't know the house. It was difficult to push the picture of the Leader in a sex-induced stupor out of her mind, but of course, she would check on him … or would that be *them*?

She could remember all too vividly the scene by the car. How embarrassing to go knocking on the door, possibly interrupt a little morning frolic … if Jia were smart she'd hide in the bathroom when Maggie got there. Oh well, she had absolutely no right to judge. It wasn't her life and, Jason or not, she shouldn't get involved. How many times would she have to repeat that little self-lecture?

She hopped out of bed. Jeans, navy cotton sweater, a brush of her hair, a bowl of dry kibble for Simon topped off with his favorite—raw chicken gizzards and she was ready to run up the road. She'd stop back by her house before going to work, maybe put on a dressier pair of slacks and give herself some eyebrows and eyelashes—but she looked okay to deliver a message.

The Jeep Grand Cherokee was parked exactly where she last remembered seeing it—even its passenger-side window was still down. So, nothing appeared to be wrong, no car trouble anyway. She left the Beemer behind the Jeep and walked up onto porch. The front door was open about a foot. Odd, but maybe he was out back. She called his name and continued around the porch to see if he might be in the garage. It appeared to be locked—a closed padlock hung from the hasp. All was quiet. Did she dare give into thinking he was just sleeping in? Perhaps, with company? She was torn by what to do. Then she turned back to the front door and again, calling his name, banged on it loudly. Absolutely nothing. No sound.

She took a deep breath and stepped inside. Nothing looked out of place. But, then, she doubted that the two had spent much time in the living room. The house was one big room with several closed doors leading off of it like spokes of a wheel. Three on one side, two on the other, kitchen across the back.

She knocked loudly on the first door to her left, then opened it. A home office and library. She pulled the door shut and moved to the next. This was a utility room, spacious for what it was, but she liked the idea of where it was—centrally located. The third door was already ajar. She knocked on the doorjamb and called out. No answer. She pushed the door fully open and stepped in.

Sometimes in life there are those moments that change your life forever. This was one. The room was dominated by a huge four-poster bed not unlike her own, but this one was resplendent in varnished, inlaid teakwood elegance. The Leader was lying on his side but his face was gone, simply mangled, his features unrecognizable. The blood had soaked through the bedding and pooled on the floor. The spattering on the headboard had left small chunks of flesh and bone as decoration, side by side with mother-of-pearl. He had been shot in the back of the head—from close range, she was sure of that—and by a caliber of bullet large enough to obliterate part of his skull.

This was a horrific crime scene. Luckily she hadn't touched anything—not even the doorknob on the room or front door. But she hadn't really expected him to be alone. Was there another body? Should she look for ... no. That was not her job. But Jia Han. She had seen her enter the house—in a somewhat compromising state of undress. She looked around. There was absolutely nothing to suggest that the Leader had not been alone. It's as if Jia had never been there. No clothing scattered about, no woman's shoes under the bed, no pair of empty wine glasses on the bed stand—then it hit her.

What if Jia was the shooter? No. Ridiculous. She was letting her imagination run away with her. But where was Jia? Closet? Bathroom? What were the chances she was still alive?

The churning of her stomach stopped her. There was

no way she could face another discovery like this. She needed to call authorities. Now—and get out of there. It was someone else's problem—people who knew what to do with the scene in front of her. Maggie backed out of the room, quickly walked to the front door and returned to her car. She moved the Beemer out of the driveway and parked along the road. There would be enough emergency vehicles needing to use the driveway without hers being in the way. She sat a minute then pulled out her phone and dialed 9-1-1. "I'm calling to report a shooting, a death …" Deep breaths. She stayed on the line and answered all the questions that she could.

Next, a quick call to the Center reporting only that the Leader had passed and it would need investigating. Yes, she had contacted local law enforcement. Yes, she would wait at the scene and offer any assistance needed. Even though she knew there was nothing she could do.

Chapter Twenty-one

His assistant, Nancy, had been the first from the Center to show up. Of course, the police wouldn't let her cross into the taped off area at the front and side of the house. A crime scene—in bucolic, rural Volusia County, Florida. The poor woman seemed beside herself, at once pacing up the drive, then back, dabbing at her eyes with a limp Kleenex, stuffing it in the pocket of her skirt, taking it out again, clenching her hands into fists, releasing, smoothing her skirt …

"Nancy, please, join me." Maggie leaned across the front seat of the Beemer and pushed open the passenger-side door, motioning for Nancy to get in.

She shook her head and waved dismissively in Maggie's direction but then seemed to change her mind. Reluctantly, she finally walked to the car and eased herself onto the seat. She still seemed too agitated to sit quietly and sat sideways, feet on the ground, a foot tapping nervously, the car's door open as wide as it would go.

"This is terrible. Just terrible. I knew I shouldn't have left him alone. And I should never have asked you to check on him. I should have sent Amos—he was finished setting out the chairs for the breakfast; he wouldn't have minded coming up here. Amos is over six feet, fit, strong—he could have lifted him. Did you try to cut him down? Was he still breathing when you found him? No, no, of course not—only a man would have been able to reach that beam in the garage and lower a body—but Amos, I think he would have been able—"

"Nancy, wait, slow down—the Leader didn't hang himself—"

"Oh, no!" Her hands flew to her mouth as she turned toward Maggie. "I knew it. I'd checked my medicine cabinet just yesterday. Two bottles of Oxycodone were gone. I should have reported it. I just didn't want to get anyone in trouble. How stupid of me. I've killed him—just as easily as if I'd handed him the prescription drugs myself." She began rocking back and forth, arms hugging her sides, eyes closed, making a soft keening sound with her chin against her chest.

Maggie leaned over and firmly placed an arm around Nancy's shoulder. "Listen to me. He was killed—not by his own hand—he was shot in the back of the head from close range. I think it's referred to as 'gangland' style."

Nancy jerked her head upright. She gasped, stared at Maggie, bit her lip and looked like she was going to pass out. "Shot?" She was gripping the seat cushion with one hand, the dash with the other to stabilize herself. "Someone did this? He didn't take his own life?"

Maggie shook her head. "Why did you assume that he had killed himself?"

A shrug. "I knew about the problems."

"At the Center?"

"He was hopelessly in debt. He'd purchased the Center some years back—the Center and several buildings on about ten acres. He overspent trying to refurbish and make additions—trying to make it enticing to those on journeys for truth. And he wanted it to be commercial—competitively so—and that meant parking facilities, bungalows at the back of the property for workers, the conference center … everything considered, the drain on money never seemed to stop."

"But the Center seems to be prospering—ninety new, full-time students, workshops sold out, a faculty of twenty plus, all the on-line activities. I really find it difficult to believe money was an issue—one serious enough to get killed over."

"Appearances were deceiving. The compound was heavily mortgaged. He was becoming despondent. I feared he would take his own life. I didn't think something like *this* would happen but I don't know details. Maybe there was money he hadn't paid back—borrowed from the people who do things like this. You said yourself it was a gang killing."

Well, that wasn't exactly what she'd said but she didn't correct Nancy. "You need to meet with the authorities and share this." And that was going to happen pretty quickly. Maggie watched as an officer in street clothes stepped off the porch. A badge was clipped to his belt, catching the light before he slipped his jacket on. He continued down the drive and ducked under the crime scene tape. He was heading directly toward the BMW.

"Yes, of course, I'll be candid if asked."

"I think you can plan on being questioned."

The officer excused the interruption then asked to speak with each woman separately, starting with Maggie. They could sit in her car if that was okay and Nancy didn't mind waiting in her own car. Nancy nodded, got out of the BMW quickly and walked toward the car parked behind Maggie's.

The officer slipped into the passenger-side seat, took out a small notebook from a buttoned vest pocket under his jacket, introduced himself as Frank Howard and corrected her use of 'officer' to detective.

"Sorry, *Detective* Howard … I'm Margaret Mahoney." Sitting in the front seat of the BMW made it difficult for a handshake but maybe that wasn't protocol. Maggie honestly didn't know; she'd never been interrogated before. He began with perfunctory questions—her full name, address, place of work, length of time she'd been a resident in the county, previous address and place of work.

"Now, tell me why you were here."

She reiterated getting a call from Nancy, the Center's Assistant Director, the woman who was waiting her turn to talk with him. Nancy had wanted her to check on the Leader. He was late for a breakfast at the Center.

"Sorry, the Leader?"

"The man who is deceased—the one who owns this house, the Director of the Center for Spiritual Learning. And if you want to know something really odd, I honestly don't know his real name."

"His name is Alex Turner. Does that sound familiar?"

"No. Not at all."

Note-taking, then, "I want you to be exact—don't leave anything out—what happened when you came here looking for Mr. Turner this morning."

Maggie told him everything, from pulling up in the driveway to pushing open the bedroom door.

"It would seem you were familiar with the house. You had been here before?"

"No, not exactly." She told him about losing Simon and seeing the Leader coming home last evening.

"Did you engage in conversation?"

"No. I saw his car pull into the drive but I was worried about my dog and needed to continue searching."

"What time was this?"

"Probably around seven."

"Was Mr. Turner by himself?"

Shit. She hadn't thought this through, about what she could say without mentioning Jia. Oh dear, she was taking too long to answer; he was staring at her.

"Do you need me to repeat the question?"

"No." A deep breath. Wasn't truth always the best path? "A young woman was with him."

"Do you know this young woman?"

"Her name is Jia Han."

"How do you know her?"

Maggie mentioned the tutoring, that Jia was a student, how she had met her through Jason who was her son's wife's son—now, *that* was confusing and terrible sounding—once or twice removed from being real family—which Jason wasn't removed from anything—he *was* family. Sometimes titles were misleading.

"Did you present yourself?"

"No."

"May I ask why not?"

"I was worried about my dog and didn't want to lose any more time."

Detective Howard turned sideways to face her. "I know how shocking this has been for you but anything you can tell us would be helpful. Is there something you're leaving out?"

"I just don't know how important this is."

"And I'll be the judge of that." The notebook now was closed and resting on his knee. She had his complete attention. She turned away to gather her thoughts. His stare was intimidating but in his line of work, wasn't it supposed to be?

She turned back to meet his stare, "I was at the edge of the woods when the Leader pulled into the drive."

"About how many feet was that?"

"Right at thirty feet from the drive and thirty-five to his car."

"Close enough to hear any conversation?"

"Not really. Well, they weren't exactly talking." Maggie then, as matter-of-factly as she could, described what she had seen.

"About how long was it from when they pulled into the drive till they went into the house?"

"Under five minutes."

"But it is your belief that you had witnessed a sexual precursor to ... uh, foreplay, if you will, that would appear to inevitably, in your opinion, lead to consensual sex? In other words, you describe the couple as laughing, playfully shedding clothing—there was no refusal on the young woman's part, attempts to get away, thwart Mr. Turner's advances—no cries for help?"

"None."

"Let me reiterate, no one seemed angry or seemed to be doing anything against his or her will?"

Maggie shook her head. She felt sick. What had she done? A little voice inside tried to assure her that she'd only told the truth. But at what cost?

A moment of note-taking, then, "I'd like you to describe Miss Han."

"Yes, of course. She's probably five foot eight, maybe nine—tall for an Asian woman—and somewhere in her twenties."

"Asian? Do you mean Chinese?"

"Yes. To the best of my knowledge. Her name would seem to indicate that. And I know that she speaks fluent Mandarin. Her hair is black, quite long, but almost always pulled back into a bun. Let me add that she's strikingly beautiful—the way she carries herself, one would think she's a model."

"But that is not her vocation? Not that you know of?"

"I don't know for certain. As I mentioned I was told she was a college student—a senior at Flagler College with a major in Ancient Architecture."

"Do you know where she's from? That is, was she born in the States?"

"I believe 'home' is California. I don't know if she was born there."

"Do you have any contact information—phone, address?"

"No. Nothing exact, I believe she lives in St. Augustine."

"But you do have the phone and address of your son's

wife's … what was that again? The young man named Jason."

"I'm not comfortable giving that information."

"Do I need to remind you that there is a penalty for obstructing justice by withholding information? Knowingly harboring a felon or possibly having knowledge of someone who is?"

Maggie felt like she'd just fallen into a pit of quicksand that was sucking her under. But there was no undoing what she'd set in motion. "Jason Linden is in St. Augustine for the holiday break. He's staying with my son, Dan Mahoney, and his wife, Elaine Mahoney—her son is Jason Linden." She opened her phone and read the address and Jason's number from her contacts. She couldn't shake the sinking feeling that enveloped her. What had she just done?

The detective took a few moments to reread his notes. "I want you to contact me if you think of anything else." He handed her a card. "*Anything*, understand? It may seem inconsequential but prove later to be important. I want to be the judge of what is useful."

Maggie nodded. He opened the door, stepped out, then leaned back into the car. "I'd like you to stop by the Sheriff's office and have your fingerprints taken, along with a sample of your DNA. This is to rule you out as having any part in the crime—not to incriminate you." He smiled. "Thanks for your time."

Chapter Twenty-two

How about lunch at Georgie's?"

"The Diner?" Elaine was bringing an overflowing clothes basket in from the garage. "Perfect. Just give me time to fold all this." She dumped the basket of towels and sheets on the bed, then walked back into the hall. "On second thought, this can wait. What if I give Jason a call? He's at the library, but he never turns down free food."

"Sure. Have him meet us there in forty-five minutes. I just need to change shirts and then we're off." Halfway to the bedroom his phone rang. "Mom, are you okay? You sound out of breath."

"I'm fine … well, not really but I need to talk with you and Elaine. I'm about twenty-five minutes from St. Augustine. I just wanted to make sure you were home. See you in half an hour."

"We're on our way to Georgie's—meet us there for lunch. Do you know where it is? If you turn east onto King from Highway 1 then take the first left It's about a half block—100 Magala Street. Got it? We'll see you in half an hour."

Dan walked back to the kitchen. "Looks like we have more company for lunch. Mom is on her way. Something's up but she wouldn't say what. Guess we'll find out.

+ + +

For once they didn't have to park on the street. The lot behind the '60s style restaurant off of King Street was half empty. Must be the holidays—people travelling or shopping. Quarter to twelve and he'd expected it to be elbow to elbow. Wasn't unusual to wait a half hour to be seated.

Dan parked near the front and saw his mother standing at the bottom of the entrance ramp to the restaurant. How could she have beaten him there? It was no family secret that she drove well over the speed limit and relied on a radar detector to keep her out of trouble, but didn't she value her safety? If not hers, then the safety of others? He didn't even want to be around when the day came to take her car—hopefully that wouldn't need to happen for another fifteen or twenty years. And, for once, he'd leave some unpleasant task to his sister Carolyn. He smiled… she'd be thrilled.

He returned Maggie's wave and was getting out of the Rover just as Jason pulled in beside him. The window on the passenger side whirred down and Jia leaned out.

"Hope you don't mind that I tagged along?"

"Of course not—good to see you again. You'll love

Georgie's if you haven't been here before." Dan locked the car before dropping the fob in his pocket.

"I haven't. I love diners, though."

"You're in the right place then."

Elaine slipped an arm through his after giving Jason and Jia each a quick hug. "This is great. I'm feeling lucky; I've seen you twice in as many days."

If Dan had taken time to think about it, he'd have thought it was odd that his mother hadn't fairly skipped across the parking lot to dole out hugs of her own. No, something was off—his mother was sending out nervous vibes from forty feet away.

Dan wasn't sure what happened next. The four of them turned to join Maggie when shrieking sirens filled the air. Three cop-cars barreled onto Magala Street, two of them roaring into the drive and a third screeching to a halt and blocking the entrance. With guns drawn, three uniformed officers surrounded them. Another steered Maggie toward them, anchoring her securely by the elbow.

"Hands in the air. All of you. Ladies, lower those purses to the ground, slow-like. Hands back up. Sir, if you're carrying, I need to know now. And same for you, young man."

"A .38 registered to me and a permit to carry are in a holster underneath the driver's seat in the Rover parked in back of me."

"Thank you. And you?" He turned to Jason.

"No gun."

"Do you own a gun?"

"No." Jason looked completely bewildered.

Dan felt irked. "What seems to be the problem?" This was unbelievable—obviously, they had the wrong people.

They'd not even asked for anyone's ID yet.

"I'm arresting Miss Jia Han for the murder of Alex Turner."

"What? No! Wait." Jia looked shocked. "I don't even know an Alex Turner."

"Oh, I think you do. You might know him as the Leader—does that ring a bell?"

"Yes, I've met the Leader. But he can't be dead."

"Sorry to say, he's very much so. Officer Burke?"

One cop stepped forward, pulled Jia's hands behind her back and snapped on cuffs, shoving her to the front of the group. "You have the right to remain silent ..."

Dan was so shocked he tuned out the rest of her rights. The Leader? Dead? Jia arrested? Cuffed?

"Jason Linden? I'm taking you in for questioning as a possible accessory—"

"Dan, do something." Elaine's strident whisper sounded utterly panicked. "We can't let them take him. And Jia? Murder? What's going on?"

"Oh my God! Stop. This young man is innocent. This is all my fault. I need to talk with your supervisor. This is a terrible mistake." Maggie rushed forward only to have the cop who cuffed Jia draw his gun, point it at her, scream for her to stop, and then quickly advance. He grabbed her by the arm before holstering his 9mm. But Maggie shook free. In the blink of an eye, the cop tackled and tripped her to the pavement, holding her down with a forearm across her back.

"Get off of me. Now! This is not what you seem to think it is. These people are innocent." Maggie struggled to sit up, clutching her right arm.

"Officers, that's my mother. You have some explaining

to do. I'm Dan Mahoney, this is my wife Elaine, Jason's mother. I want answers and an apology. If you insist on taking them in, we'll follow you to the station and sort this out. But there's no need for force. I'm sure there's been some error. Mom, are you all right?"

"I've been better." The officer had released her and Maggie was rubbing her right elbow.

"Do we need to go to the Emergency Room? Is your arm OK?" Elaine asked.

Maggie shook her head. "No emergency room. I'll live—just a little bruised and sore."

"All right. As you wish. Mr. Linden, Miss Han, and Ms. Mahoney will come with us. You're free to pick up your belongings."

Elaine quickly picked up the three purses. She watched as Jason was placed in the back of a squad car, Maggie seated beside him. Jia had already been pushed to sit in the backseat of the car blocking the entrance. As she turned to get into the Rover, a flash caught her eye. A man directly across the street from the restaurant was taking pictures. Oh good grief! Was there anything in today's world that wasn't recorded? She hoped she wouldn't see herself on You Tube but she'd deal with it later. The three cruisers started up and pulled out of the driveway. At the corner of King and Magala, they all turned left with the Rover close behind.

Elaine sank into her seat. "What do you think Maggie meant when she said Jia's arrest was all her fault? I'm confused."

"You know as much as I do, but I'm sure she'll tell us." He knew better than to second-guess his mother, but why did she always turn out to be a pain in his elbow? To put it nicely. "An arrest on a charge of murder is serious—I *really* hope there's a simple explanation."

The squad cars pulled into the parking lot at the municipal building and continued around to the back. Dan took a spot in front, turned off the Rover, and waited for Elaine to gather up her purse and Jia's before getting out, then turning back to retrieve Maggie's from the floorboards. What a way to blow off lunch and spend an afternoon. Yet, he was shocked —the Leader murdered? That in itself was bad enough, but how in the world did Jia and Jason figure into all this? And to top it off, his mother?

His mind whirled. In the past couple weeks, a somewhat simple case of stolen relics had led to child-slave trafficking, a dead supposed nun, and a drowned young girl; Elaine had gotten beaten up by what could have been a victim of the traffickers; and now, a family friend had been charged with murder; while his mother and stepson were being questioned as accomplices. Craziness.

He had the name of Max Smirnov and probable proof of who stole the relics—*if* the name was real; but now there was a third death—probably a third murder. Could they all be connected? They might be. But he knew he was not much closer to making sense of any of it.

They were met at the front door by the arresting officer. "Follow me. I'd like us all to meet in the conference room."

"Coffee? Iced tea? Bottle of water?" The receptionist stuck her head in the door after they were seated. There were no takers. Elaine and Dan were both focused on the situation, not beverages, but they thanked the woman. Odd. An arrest was made in a murder and suddenly it seemed more like a tea party. What was next, crumpets? Dan was losing patience.

The door opened again and this time Chief Rob Mitchell stepped into the room.

"Mr. Mahoney. Good to see you again."

Dan acknowledged the greeting and introduced the chief to Elaine. "It's my mother and my wife's son that you're holding."

"Yes, Jason already shared that with me. Sharp kid. When some of this isn't so pressing, we're going to put our heads together over a chessboard."

"Good luck. You'll be challenged."

"I can believe that. And I want to say I'm sorry about the force used with your mother. I'm sure you understand that my men were just following orders. Your mother's quite a handful."

"You're telling me." But why detain her? This certainly wasn't like any interrogation that he'd ever sat in on.

The Chief smiled and leaned against the table, hands gripping the edges for balance. "Before I bring in Miss Han, Ms. Mahoney, and Mr. Linden, I want to go on record as saying I don't think this is a good idea. You are going to be made privy to information which, at the very least, is classified police work. I might add that the investigation is international in scope and possibly could put you in an extremely dangerous position. I'm truly sorry that your mother has gotten involved. Sometimes not knowing is safety in itself. So, I'll offer you the opportunity to pass on being briefed."

"Absolutely not. I have every right to know what my son is involved in or why he's suspected of being a part of whatever this is."

"I think we're in agreement here. I have a portion of the missing relics puzzle solved, but finding them appears to overlap your investigation—I guess I'm trying to say that I already feel involved. Just part of my job," Dan added.

"All right, we'll proceed." Chief Mitchell opened the door and stood aside as Jia, Maggie, and Jason entered the room.

"I told you she'd play the 'mom card'." Jason and the chief exchanged smiles.

Dan had been a part of multiple arrests and bookings in his lifetime but for arrests to have been made or people being held for questioning, in this case, something wasn't right. Everyone seemed just a little too relaxed and jovial for the severity of the charges, Dan thought.

Jia stepped forward. "I've talked with Chief Mitchell and have some things to share—he's given me the go ahead." Jia pulled out a chair at the head of the table and sat down. Maggie and Jason took seats also at the nod from Chief Mitchell.

"Before we start, you should know my birth name was Cai Ling Tran. But I prefer to use the name you know me by, Jia Han. " She turned to Elaine. "I think you were close to figuring some things out. You were right when you said Lila Tran and I looked alike. We were twins. "

"Whoa. A little too fast for me. Is there a beginning to all this?" If Dan felt relieved it was because no one seemed to be under arrest. But confused as to the sudden change in direction? Yes. So far this all appeared to be just a friendly group chat.

"If I could have my purse." Elaine scooted it across the table. Jia unzipped a side pocket and pulled out a badge, placing it on the table. "I'm CIA but currently assigned to Interpol."

"Interpol?" Elaine sounded impressed.

"Long story—but I think you might be interested."

"Why don't we work backward. I'm assuming you are not being charged in the Leader's murder? You are an undercover agent?" Dan could see that his mother was relieved and seemed downright cheery if he could read body language correctly.

"No, I'm not being charged and, yes, I have been working undercover. I can't believe Maggie saw me … what should I call it … auditioning for a call girl's position. I'm truly sorry about that. I would have reached the same conclusions and reported me once you found the Leader had been murdered. You had no idea what was going on. In truth, I was literally attempting to infiltrate the sex trafficking underground as part of my assignment."

"Now things are getting interesting," Dan whispered as Elaine kicked him under the table.

"But let me back-track. Some of my story you already know, but I'll go back to the beginning." Jia paused to open the bottle of water in front of her. "The biographical history the Basilica received from Boston College is legit—my father was a professor in the Department of Engineering. I completed three years of study. And, yes, I was in the Theology Department. I was not, however, seeking employment or fulfillment as a nun. I went to parochial schools through high school and was probably a model Catholic, but that was about it. My major in school was ecclesiastical literature.

I had also shared with you that I was a tourist baby. Only I was born in Boston, not Los Angeles. What I didn't know about my own birth, I learned on the trip to Yunnan the year before I was to graduate from BC. I had just lost my adoptive mother, and my father wanted me to know my birth mother—the surrogate that Dr. and Mrs. Tran hired to give them a family. It was a bittersweet meeting. I had no idea I had been a twin. My adoptive mother refused two babies—she worked and didn't want the extra responsibility. Secretly, I think it was my father who wanted a family.

I have no idea how I was chosen—maybe they flipped a coin—but I stayed in Boston and the baby later known as Lila was sent on. I believed my father when he said he'd lost track of her. But I was angry, very angry—at a dead adoptive mother too selfish to think of anyone but herself and at a hen-pecked father who gave into her and didn't even try to find my sister. And neither of them ever told me about her. If I knew then what I know now, I would have been doubly incensed—Lila's life was anything but easy. She did not have the opportunities I had. You may now better understand my decision to keep the name of Jia Han. It represents a new start for me. There is just too much sadness connected with the twin who took my birth name and lost her life so violently.

My father's passion in life was climbing. Taking me to meet my biological mother and ascending the local mountain was doubly rewarding—a shame it had such a tragic ending. Both my father and his guide were presumed lost. Ceremonies were held, the dead celebrated in absentia, and the mountain was deemed too dangerous for future climbs. Life in that part of the world returned to normal. And I longed to be a part of that 'normal'.

For me, that year had been life-altering, tumultuous— the loss of both parents, the existence of a sister I might not ever meet ... I felt anger and stultifying grief rolled into one. I chose to stay with my biological mother in

Yunnan. I had uncles and aunts, a grandmother, even two half-brothers. It was the family I never had. After a year I even became engaged to the local mayor, some fifteen years older but well established in the village. At first I thought it was the stability I wanted—needed—for healing. But by the end of the second year, I realized only too clearly that I was an American. The village, the way of life, what was expected of me, bound me just as tightly as if I had been in chains.

At about this same time, I was contacted by a representative from Interpol with even more shocking information to share. My father had probably been murdered, and his guide, Max Walters, had resurfaced. And, oh yes, my identity had been stolen and was being used by a young woman who was probably my twin sister—*and* she was involved in slave trafficking. And did I leave out that she was posing as a nun? Is it any wonder that I welcomed the new identity that was offered and also the chance to avenge so many wrongs?"

Jia paused and took a sip of water. "Maggie, you may have done the investigation into the murder of the Leader a big favor. If I'm presumed to be the killer and as far as anyone knows I'm kept incarcerated, the real killer or killers will feel safe to surface. Please, do not beat yourself up, thinking you've caused me harm in any way. Chief Mitchell was in contact with Interpol and my bosses—he knew I was in St. Augustine. This may be a better outcome than we could have planned."

"But it's not just the Leader's death that I don't understand. I still can't make sense out of Lila's murder," Dan interjected. "She had the perfect cover. I can't believe an organized group would throw that away."

Chief Mitchell leaned forward, "I agree. The Leader's death might make more sense. He was an inland fencing agent for the Yacht Club guys out of Miami. We were getting close but he was good. We could never prove our suspicions—we were never at the right place at the right time. The idea was for Jia to infiltrate the ranks, so to speak—take over where Lila left off—excluding posing as a nun. The setup would have given us what we wanted and not just the Leader. I think we would have been in a position to bring in some others.

"It's maddening that the Leader could have eluded us for so long. But he kept his head down, and that's a tough crowd. And there's big money to be made. I can see someone jockeying for position and deciding to replace him—still, he had excellent cover. And he brought in the money through his Spiritual Camp—there seems to be a fortune to be made in the occult. It wasn't like he needed to dabble in human trafficking."

"I feel badly that I got any of you involved." She turned to Maggie, "I joined your online following just to send you a warning email but tutoring Jason was the perfect job. Seriously, just the cover I needed. I felt I had to take advantage of it."

"And my Mandarin is getting pretty good."

Elaine was watching Jason. He didn't seem surprised by any of it—did that mean he'd heard some or all of it before?

"Were you able to meet Lila?" Elaine asked.

"Not face-to-face. We texted. I was able to fill her in on her family in Yunnan. I sent pictures of her mother. I know she appreciated that. She trusted me. She knew she was in constant danger if she didn't play the game, but her conscience was dictating she get out. I was on her bank account, and at her death I transferred her money to authorities, keeping it from falling into the wrong hands. It will always be one of my biggest regrets that we didn't meet."

"And the man who calls himself Max Walters?" Dan asked.

"Disappeared. Again, I might add. I concur with Mr. Mahoney; there seems to be fairly conclusive evidence—circumstantial, but rock solid—that he's the thief of the Basilica's relics. And the mystery here is that they have not appeared on the international antiquities market. I don't rule out that they are still local or, at least, still in the States. I've petitioned Interpol to make our database available to Mr. Mahoney if he's interested."

"Absolutely. Thank you. So what's next? Chief, I'm assuming you've searched the Leader's house?"

"Served warrants for both his house and his office at the Center two hours ago. Nothing. Wiped clean. Actually, a little too neat and tidy, given the timeframe of the murder to time of reporting. Your mother reported finding the body at six-thirty. The area was secured at roughly seven fifteen. We had a team on the scene within an hour. There was nothing out of place. Even the safe at the Center held only a modest amount of cash. Office records, bank statements, correspondence—all in order and nothing even remotely suspicious. That supports my theory of pre-planning. The Leader's death was not a spur-of-the-moment knee-jerk reaction. It was premeditated. It follows that no one knew about Jia. She almost got in the way but, luckily, decided to leave after the Leader had a few vodkas and passed out."

"I borrowed his mountain bike and had a rather chilly ride back to civilization. But obviously it was one of the smartest decisions I've ever made."

"Now for what we'll do going forward. We'll announce that we've arrested a suspect. We can't keep reporters from tapping into police scanners and I saw someone taking a few pictures across the street from the diner during the arrest. I'll bet we make the *Record's* front page tomorrow... we'll offer them a news release this afternoon. It will be worded a little vaguely ... 'last person to see him alive, reason to believe there was an altercation, suspect being held without bail, on-going investigation' ... that sort of thing. In the meantime, Ms. Han will be refusing all interviews because she won't be in the area. We'll transfer her to Jacksonville on the QT; she'll be working with the FBI's office there. "

"Good plan." And Dan meant it. He doubted Jia Han would be safe if she stayed in the area. The best-case scenario would be the real killer or killers would believe the ruse and decide they were in the clear. But just as likely, they could try to eliminate her, fearing she might have damaging information. They would really have to be wondering what she'd seen or heard. They might assume she'd been hiding in the closet.

"I think everyone needs to be on his or her toes. Margaret Mahoney, Jason, be especially careful. Our stories have to be in sync. Jia Han appears to be the one who murdered the Leader. You can go so far as to suggest that certain items found on the premises were being tested for DNA but nothing as yet is conclusive. I don't want to put either one of you in harm's way but, Margaret, you'll be in a prime position to hear or see something that might implicate the real killers. I use the plural here because I'm convinced that more than one person was in on this."

"Have you found anything to indicate that the Leader was insolvent?" Maggie asked.

"No, exactly the opposite. In fact, the Center is bringing in money hand over fist. They pay some hefty taxes to the township, but these payments are well within their means. There's some indication that start-up monies—the sum to acquire the original acreage and erect several of the Center's buildings might have been supported by illicit funds but, if so, those debts have long been paid off. And we only had suspicions, never proof. Was there some reason you asked?"

Maggie shared Nancy's rather convincing argument that the Leader's murder might have happened because certain loans had not been repaid to members of organized crime. Nancy had thought the Leader was despondent over money problems and, before she realized it had been murder, had insisted the Leader had taken his own life.

"Nothing that we've found would indicate that, and we've been keeping close tabs on the Leader for quite a few years now. But maybe it's an avenue we need to revisit. It's exactly this type of hearsay that I'd like you to share."

"I've twisted Maggie's arm into letting me come visit for a few days. Simon needs a playmate." Jason looked directly at his mother.

"I don't think that's a good—"

"It's settled, Mom. I'll be careful."

"If I can weigh in here," the Chief added, "I believe in strength in numbers. I don't think we'll have long to wait before the real murderers show themselves. I imagine they're feeling pretty safe about now—and safety can lead to errors. I've briefed Margaret and Jason on exactly the kind of evidence we'd need. Notes should include exact location, time, and accompanying dialogue—recorded, if possible—of any incident that either of them feels might further our investigation. For starters, I'd like to know who takes over for the Leader. Who inherits? Monetarily, that person has a lot to gain. And don't rule out jealousy. Did he make promises he didn't keep? Was someone vying for power? Did he double-cross or cheat a benefactor in some way? I understand he had quite the reputation with women. Did a tryst turn ugly? Of course, all of us probably think his death was directly related to a sex trafficking ring but that link isn't exactly clear at the moment. Knowing Lila Tran isn't conclusive evidence of anything, but it does seem to be the suggestion of a connection. Let me add, the use of a hit man makes that the most plausible."

"That's a lot of possibilities." Dan shared his thoughts. "The Center could be a front for a lot of activities. For starters, it's perfectly set up to launder very large sums from foreign clients in the sex trade."

"Exactly. But I'm not at liberty to say anymore. So, any questions? I'm a call or text away. And nothing is inconsequential if it catches your attention. Be on the lookout, but be safe."

Chapter Twenty-three

Moving her office desk and chair from the spare bedroom into the dining room wouldn't have been a chore had it not been for Simon simply gluing himself to Jason and getting underfoot. Maggie tried putting him outdoors but he sat by the back door and howled—that hair-raising kind of 'you're killing me' howl. So, back in he came and Maggie swore he was smirking. Yes, he'd gotten his way. He'd even passed up a meaty shank bone to be with his new friend. It appeared he was starved for companionship, and that made her feel guilty.

"As soon as we finish up here, I'm going to run into the office for an hour or two. I feel like I've been gone a week not just a couple days. Anything I can bring you?"

"No, I'm fine. I'll take Simon for a walk and get caught up on some reading."

"You have my number if you think of something."

+ + +

Secretly, she was thrilled that Jason was going to spend some time at Dragon's Bend. Was she frightened after the Leader's violent death? A little. She had quite by accident gotten way too involved. She could leave all of the 'whodunit' stuff to her son and never miss it. Still, being on the lookout for clues was kind of exciting, she had to admit. She just hoped she'd recognize something important if she stumbled upon it.

The parking lot was full—the sides and back of the building overflowing with cars. Clients? The curious? Probably both, she decided. She squeezed the Beemer in beside the dumpster in back and placed her employee card on the dash. Garbage day was yesterday so the spot was safe. She walked in the back door and stopped in the lounge long enough to pour and doctor a paper cup full of coffee.

"Maggie. I'm so glad you're here. Do you have a few minutes to talk?" Nancy stood in the doorway.

"Sure. I don't have an appointment until later."

"Great. Bring your coffee. We'll meet in my office."

Maggie gathered up purse and jacket and, carefully balancing her coffee, followed Nancy down the hall.

Indicating that Maggie take the chair in front of her desk, Nancy moved behind her to close the office door. "There. Finally some privacy. I don't have to tell you this place has been a madhouse."

"I can't even imagine."

Nancy pulled her desk chair out and sat down, leaning forward forming a more intimate space. "Maggie, I just want to say thank you for your bravery. You came forward with what you saw at the Leader's house and it led to an arrest. I'm sorry there's no reward. So few people do the right thing anymore. And I understand the young woman was known to you? A friend of the family?"

"Not exactly. She was my step-grandson's tutor. But, yes, I had met her before."

"Well, it was the right thing to do. I think these things are best handled by the authorities but they need our help sometimes. I'm only sorry the press had to take those awful pictures. It was such an invasion of your privacy when you were only trying to help."

Maggie nodded. She and family had graced the front page of the *Record* in somewhat compromising positions— exactly like Chief Mitchel warned. Unfortunately, the photo of her being restrained did not do her any favors, but the article and follow-up the next day exonerated her and the others as it zeroed in on Jia Han. At best, the feature writer had made it seem as though they all had been duped—entirely innocently taken in by what was hinted at as a woman with a dark, nefarious past who was possibly linked to a criminal underground and an international ring of thieves. No mention of how this might implicate the Leader.

"Law enforcement had to make certain I was who I said I was and I had just reported what I had seen and wasn't an accomplice in any way. The same for Jason. His only part in all this was having a direct connection to Jia Han, his tutor of the last few weeks."

"Well, there couldn't have been such a swift arrest without you, and for that I'm thankful. There will be a ceremony of life for the Leader tonight at the Center with a reception following. I would like to pay tribute to your helpfulness. I'm assuming I can count on you to attend?"

"Yes, I'll be there. My step-grandson will be staying with me for a week or so, may I bring him?"

"Of course." Nancy sat back in her chair, looking pensive. "Interesting. You know, this gives me an idea. I'm having a terrible time finding good help over the holidays. We're just a little too far out in the country. I'm in desperate need of someone to help me with the petting zoo."

"I had no idea we had such a thing."

"Well, it's a small herd of twelve Nigerian Dwarf Goats that Rosy uses in her yoga class—goat yoga is all the rage out west—and when the goats aren't 'working', they're a wonderful addition for attracting children. The Leader turned their home behind the barn into a petting zoo. But they are rather demanding—they like warm water in the morning, an alfalfa-grass mix plus mash twice a day ... well, you get the picture, it's simply more than the staff can keep up with. Rosy would do it but she only has classes here three times a week.

"There would be other duties—setting up tables and chairs for meetings and then taking them down ... I suppose a job description would read general maintenance; that would cover everything. If he can drive a tractor, he might be called on to supervise the hayride tours of the property. They're always popular this time of year. Do you think your step-grandson would be interested? We pay twelve-fifty an hour with generous overtime for weekends."

"I'll ask. His name is Jason Linden."

"It would just be for the holidays when the schedule is so hectic. If he's interested, have him stop by and fill out an application. And, the sooner the better."

Maggie texted Jason the minute she got back to the lounge for a second cup of coffee, and as she had guessed, he was interested and would run by the Center that afternoon.

+ + +

He'd be the first to admit that the major perk of any vacation from school was sleeping in, not getting up at five a.m. to go to work—in this case to feed some dozen or so goats. Jason carefully put the two five-gallon buckets of warm water down and slipped the padlock off of the chain-link gate. Yes, he'd tested the water with his elbow and the buckets were each baby-bottle perfect.

His audience of kids and nannies lined the fence in front of him. From the intensity of the bleating, he was facing a pretty hungry mob. He doubted all that noise was just a welcoming chant. He eased open the gate and set one bucket at a time inside the corral. There was a lot of pushing and shoving but finally everyone seemed to have had her turn to drink. They were all small, tinier than he had imagined. He was wondering what part of Nigerian 'dwarf' he hadn't understood—not one animal even came up to his knees. Their size, and the fact goats weren't supposed to bite, would be non-threatening to children—and they'd all been dehorned. That was a plus.

And from what he'd read about males, he understood why there were only females. From the bucks' musky smells to a nasty habit of butting things that got in their way, not to mention pretty randy habits, females were by far preferred. Keeping a buck was just too problematic. Even breeding was best done by taking the does to the bucks. He'd be back in school before that spring event. He could only imagine taking a carload of goats somewhere for a one-night stand.

He walked back to the barn and couldn't help but notice there were no goat toys. He'd Googled goat care at midnight last night and every picture of a goat enclosure had some sort of jungle-gym apparatus in the center. Maybe if he dragged a few bales of straw out of the barn and creatively stacked them, it would give them something to climb on and jump off of until he could build a more permanent structure. He'd seen some old wooden pallets and storage crates leaning against a back wall and thought he could cobble together a fairly respectable ramp with varying heights of landing areas. Jumping off of things seemed to be a favorite thing to do.

He'd been given the go-ahead to make sure the goats were well taken care of—he hoped that included exercise and challenging activities. No one else really had stepped up, at least not since the Leader was no longer around. Jason couldn't imagine that they received all the exercise they needed by jumping over and onto the backs of middle-aged women in various yoga poses. There were some pretty hilarious You Tube videos. He wondered how many women had really seen themselves online.

Jason continued to the back of the corral with several frolicking escorts in tow. They were curious and seemed to find him fascinating. The building had been portioned off into an area for the goats to get out of the weather, with a protected feeding stall containing two small hay racks, feed storage in four covered fifty gallon barrels, and a partitioned area that held alfalfa with a loft overhead. Heading toward the main part of the barn he found a couple work areas with benches, an indoor tool shed the size of a large closet, and an open area where more than half of the large building housed a tractor, attachments for mowing, a flatbed trailer, a horse trailer, and a pick-up truck.

But most alarming was the fact that the goats were out of food. A couple empty bags of goat chow, a quarter of a bale of alfalfa grass mix, and maybe a coffee can of grain at the bottom of one of the fifty gallon barrels—and that was it. He scattered the remaining hay and divided the grain between two feed pans and walked back up to the Center.

+ + +

Nancy was happy to see him. "Oh, I'm so glad you could help us out. I know nothing about goats. The Leader fed them morning and night and even walked them in the woods twice a week when he could get away. He found it therapeutic. Frankly, I don't even understand what he was talking about. I find them strange, demanding little nuisances but in a short time, they've become a fixture at the Center. At least they don't bite children.

"However, I'm not surprised that they're out of food. No one has really stepped up to take on their responsibility. I have Amos busy until lunch, helping me lay carpet in the entry. Would you mind picking up their food? You'll have to go into DeLand. We run a tab at one of the feed stores. They'll know what we usually get. I'll get directions."

"That's fine, not a problem."

Nancy looked harried. But then it hadn't exactly been an easy few days. She began rummaging around in one of the desk drawers.

"Here are the truck keys. And here's an invoice from a feed store in DeLand. I imagine we'll need more of everything that's on this list—looks like we haven't purchased supplies for almost three weeks. In fact, go ahead and pick up at least ten bales of grass mix, a dozen or more if it's good quality. Oh, and here's a credit card. I have no idea how much gas is in the truck—and treat yourself to lunch."

Jason assured her he'd take care of everything and he headed back to the barn. The pickup had a quarter tank of gas so he'd have to fill up before going too far. Round trip was going to be over a hundred and twenty miles. At least the truck started right away. Someone must drive it fairly often. He cut across the back of the parking lot and paused before pulling out onto the highway. There was Maggie getting out of her BMW at the entrance.

He pulled up alongside her and lowered the window. "I'm off to DeLand to pick up supplies. I have no idea when I'll be back; don't plan on me for dinner."

"Whose truck is that?"

"Belongs to the Center, why?"

"Let me check something." Maggie walked around the back of the truck and then returned to the driver's side. "There's mud covering the license tag. I know this truck. And I completely forgot about it."

She quickly filled Jason in on the night of the murder—a truck, no, *this* truck going too fast, heading south and forty-five minutes later coming back north, still breaking the speed limit for a gravel road at night. What were they doing? She'd thought it was kids, out too late, driving too fast. But this must have been someone from the Center. If the truck's occupant or occupants were in the clear, at the very least, maybe they saw something. They should be questioned. There must be some sort of sign-out sheet. Someone at the Center would know who had checked out this truck on that date.

"Give me a minute." Maggie leaned against the door. "I need to call Detective Frank Howard and see if he thinks the information is worth taking a look at. It might not be too late to check for prints."

She found his card in her purse and dialed his cell—better than explaining everything to a receptionist. At the very least, she could leave a direct message. But he answered on the second ring. A quick explanation and his response was just as quick—yes. Have Jason meet him at the Sheriff's office in DeLand, directly, before he did any shopping. He'd have his team go over the car. Checking for prints was a good idea, but he couldn't promise a quick turnaround. They were short-staffed because of the holidays. But he believed this was worth throwing some man-hours at. He stopped just short of saying they were grasping at straws. But the indication was that they were no further along now than they'd been a few days ago.

Maggie found a couple plastic bags in her car and insisted Jason put them over his hands. Awkward, but the steering wheel, gearshift and the dash, in general, would be the most common places to find prints.

"You know, this may be absolutely nothing, but thanks for being willing to take the time."

"I'll let you know how it goes." With that, Jason pulled out and headed to DeLand.

+ + +

It amazed him that fifteen miles away from the coast, traveling inland, his surroundings suddenly looked like Kansas. Farmland, two-lane roads, sparsely scattered houses, and signs for U-Pick berries—black, blue, or strawberry. The state was an enigma with the north and central parts totally different than one would imagine—the area was more than white-haired old people with plastic flamingo lawn ornaments.

Detective Howard met him in the parking lot in front of the Volusia Court House and directed him to the back where two technicians waited in one end of the county maintenance building.

"It's going to take these guys awhile. Did Ms. Mahoney say you were in town to get supplies for the Center?"

Jason explained that he was basically on a feed store run with maybe a stop at Ace Hardware.

"Then let's not waste your time or raise any suspicions at the Center by you getting back late. Why don't you take one of the County trucks and do your running around? We'll swap back out and get you on your way without any downtime. Sound okay?"

"Sounds perfect." Other than loading and unloading a dozen seventy pound bales of hay twice, it was the best plan.

DeLand was a small town—"the Athens of Florida"—if he could believe the advertising, and he immediately liked it. Aside from farming and retirement, it was the home of Stetson University (go, Hatters!) and reminded him a lot of Las Cruces, New Mexico. Main Street lived up to its name—it was the center of town and everything of any importance was in close proximity. Jason had no trouble finding the store he wanted.

He backed up to the loading ramp of Harrison's Feed

and Seed and went inside.

The guy behind the counter wanted to hear the latest on the Leader's death, but Jason feigned ignorance— touted the fact that he was just a hired hand. But the topic seemed to be on everyone's mind. The Center seemed to have a mixed group of supporters—some believers, some naysayers. But everyone seemed thrilled with the amount of business it brought into the county. Numbers were up for the Stetson Mansion Christmas tour, likewise for the live nativity on the Episcopal Church lawn (with homemade cookies and cocoa for all visitors). DeLand really knew how to celebrate the holidays. With a population of a little over thirty thousand, the town would never lose its small town feel—Jason was sure of that. He'd put money on everybody knowing everybody. But neighbor helping neighbor also came to mind. This looked like modern small-town living at its best.

Supporting that idea, the feed store personnel were super helpful. The manager was some sort of goat specialist and talked him into a mineral block for outdoor placement in the corral, and a vitamin crumble to be mixed with the goats' mash. That is, if he wanted a successful breeding season in the spring. Jason wasn't sure but figured vitamins couldn't hurt.

He also purchased twelve bales of barn-stored Timothy/orchard grass mix—the last on hand before the truck came in after Christmas. He added ten bags of goat chow—fifty pounds each. A couple curry combs and stiff-bristled brushes rounded out the order. The articles he'd read said all goats liked to be groomed. Guess he'd find out.

He watched two young men fill the back of the pickup.

There was a lot. Still, all of the food was only going to feed twelve goats for a couple weeks—maybe a bit longer if he took them out once a day to forage in the woods. And he'd just put a few hundred dollars on the Center's tab. He hoped goat yoga was lucrative.

He'd stopped at the hardware store earlier and added a couple boxes of ten-penny nails, hinges, and four rolls of one hundred foot, sixty inch, wire horse fence. Movable, temporary enclosures would help with weeding and with the cost of food; he'd have to make certain he allowed time every day to move the herd around the grounds. From learning Mandarin to goat management, there hadn't been much of a transition; the learning curve on each had been perpendicular. But he'd be the first to admit he wasn't bored. In fact, he was rather pleased with himself—twelve small goats didn't know it yet but he was about to give them a Merry Christmas. If he acted quickly, he could put their temporary playground in place this evening.

He was back at the County jail and Sheriff's office in an hour and a half. Detective Howard met him at the maintenance garage. "Thank Ms. Mahoney again for giving me a call. Stuff like this gets forgotten when it could make a big difference. I'm not guaranteeing a quick turn-around with the holidays and all, but I think the lab may have some positive results for us by the end of the week. Happy holidays to you and your family."

Jason returned the best wishes and helped switch trucks, reloading all the feed before heading back to the Center. He wasn't sure he'd have help unloading once he got there. In reality he could be facing one long afternoon of hard work. And add a couple evening hours to that. He still needed to work on the goat gym.

Chapter Twenty-four

This is Christmas week," Elaine poured two cups of coffee, walked to the table and handed one to Dan "I've been thinking. Let's take our presents over to Maggie's after dinner and spend a couple days, maybe even Christmas Eve, at the Center. I think Maggie works that night, and I don't want them having to drive over here afterward. It would just be too late. Plus, I think the Center is crazy busy between Christmas and New Year's. You know, people wanting predictions for the upcoming year. We're good at amusing ourselves. We could take in the festivities at DeLand. It's fairly close. I understand they have fireworks on Christmas day."

"Hey, I'm convinced. Count me in. But fireworks?

Why didn't you say that first? That's an easy sell."

"Stop teasing. I'm serious."

Dan leaned across the table and put a hand on Elaine's arm. "Do I detect a little concern for Jason?"

"Honestly? I worry about both of them. I'm not feeling very confident that they're not in danger."

"Okay. Let's go. Call Mom, then see if you can find a room somewhere. On second thought, I don't want Maggie insisting on sleeping on the couch so better nail down a room first. She can be pretty persuasive."

A room at the Hampton Inn in DeLand was the best and closest accommodations Elaine could find, so with that out of the way, she checked her to-do list before calling Maggie. Gifts were wrapped—the newest, greatest iPhone for Dan. Jason's gift was one he knew about. She and Dan had offered to pay for a full six-week workshop, including travel in China during the summer on a university-sponsored tour. He was on a full scholarship but it didn't allow for extras. For Maggie, six months' worth of once-a-month facials and/or massages from someone at the Center named Annabel. And Simon? Twelve months of fresh, dog-approved, liver jerky treats delivered to the door.

She'd overspent her budget but Dan had generously chipped in for Maggie's gift and insisted on dividing the cost of Jason's tour. She thought the gifts were good choices. In half an hour the Rover was packed and they would be on the road by seven. Maggie was, of course, beside herself and promised all sorts of Christmas treats. But she absolutely refused to think of them staying at some motel miles away. No. She had a day bed and would set it up in the foyer for Jason. There were two bathrooms and two TV sets—what more would they need? She'd start on the cookies this very afternoon. Elaine smiled. There was nothing like forcing a woman into mom-mode. She had a feeling this would be one of the best Christmases she'd had in a long time—her first Christmas as the other Ms. Mahoney. Fingers crossed that everyone would be safe.

+ + +

Jason expertly backed the loaded truck into the barn behind the Center. He'd just finished unloading the goat chow and grain when Amos walked in to offer help with the hay.

"Let's put at least half of this load in the loft, including the goat chow and grain."

Putting anything in the loft meant pulling down the fold-up steps and dragging some pretty heavy, awkward-sized items up one story and then stacking them. And Jason knew who would be doing the bulk of the work. Amos was probably pushing seventy and complained loudly about having arthritic knees, to anyone who would listen. No, this was going to be Jason's exercise. To think he had bemoaned missed trips to the gym over the holidays.

He pulled down the steps and secured them before climbing up to survey the storage area. Half of the loft was already filled with bales of straw, stacked to the roof across the back wall. He knew he wanted to use at least six for the temporary goat jungle gym. He dislodged a couple bales and carried them to the loft's edge.

"I'm going to toss these bales down. Watch yourself."

It was the loosening of the fourth bale that revealed the hide-out. The stack didn't reach the wall or the ceiling in the corner. Fortified by pieces of plywood, including one across the top, a completely hidden bunk area was exposed. Judging from the sleeping bag, wadded Whopper wrappers, and empty soda cans, the area could and apparently did offer shelter to one person. Was it occupied during the day? Or maybe only at night? It was difficult to tell, but he didn't have the feeling that he'd uncovered something not being used. This was current. No dust, and the sleeping bag looked freshly washed.

He was careful not to touch anything, and he quickly rearranged several bales of straw to hide his discovery. He dug his phone out of his pocket and took pictures. Then, with Amos steadying the steps and helping to guide the heavy bales, Jason carried all the new purchases up to the loft. An hour and a half later he was emptying the last of the grain into covered barrels; with Amos's help he fed the goats their evening meal. He was tired. And hungry— it didn't pay to skip lunch. He would come early in the morning to complete the jungle gym and get started on a more permanent one.

Then out of curiosity he asked, "Do you ever have an issue with transients out here?"

Amos paused a minute to think, "I can't remember anything recent. 'Bout a year back, I found three girls hiding in the barn."

"What happened?"

"Seems they had ditched some school tour thing and decided to run away."

"They sound young."

"Yeah, teenagers. I hate that age. They don't listen to reason. They know everything."

Jason smiled, "Did these girls 'know everything'?"

"Who could tell? They didn't speak any language I

could understand. Miss Nancy was the one who explained who they were."

"Do you know where they were from?"

"Nobody said. I'm gonna guess Nam or one of those countries."

"What happened to them?"

"The Leader took care of it. Last I saw of them, all three were in the back seat of his car heading out of here."

"Nothing since?"

"Naw. Don't know of anything anyway. We're pretty isolated out here. Makes the Leader's murder all the more shocking."

Jason certainly wasn't going to mention the present loft hide-out. But he'd keep an eye on the place. He had an excuse to spend some time up there now. His stomach growled. He wasn't keeping track of time but the sun had set some hour or so before. He hadn't counted on Nancy leaving a list of chores. Looked like he still had work to do. He'd washed the porch at the Center, put up a wreath that had been knocked down, unplugged a water fountain, and painted the dividing stripes on five new handicap parking spots next to the entrance. He was just now sweeping out the bed of the truck. It'd been a long first day on the job but in another ten minutes, he'd be heading out. He apologized to his twelve new friends and promised an early start in the morning.

Simon went berserk the minute Jason turned into the drive. Luckily a six-foot fence kept the dog safe in the back yard but he needed some attention. And Jason needed some food. The house smelled fantastic—something with garlic and butter, maybe sausage. His favorite combination, even if it probably wasn't pizza.

"Aren't you excited?" Maggie stood in the kitchen door with a French baguette in one hand and a package of spaghetti in the other.

"About?"

"Come on, you can't tell me your mother didn't call or text. Unless you already knew they were coming tonight and staying for Christmas Eve and Christmas Day. They should be here in about an hour."

"I had no idea. It's weird she didn't call." Jason reached in his pocket. "Dammit."

"What?"

"I left my phone at work. I gotta go back. I can't lose my phone."

"Not before dinner. The sauce is simmering and I just need to cook the spaghetti and throw the garlic toast under the broiler—then we eat. You look starved. Your folks have already eaten, so it's just us. The phone will wait on you, I'm sure."

"You're probably right. Mind if I get a beer?"

"Help yourself."

Dinner was delicious and the second helping was followed by a third. When they were finished, Jason carried plates and bowls into the kitchen, rinsed the worst of the tomato sauce off and stacked everything in the dishwasher.

"I'm going to be spoiled. Thank you. I really appreciate the help. Still going to pick up your phone?" Jason nodded. "Then why don't you give Simon a ride? He loves car rides but, I warn you, he prefers shotgun."

"Think he'd be okay around a bunch of goats?"

"I don't see why not. Rotties are guard dogs, and I'm pretty sure somewhere in their background that included livestock. He'd love the outing."

Maggie wasn't kidding about riding shotgun. He tried to lure Simon into the back seat with a treat, but nothing doing. Simon sat stoically by the passenger-side front. The minute Jason touched the door handle, he went into his frenzied happy-dance and squeezed into the seat, turning to look out the window. Shotgun meant that Jason had absolutely no view from the right side mirror. But he had a happy dog.

Ten minutes later, he was pulling into the Center. The front parking lot was full so he pulled around behind the barn. Must be a workshop night. There could easily be a couple hundred people there. The barn was dark and the goats were quiet. He slipped a leash on Simon, told him to 'wait' and walked around to open his door. The dog hopped out and couldn't stop sniffing—the ground in front of him, the air, the tires on the car he'd just gotten out of—he was obviously being assailed by new smells.

"Let's go meet some goats." Jason commanded Simon to 'sit' and then he opened the gate to the corral, went in with Simon glued to his side and waited for the goats, ever curious, to come out of the barn.

The goats were less than pleased. They came tumbling out, then stopped, jumped, bleated, ran back toward the barn, and fell over one another getting to safety before turning to stand in the doorway with their heads poking out. Slowly, the largest and probably oldest nanny ventured forward. Simon who had started to explore the corral literally hit the ground. Jason had never seen a dog simply fall to a 'down' position and freeze.

Simon did not move. Not sensing a threat any more, one by one the goats came back out and slowly circled him. Still not a muscle on the dog twitched. Growing braver, four goats came forward to sniff him and finally all twelve gathered around—pushing, shoving, and bleating in excitement—not running away when Simon stood. Jason was impressed that Simon seemed to intuitively know what to do so as not to panic them. The goats by now wanted to follow them anywhere. He closed them off from the center part of the barn and walked to the loft, letting Simon tag along after him.

"Okay, pal, you're going to have to wait here." He probably didn't have to worry about the dog bounding after him. He vaguely remembered Maggie saying Simon didn't like stairs. Jason pulled down the steps and Simon sat quietly. Now to find the phone. He'd taken it out to snap pictures and didn't remember putting it back in his pocket. It should be on top of the second stack of straw along the back wall.

Below, the goats were ticked and voicing their displeasure at being locked out. Simon's low growl alerted him to something more. Jason moved quickly toward the back, feeling around in the dark he found his phone exactly where he remembered putting it—on top of a straw bale. He pressed the flashlight app and did a quick scan of the hideout corner. And then he heard it, too. Someone was crying—stifled, with lots of sniffling, definitely muted sobs.

He moved toward the corner just as the make-shift plywood roof over the hiding place shifted. He yanked it aside and shined the light inside.

"Su Lin?" The girl huddled in the small shelter looked wild-eyed. She was dirty, her hair was matted and her t-shirt torn.

"Please, don't hurt me." It was more of a whimper

before she sank to the ground. "Don't let them take me."

Jason moved two bales of straw and sat down beside her. "No one's going to hurt you. I won't let anyone take you, but we need to get you out of here." Did he lie to her? *Could* he get her out?

He was appalled at her condition. She was emaciated in addition to being dirty. She certainly hadn't been fed regularly in the last couple weeks. He took her hand to reassure her and she felt hot to the touch. She could be ill. Could he sneak her out to the car without anyone seeing?

He helped her stand and carried her down the stairs to the barn floor where he helped her to sit on a bench along the wall. She couldn't weigh more than a hundred pounds, probably less. The car was parked behind the barn—that was a stroke of luck, but he still had to get her through the barn and out the corral gate.

He found a horse blanket in a former tack room and wrapped it around her. She was shivering but had stopped crying. He'd take Simon out to the car first then come back for Su Lin, carrying her if he had to, and put her in the back seat and cover her with the blanket. He doubted anyone would be out this late—at least not this far from the Center itself. It was nine and most events ran until ten.

He didn't turn on any lights but again used his phone as a flashlight to take Simon to the car. He was just opening the door when Simon growled, then spun around and barked, pulling the leash taut as he lunged at something behind them.

"Hey, that you Jason? Don't let that dog loose." Amos was outside the gate and didn't seem to be in any hurry to come into the corral.

"Amos, I didn't see you walk up. This is Simon."

"He's one big mother, ain't he? You keep a hold of that leash; I don't want to wrestle with that one. He mean?"

"I've got him. He's not too friendly when he's in a strange place." That was sort of a lie, but maybe it would discourage Amos from hanging around.

"You getting a head start on that exercise stuff for the goats?"

Jason laughed and held out his phone. "No, left my phone in the loft. Can't survive overnight without it."

"You sound like my kids. And they're a lot older than you. You be careful now. I'm taking off a couple days so if I don't see you before Christmas, you have a good one." With that he backed away from the gate but kept an eye on Simon and didn't turn around until he was on the path back to the Center. Jason waited until he could no longer see him before putting Simon in the front seat, closing the door and returning to the barn to retrieve Su Lin.

Jason didn't take any chances. Once Su Lin was tucked under the blanket in the back seat, he drove across the field away from the barn and crossed a culvert to meet up with an adjoining county road. No rolling through the parking lot, just in case he would run into someone curious as to why he was there so late. It was out of his way but so much safer.

He was relieved to see Dan and Elaine's car in Maggie's driveway. Sometimes his Mom was better at figuring out what to do—and this was definitely one of those times. But he needed to tell Su Lin that Elaine was there. He could only imagine the panic a meeting might cause.

"She doesn't blame you. You were cornered, afraid. She didn't call the cops. In fact, when they interviewed her in the hospital, she let them believe that it was a botched burglary. She thought the person who had followed her into the house and attacked her was a man. Trust me. You have nothing to worry about. I know my Mom—she'll want to help. Okay?" A weak nod but Su Lin didn't look convinced.

Elaine looked stunned when he stepped through the door, an arm around Su Lin. A second later, the girl twisted away and fell prostate on the floor, crying over and over, "I'm so sorry, I'm so sorry, I'm so sorry."

Elaine rushed to her side, knelt and helped her to a sitting position. "It's all right. You were frightened—you meant to get away, not hurt me." Another nod, she quieted, but didn't raise her head. The sobs had turned into hiccups and she seemed to have lost any strength she might have had and slumped against Elaine.

"Dan, she's ill. She has a fever. Help me get her to the couch. Maggie, maybe a glass of water?"

"We really need to get her to an ER—is the hospital in Deland the closest?" Dan directed the question to his mother.

"The closest and the best—even for a small town. I always find emergency services to be well-staffed in a college town. I'll call ahead." Maggie handed off a glass of water and picked up her cell. "I'd feel better if law enforcement were advised. Someone has brutalized this child—look at the bruising, the chafing around her wrists—I don't think she's been fed or had access to clean clothing. I'm going to pack her a bag. Just a few toiletries, a clean t-shirt, maybe a pair of yoga pants."

"Thanks, Mom. I totally agree—we're looking at criminal abuse, not just neglect. Let Detective Howard know we're on our way. Jason, keep Maggie company. Lock the doors, check the windows, and bring Simon inside. I'm hoping no one saw you but you two be careful. I'll let you know what they say at the hospital."

Chapter Twenty-five

Two nights before Christmas and the Emergency Room was next to empty. Students weren't on campus so the entire town seemed to be snoozing. Two orderlies met them at the door, strapped Su Lin to a gurney and rushed her down the hall to an exam room. Dan and Elaine took seats in the admitting area, and a woman got up from behind the information desk and approached with paperwork—three or four pages on a clipboard. Elaine explained the situation and said she would fill out as much as she knew about the young woman but her information would not be complete. Barely fifteen minutes had passed before Detective Howard walked in with two deputies in tow.

"Mr. and Ms. Mahoney, good to see you again. Your mother filled me in on how your son found this young woman at the Center. I agree, she just may be the break we've been looking for. My friend, Chief Mitchell, up in St. John's County is more than a little interested and thinks she might be a link to the Lila Tran case. We'll see, I guess. I'm going to try to talk with her now." With that he walked back to the first exam room.

Dan was trying not to get his hopes up, but maybe Su Lin could offer the first solid piece of evidence that Lila Tran had solicited young women for human trafficking, that Lila was part of a very lucrative slave trade ring that reached to, and included, the Leader. At the very least, he hoped she could identify those who had kept her captive and mistreated her. Hadn't Elaine mentioned that Su Lin approached Sr. Rachel in search of Sr. Leah, aka Lila?

"You know, I think Su Lin might have a lot of answers," Elaine said.

"I was just thinking that. I don't think she's the first to be held at the Center before being moved or sold."

"Could be a long evening. Want a soda? I noticed a vending machine around the corner."

"I'm fine. Looks like Detective Howard had a very short interview." The detective was walking back down the hall in their direction.

"They're taking her up to surgery."

"Surgery? What's wrong?"

"Some kind of intestinal blockage for one thing, a severely sprained wrist with pulled ligaments, rape—the kid has had it rough. I'll be back in the morning, but in the meantime just to be on the safe side I'm leaving one of my deputies here."

"Great idea. I feel better." And Dan meant it. If those in control found out where she was, they might try to remove her, or worse.

"I'd like one of you to meet me here in the morning. I think I'll get more useful information and it will put less stress on Miss Su Lin if a familiar face is present."

"Of course. I think you're right." Having a woman present made sense, Elaine thought. Thinking of Su Lin being raped made her sick. "I'll be here."

"Let's say ten?"

"Perfect."

"Otherwise, stick with business as usual. I'd like Jason to go into work. If anyone mentions Su Lin, he's going to say he thought she was a transient and he helped her get back on the street. But tell Margaret and Jason both to keep their eyes open and be careful."

Chapter Twenty-six

The day was cloudy but no rain was forecast. Jason really needed to work outdoors. He hoped there wasn't a to-do list waiting for him from Nancy so he could give all his attention to the goats' new toy. Dan walked into the dining room carrying a cup of coffee in a to-go cup. Breakfast had been toaster waffles or cereal, nothing fancy or time consuming. There was a real, palpable sense of anticipation. If the day went as planned, there could be a lot of questions answered. He knew Dan and Maggie both were hoping the lab results from the truck would prove helpful and that they might hear something soon.

"Jason, I'm going to let your Mom take the Rover to the hospital and I'd like to go in to work with you and Maggie. I could always help put together that goat gym you were talking about."

"Great idea. I'd like to get in early. Could we leave before eight?" Jason checked his phone, seven-thirty. "Would that work for you, Maggie?"

"Sure. Let me get a jacket."

+ + +

This was the first day the parking lot wasn't jammed. Still, there were at least fifty cars behind the center and a few lining both sides of the street. Last minute shoppers, Dan guessed. The gift shop was popular and, as Maggie pointed out, gift certificates for New Year readings were the most sought after. She had personally already sold twenty-two.

Unlike years in the past, his shopping was done. By the time Elaine returned from the hospital, there would be a new Mini-Cooper in Maggie's drive. He didn't mind sharing the Rover, it was just awkward—too much synchronizing of schedules for his liking. And she'd always wanted one. The dealership was outfitting it with a huge bow and driving it over from Orlando. White hood-stripes on the red body of a super-charged, stick shift convertible. Yeah, he could probably put money on the fact that it wouldn't be going back and pretty certain he'd score some points for this gift.

Dan and Jason said good-bye to Maggie at the back door of the Center and headed across the parking lot to the barn.

"Want to help me feed?"

"Sure." Twelve bleating goats made it pretty difficult to refuse.

He followed Jason to the main part of the barn,

helping him push open the double, sliding doors in front of the parked truck to make it easier to drag out a half bale of Timothy and a half bale of orchard grass. That would keep the goats busy for a while. Jason had told him an adult Nigerian would eat about five pounds of roughage a day, almost all of a seventy-pound bale for the twelve of these guys. Dan was glad he wasn't picking up the tab. Best to have a hobby that didn't eat, but then the boat he'd had a few years back came to mind. That was a money-pit, too, and a hell of a lot of work. If he had a choice, he'd go with cute. These little guys had that in spades.

Dan mixed the grass from the two half bales in a wheelbarrow, unlocked the side gate to the goats' corral, and filled the two-sided hayracks in their exercise area. They were noisy and demanding but finally settled down to eat. Food would keep them out from underfoot for a while. He went out the side entrance to their corral and closed the gate behind him. There was a distinct feeling of being in the land of the Lilliputians. Probably not one goat weighed more than seventy pounds.

"They like you." Jason had been watching the goats jump around Dan.

"I don't think it's personal—they just like food."

"Well, this will *really* make you popular. They're push-overs for a drink of warm water in the morning. There's a double gardener's sink in the back. I need two five gallon buckets, each half full. And I'm not kidding, let it get warm. The little guys are particular. I'm going to stack all of the pallets and boards outside here on the driveway. And thanks for your help. This gives me a head start on chores." Jason was dragging a wooden-slat pallet out the open door.

Dan picked up a couple five gallon white buckets and started toward the back of the barn.

"Jason?" A female voice.

Dan turned back. Nancy was walking up the drive. Dan put the buckets down and walked back to the entrance where Jason was standing.

"Nancy, I'd like you to meet my step-dad, Dan Mahoney."

"Of course, Maggie's son. Thanks for helping out. We're always understaffed over the holidays. But I have a couple questions for Jason. Amos said you were here late last night." A little accusatory Dan thought but Jason seemed unruffled.

"I'd left my phone and came back for it."

"And you found someone in the loft? Amos overheard you talking to them."

"Yeah, a kid, a girl from the street. She wanted a ride into Deland. I gave her a horse blanket from the tack room. I'll replace it or pay for it, but it was cold last night."

"And you gave her a ride?"

Jason nodded. "She had friends in town."

"Well, thank you for going out of your way to show kindness. We get transients out this way every once in awhile. It's always nice to demonstrate a true Christmas spirit."

Dan thought she seemed convinced Jason was telling the truth, but he doubted Amos had been the tattle-tale. It was more likely Nancy not finding Su Lin and concluding she'd been discovered. He didn't expect to hear from Elaine before lunch, but he suspected Su Lin was going to be very helpful.

"I hope you don't mind my using up this old wood.

I was clearing out the barn and thought I could put it to good use."

"Not at all. I'm thankful the barn is getting cleaned. Stop by my office before you leave today. I'm handing out a few Christmas bonuses."

Dan turned to pick up his buckets beside the truck and saw a flicker of movement in the cab.

"Jump!" He literally screamed it just as the truck roared into motion.

Jason and Nancy were standing directly in its path. With the reflexes of the young, Jason threw himself clear of the vehicle. But the driver, floor-boarding it out of the barn, squarely struck Nancy, dragging her underneath the chassis. Dan felt as if his heart stopped.

The rest seemed to happen in slow motion. The driver swerved to miss the two squad cars pulling into the drive, and the truck flipped onto its side as the driver tried to clear the drainage ditch. Four cops with guns drawn rushed the overturned pickup and dragged the driver out, throwing him to the ground and cuffing him.

Jason and Dan both ran to Nancy, who had been dislodged when the truck flipped. There were zero vital signs but Dan started CPR.

"Let me do that. I have an ambulance on the way." Dan stood up and let the young cop take over, but he didn't hold out any hope that Nancy could be revived. She had taken a direct hit to the upper body and her chest appeared crushed.

"I wonder who the driver is." Jason looked shaken but the kid hadn't panicked. Dan was impressed.

"Looks like we're going to find out." Dan pointed toward Detective Howard and Chief Mitchell, who were walking toward them.

"Great to see you guys uninjured. Let me finish up here and then let's meet at the Center. Your wife is there now with Jia Han and Su Lin." Chief Mitchell shook hands with Dan and Jason as Detective Howard waved toward the ambulance that had just pulled up.

"Su Lin? I thought she had surgery." Had Dan heard correctly?

"Long story," then Chief Mitchell added, "Let me just say, surgery was averted. Go on up. The crime lab will be going over things here. They'll need your statements, but that can take place later. We need to get some tape up, keep out the curious and make sure Mrs. Turner has a ride to the morgue."

"*Mrs.* Turner?" Now Dan was confused.

"The Leader's wife. I guess former wife would be more appropriate. Interesting how one white pickup blew this case wide open, but I'll get to the details later. I have some work ahead of me here."

+ + +

Maggie was on her third cup of coffee, but who was counting? Her family was safe! She kept repeating it like a mantra. The morning had turned simply crazy. The police had shut down the Center but not before holding several workers for questioning. They took extra time with Jia and Su Lin. Maggie was thankful someone had the presence of mind to bring Jia down from Jacksonville to be with Su Lin during questioning at the hospital. She could only imagine how much that meant to the young girl. And thank god she hadn't had to go through surgery. She had bruising and had obviously endured trauma but Maggie felt good about her recovery. She was resilient—Maggie could just tell.

When word came from the barn that someone had been killed, it had scared everyone half to death. It seemed like days before a uniformed officer came up from the area to tell them what had happened and assure that Dan and Jason were all right. The person who had lost her life was the Center's Director. Nancy? That raised a lot of questions that the officer was 'not at liberty to answer'. Such a stock reply, but they would have to wait for a debriefing by Detective Howard and Chief Mitchell. And, oh yes, no one was to leave the Center. As if wild horses could drag anyone away.

A Search Warrant legally gave law enforcement the right to search the premises, and a crew had been in Nancy's office for more than an hour. During the same time, Maggie, Elaine, and the two young Chinese women had been waiting in the lounge in relative privacy. Apparently Dan and Jason were being detained.

The ambulance finally left with sirens wailing as it backtracked up the road and eventually pulled onto the highway. Was there anything as mournful or foreboding as a siren? The sound seemed to hang in the air long after it had left the premises. At one point Maggie actually wanted to hold her hands over her ears. She really didn't care how childish it might look.

A young officer stopped by to reassure them that Mr. Mahoney and Mr. Linden would be with them shortly. Then they learned that someone had been arrested. But the officer didn't mention a name. Said he wasn't allowed to divulge information. He was obviously a rookie/ flunky without clout, so maybe he really didn't know the name. They watched as computers and file cabinets were removed from the main office, taken past the lounge and out the back door. Seemed like this had turned into a big operation.

"I wonder what they've found?" Elaine asked. "Did you know Nancy well?"

"Really, not at all. I always got the idea she ran things—the brains behind the throne, so to speak. Su Lin, what was your impression?"

"She was mean." Su Lin looked at the ground and didn't offer anything else.

"So we have no idea who the driver is? He was arrested; I wonder if he struck Nancy on purpose?" Jia asked.

"I know you have a lot of questions, and I think I can help you with some answers but thought you'd like to see these guys first." Detective Howard stepped aside as Dan and Jason walked into the lounge.

"Dan, Jason …" Elaine hurried to hug each one. "You can't imagine how good it is to see you."

"You might say it's been a busy morning." Dan grinned as he put his arm around Elaine. "And that, I think, is an understatement."

"So, what's the first question?" Chief Mitchell stepped forward.

"Before we get started with the answers, let me say we wouldn't have any if it hadn't been for Maggie Mahoney having reported one light-colored pick-up truck." Detective Howard interjected, "DNA and fingerprints found in the vehicle put some pieces of the puzzle together that we otherwise may not have figured out. At least not this quickly. I badgered our labs to go beyond priority and get us some answers today. Their quick work, running the evidence through the international base, identified Max Smirnov and his sister, Martina Smirnov or Nancy Turner as everyone here knew her."

"Wait. Max Smirnov? The one who killed my sister? And maybe the Leader?"

"Yes, and I'd say *definitely* the Leader, too. Blood was found in the pickup that matched Alex Turner and put the driver at the scene. Bloody clothing belonging to Mr. Smirnov also contained the Leader's blood and was found behind the driver's seat."

"But why? Why was Lila Tran killed? And the Leader?" This from Jia.

"As far as we can determine, Max's sister was the master-mind. And she was simply tired of her husband's philandering. He wanted a divorce but she wasn't going to give up what they had built together at Dragon's Bend. The Leader wanted to replace her with Lila Tran. Unlike what appeared to be several dalliances over the years, he was completely smitten with Lila. Martina, that is, Nancy found out that Lila wanted out and under that guise, she had her brother kill her.

"The Leader was devastated but Nancy had gotten what she wanted. So the afternoon of the open house when you showed up looking very much like your twin, Nancy watched her husband fall all over himself to talk to you—I think it was the last straw. Nancy saw that she was losing him once again. There was only one answer; he had to be killed. Getting rid of him would give everything to her—a very lucrative business in the occult *and* the network to provide young women for the slave trade.

"But this is where it gets interesting. According to a very carefully laid out plot, Nancy had been setting up the books here at the Center to appear they were heading toward bankruptcy. Of consequence, a despondent Leader was going to appear to take his own life. A suicide note was found in the office with what I'm sure is a forged signature."

"No wonder she found it so difficult to believe he'd been shot." Maggie interjected.

"Exactly. She had given her brother explicit orders to strangle him by hanging the body from the beam in the garage. Max got sloppy or at least thought he'd do it a simpler way. I can only imagine how relieved they both were when Jia was arrested. I don't think that even being a close relative would have protected Max from his sister's anger." Chief Mitchell summed up by thanking everyone present for his or her support. "We couldn't have done it without you."

Detective Howard added, "I can't believe that an international cartel of human traffickers was foiled by a jealous, greedy woman."

"Did Max run over his sister on purpose?" Elaine asked.

"Not sure we'll ever know."

"We do know that Max," Jia continued, "was the one who had been doing the cartel's dirty work for years. He's a person who truly has no conscience. We'll never have proof he killed my father, but I'm sure he did. Perhaps, only to steal my identity. I was lucky to have escaped him but I'm certain he thought I would stay in China. Apparently Lila was already working in Miami. Our being twins made borrowing my identity easy." She paused. "There is one last bit of good news." Jia turned to Su Lin, "Ready to share?"

A nod, then Su Lin held out a closed fist to Dan,

turned it over, and opened her fingers. There was another of the thumbnail sized cabochon rubies from the top of the wooden relics box.

"Su Lin, where did you find this?" Dan was shocked.

"I took it off of an old box that I found in the barn. It had some bones in it. I thought this looked like a real jewel, so I swallowed it to take it with me when I ran away. But it got stuck."

"The blockage is what made her sick. The good news is that nature had a way of 'moving' things along and surgery wasn't needed," Elaine pointed out, trying hard not to smile as she watched Dan quickly and gingerly place it on the table.

"Where is this box now?"

"Right here." Detective Howard set a cardboard carton on the table, opened it and withdrew the elder bark container. "It's evidence but I think we can get it back to you by the first of the year. I'm sure Father Pete will be thrilled."

"You know, I distinctly remember there being a reward for the return of the relics' container. Dan, wasn't it your company that made the offer?" Elaine asked.

"Yes, fifty thousand dollars. I'd say you qualify, Su Lin."

Overcome, Su Lin put her hands over her face and burst into tears. Elaine quickly put an arm around her. "I think this changes a lot of things, don't you?"

Su Lin nodded and whispered, "Thank you."

"Do you remember what the cards said when I did your reading?" Maggie asked, turning to Elaine.

"They were absolutely correct."

"Why am I not surprised?" Dan offered.

Maggie couldn't tell if he was being truthful or just

pulling her leg, but she didn't care. She might even give Gert and Theo a shout out—maybe they were looking out for her after all. Who was to say this happy ending didn't have some extraterrestrial help? She couldn't wait to consult the cards.

Chapter Twenty-seven

Jason had washed his mother's Mini Cooper three times in the week after New Years in fifty-five degree temps no less. Twice at Maggie's with Simon biting at the spray of water coming out of the hose and getting thoroughly soaked and later at the condo in St. Augustine. Dan pushed his luck and offered a trade—wash the Rover and take it for the evening. Jia was leaving for CIA headquarters in McLean, Virginia Thursday morning and Jason was headed back to college the next day. Dinner was going to be something special—just the two of them at St Augustine's Olde House Restaurant. The least Dan could do is offer a decent ride for their last date. They were going in opposite directions but Dan overheard talk of their meeting in China during Jason's summer tour. He was glad they were keeping in touch.

But it was his mother who seemed to have scored big time. She'd been asked to step in as the temporary Director of Affairs for the Center. According to her, 'a plum of a job.' New house, new job, new future. He was thrilled for her and knew whoever chose her recognized a talented and tireless worker.

In the meantime he was trying to stay out of Elaine's way. Putting the final touches on her January sixth talk required quiet, two computers and at least ten volumes of Church history spread out across the office floor. The Sunday start to the series would follow an after-church celebration and rededication of the relics. Dan was picking up the box holding the bones of Saint Bonaventure from Chief Mitchell's office that afternoon and returning it to the church.

Father Pete was beside himself. He made a special effort to make certain everyone who had anything to do with the recovery of the relics was thanked and invited to attend the special Epiphany mass and feast. This year there was far more to celebrate than just the visit of the Magi.

Elaine insisted on driving the Mini Cooper to the Basilica on Sunday morning. Maggie would drive up from Devil's Bend and meet them there. The weather, a chilly forty-seven degrees, precluded driving with the top down but that was the only hiccup in an otherwise Florida-perfect winter day.

Holiday decorations were still in place at the church, and the pine wreaths with red bows at the ends of each pew offered a matching accent to the huge, red poinsettias that outlined the dais, altar, and front of the choir loft. Even the double front doors to the street held enormous bright, green wreaths with red bows. But it was the front of the nave that held everyone's attention. A crèche of life-sized figures included two small sheep and a donkey and a plaster of Paris baby Jesus, perfectly serene in his rough, wooden manger. And to his right with garlands of looped gold tinsel caught at the center with a small red bow was the display case safe. The elder bark box lid was slightly ajar revealing the sacred bones of Saint Bonaventure.

Father began the mass by holding the box of relics above his head and asked for God's blessing on the dozen or so men and women who were connected even fleetingly in its return. Dan got the idea that what he would call good detective work was suddenly being attributed to God. But then who was he to question? Father Pete just might be onto something.

Thank you for taking the time to read *Epiphany*. If you enjoyed it, please consider telling your friends or posting a short review. Word of mouth is an author's best friend and is much appreciated.
Thank you,

Susan Slater

+ + +

Get another Susan Slater book FREE—visit her website to find out how!

Visit Susan's website at **susansslater.com** where you can sign up for her free mystery newsletter and a chance to win some very cool stuff.

Contact Susan: susan@susansslater.com
Follow Susan on Facebook

Books by Susan Slater

The Ben Pecos Mystery Series
The Pumpkin Seed Massacre
Yellow Lies
Thunderbird
Fire Dancer
Under A Mulberry Moon
A Way to the Manger (a Christmas novella)

The Dan Mahoney Mystery Series
Flash Flood
Rollover
Hair of the Dog
Epiphany

Standalone Novels
0-60
Five O'Clock Shadow